THE CRAZY KILL

CHARLES HAMBLETT

The Crazy Kill

A FANTASY

SIDGWICK & JACKSON

LONDON

First published in 1956

MADE AND PRINTED IN GREAT BRITAIN BY
THE GARDEN CITY PRESS LIMITED,
LETCHWORTH, HERTFORDSHIRE

For
JOYCE

Contents

Prologue

by John Huston

I FIRST MET Charles Hamblett in Ireland when we were making early land shots for my film of *Moby Dick*. He stayed with us a while, during which we discovered mutual interests in whisky, horses and modes of living. By the time we set off for the Canaries for the final sequences it seemed natural enough for him to come along; he had become one of the family.

I knew, we all knew, that Charlie was writing a book, but none of us gave it much thought. Film people are used to writers, and there is, perhaps, a typical flaw in our attitude towards them—overrating the famous and underrating the not so famous.

Now that my film is finished and I can read this curiously evocation story, I have a chastening thought: all the while I was in the Canaries working out my own salvation with *Moby* and being in the centre of what was happening, Charlie was in the heart of it, too, going through it all with equal intensity, but barely noticed. (But then this is one of the finest possible gifts for the making of good writing.)

He has called his book a fantasy; thinking in terms of painting, as I often do, I would call it impressionistic. I am reminded of a story about a peasant woman's comments on Cézanne. 'There it is all the time,' she said, 'but you don't see it. Then he paints it and you see it.' There are times when fiction is truer than truth.

Charlie Hamblett saw something in the Canaries that none

9

of us saw, and we were looking hard. His book, which strikes many off-beat chords in the mind, must therefore be regarded as a work of fiction. But is it just that? Next time we meet I shall ask him for a map of the Budgerigar Islands. I may want to direct a picture there sometime.

Paris, March 1956.

THE CRAZY KILL

CHAPTER ONE

The Flight

SOMETHING WAS GOING to happen, down there in the Budgerigars; something strange and cathartic and perhaps even wonderful. You know how it is down there, with the drivers of the lemon carts cursing their burros, and the burros burrowing, and the bums borrowing lemons from the burros; and storekeepers keeping store, and barkeeps scrubbing out and sanding over the stone floors of the bars, and the kept women just about keeping alive. And then those fishermen with blue swollen feet sleeping on the beaches by their boats. Those cute little boats. Those cute fishermen. Primitive. Sleeping. *You* know how it is.

It was the fishers, really, that started it. We knew that the moment Simpson saw them it would be the start of something. Or the end of something. Or something. For with fishermen you either have or have not. And Simpson has it with fishers, just as he has it with hunters and boxers and jockeys. You know how it is with Simpson. Call him that. Call him a film director. Call him a genius. Call him a cab. Call me madame. Well, that is how it was and how it really started. With the fishermen.

We tried, mind. Especially Perdita. Perdita Murray, the stranded sailor's friend. Gee, how that chick tried. Perdita was helping out on the production. Sewing buttons on, fixing false eyelashes, sending cables—that sort of thing. She managed as near as anyone to manage Simpson that year,

and all that time we were hunting whales. A great little chick,
Perdita; Indonesian-Irish, with a dash of pure Hungarian.
What a dish that dash made her, and what a heart that kid
had. Yeah, Simpson had her around all the while, along with
a battery of secretaries and female wrestlers and what have
you. He needed her around, apart from the costumes, in case
he wanted shots of a chick waving goodbye to the crew. With
her slant eyes and ginger pigtails she was just the doll you
needed around for farewells on a rain-swept jetty. And Perdita
managed Simpson like a champion. But it was different when
the fishers got into the act.

You must try to understand how it was down there, in a
tropical setting after months in cold waters with attempted
mutinies, boat casualties, guys going berserk with belaying-
pins; after frostbite, trench foot, hotfoot, chickenpox, small-
pox, bigpox, and all the little poxes that flesh is heir to. We
knew what we were doing when we signed on with Simpson,
mind. Or most of us did. A Simpson production is never a
picnic. You know how it is in movies—the public wants
snowstorms, hurricanes, fires, shipwrecks, floods, bashed-in
heads, blood everywhere. Well, Simpson does all this, but with
handles and with great artistry. In a world where blood is
argument and the bell tolls for rich and poor alike (only with
the rich it has a different tone) Simpson is the boy wonder of
them all. In the places where hombres congregate to talk of
bulls and baseball and dolls and great racehorses and spectacular jags and how Dempsey was the whitest fighter of the
century, and how El Gallo and Juan Belmonte and Josélito
were head and cojones superior to these kids they have
now who louse themselves up for the favours of the first broad
from Hollywood who tosses them a look. In places like Jim
Glennon's or Costellos on Third Avenue, Paddy Kennedy's
Star or the Wig in London, the Lancaster in Paris, or Harry's
in Venice; in places where waiters will give you the world if

they learn that you knew Bob Capa, or in places where
gamblers assemble and remember past coups the way fishermen remember catches, the coup or the catch getting bigger
with each telling, in such places you will see ugly beat-up
pusses shine like a lucky dollar at the mention of Simpson.
And someone will tell you how he shook down a couple of
lilies and placed the proceeds on an eight-to-one winner at
Longchamps and lost it all to some dame he had been shacked
up with; and someone else will tell how, when every major
studio on the Coast had turned down his idea to film
Finnegan's Wake on location in Dublin, he charmed Sol
Bleistein into financing *Death in Acapulco*, which he had
been preparing all along while kidding the others about the
Dublin project. Man, he's a modern da Vinci, but cool. As
a writer said about another great and original director of our
time, the secret of his direction is that it is sensitive and
artistic without being self-consciously arty. There is always
much thought, much *concentration* of thought, behind each
of his shots. But he never hams with a camera, never sacrifices
perception for mere virtuosity. When actually filming,
Simpson is just about the most integrated guy in the business.
But when he's off duty, oh brother!

Take the fishermen. Mind, at first we thought we had the
whole deal wrapped up. But Simpson is smart. You try to
kid him, kid, and, believe me, kid, you soon wonder who is
kidding who and the hell with grammar.

You don't have to twist my arm for me to tell you why we
were there in the first place. I'll tell you for free. We had gone
down to them Budgerigars for shooting final sequences of
Simpson's masterpiece, *The White Whale*. We? Well, I wasn't
there for fun, kid. I'd been hired to write additional dialogue.
For the whale. Yeah, I said the whale. A big, prestige job. I
got a good agent.

So we set out. Pan to a moonless night in damp December.

To a coach roaring down the main London-Southampton road. Inside : a mob of technicians, cameramen, sound-mixers, cement-mixers, good-mixers, bad-mixers, cashiers, footpads, panhandlers, three studio plasterers and a writer, also plastered. We are the advance crew, the spearhead, though one or two others have gone ahead to build whales and soften up the natives with gifts of beads and shaving mirrors and other gewgaws. A second party was due to fly from the same base the next day, a mob consisting largely of actors and stuntmen, plastered or otherwise. Simpson and the star of the film, Gregory Pinch, were travelling separately by way of Paris and Madrid. Boy, do those two love Paris. Boy, do they love Madrid. And, boy, does Paris love them. And, boy, does Madrid love them. And if you go Air France it's champagne, champagne all the way. Shall we continue? Or shall we join the ladies?

We got into a flying-boat, fastened our safety belts, leaned back, and crunched boiled sweets. (Note the eye for insignificant detail, the excruciating plodding over well-worn trails. Kid, I've wrassled with Mister Hemingway, I've wrassled with Mister Saroyan, I've wrassled with Mister Perelman and I'd wrassle with Mister de Maupassant if he was still around.) The craft moved forward. The floats under the wings stroked the water. A technician stroked the air hostess's moustache. Nick stroked the cat. The cat bit Nick and Nick bit the bullet. He's rugged, is Nick.

During the next few hours we dreamed in snatches. Of home. Of palms and camels. Of the whales we had lost at sea during the summer locations off Heligoland. Of time and the river. Of Portugal. Of April in Portugal. And of how it would be down there in the Budgerigars. The Budgerigar, kid, with handles. Win, lose or draw, you can't kill a guy's dreams. And down there there would be another kill; *the final killing of Simpson's long dream of making a whale film.*

It was cold in the aircraft, and we huddled under woollen blankets; damned souls in a green aquatint of hell. Then, gradually, the dawn began to stand up in the east like a swollen tonsil. (Steady, Mack, watch your similes or you'll lose them and then where will you be? Ever seen a writer without his similes?)

People stirred and muttered.

'I'd give anything for a cup of cawfee!'

'I'm frozen!'

'Yeah, it's hell, bub!'

'You said it.'

Scintillating dialogue. Who said TV is killing good talk?

The dawn climbed higher over the map of clouds that obliterated the Iberian peninsula. Then higher. Then higher still. Us in that aircraft watching it. Then, at the tip of Portugal, the cloud formations broke a little and you could see below the white-and-red towns and tiny bullrings and long volcanic hills like strips of leather drying in the new sunlight. Things looked fine down there. Particularly the bullrings. Bullrings look fine whichever way you look at them, even Portuguese bullrings. And we were looking at them from a really fine angle. The composition was great, kid. Simply great.

We began to lose height, dropping lightly to make a feathery landing on the warm-looking December water of the Tagus. The engines stopped roaring. The technician stopped stroking the hostess's moustache. Nick took a powder. The cat sat on the mat. And we all got out and had breakfast ashore while they refuelled the aircraft. Eggs and fundador. Wonderful.

Long distance from Madrid. For me. I took up the receiver.

'Slim?'

'Yeah.'

'John here.'

'Why, you old son of a bitch.'

I shadow-boxed for a minute or two.

'How's the boy?'

'Fine.'

'Listen, kid. I've just been having a nightcap with two or three bullfighters at Chicote's and they tell me there's some of the world's best fishing off the Budgerigars. Big stuff. I want you to fix up all the tackle we need. And bait. Baskets of the stuff. And nose out the best fishermen. Get them on the payroll if necessary. Line it up, kid.'

'Sure, but——'

'Have it all ready for when I arrive. And, kid——'

'Yeah?'

'Don't tell Perdita anything.'

The line went cold. I went back to the breakfast room. I did not say anything to the others. For that matter, the others didn't say anything to me. Then we went back into the flying-boat.

For several hours after refuelling we thrust south, high above cloud-banks. Once, far away over the hazed sea, the giant snow-capped ridges of the Atlas Mountains reared over a world of cloud, and, for a while, you could feel Africa (you could feel the mystery, kid), and then, on our right, we saw the Canary Islands strung across the sun-polished parquetry of the afternoon sea and then we nosed farther south. But mostly it was haze and clouds and occasional naps and Scotch and bottled beer and sliced airways ham on cardboard platters. Real ham. Orson was over in Paris. (Paris, kid. Paris, France.) Then, suddenly over the sea on the starboard side, we saw a long, mountainous stretch of sunbaked land.

'We're there,' someone announced, but brilliantly.

The seaplane flew over a harbour with little ships in and a strip of land covered with square white houses, the land dividing two bays and joining the main island to a smaller one. We flew in between the steep bare hills and turned and nosed gently down in the harbour.

'Holy cow,' someone said. 'It looks exactly like Alcatraz.'

Yeah, I thought, but profoundly. With handles.

That was before the fishermen.

.   .   .   .

It was a big bare brute of an island.

Hills like slag-heaps in coal country overhung the dusty palms and patios, the harbour arm, the narrow Moorish-looking streets. A soft wind from Africa puffed the fine sands of these hills into slanting knives of dust, descending like fine rain across the bay and town. This was the main island of the Budgerigar archipelago. Harsh, primitive, decadent. Backward, too. They make their own Coca-Cola.

We jolted along the waterfront between the Puerto de la Fez and the residential and shopping centres of Los Tropicos. At one point we were held up by a long funeral procession.

'Incredible lu-lot,' Kevin o' the Bog said. 'Mum-moment anybody dies the whole bub-bloody population turns out for the fu-fu-fu-fu—, the burial.'

Kevin was chief fixer of boats and whales. Kevin is Irish. He stutters occasionally.

'How's the whale?' I asked Kevin. He had been there a fortnight getting local ship builders building the new whale.

'In the pup-pink, old boy.'

'Is he seaborne yet?'

'Lord, no. But he's coming along nicely.'

This was to be the last of several whales built for the film. You know how it is with whales. Lose one or two, and what happens? You get the boys to build another. Preferably at the opposite end of the world. Preferably with handles. Big handles. And plenty of them. Only this was to be the last;

the guys who were financing this little old epic had made that quite clear.

Well, we had arrived. And I had a mission. With the fishermen.

.   .   .   .   .

We drove up to the hotel, the usual Babylonian bore. You know, the sort of shack that naturally attracts elderly hypochondriacs with the twitches, fussy women with paid companions, expensive tarts roving around with roving executives, rich tradespeople with arty tutors and massive Swedish maids with goitre, and thin-lipped men with strait-jackets in their suitcases. And then the waiters, looking like refugees from the nearest nuthouse. You know the kind : Lissen, bub, if I were *you* and I think I *yam*. . . . Still, it was a place to rest one's head, and I settled into my monk's cell, stabled my dromedaries, combed my venerable beard, and set off for the port and the taverns where the fishermen were most likely to be drinking the wine of the country.

My researches led me eventually to the Green Dolphin Bar, where you couldn't swing a pickled herring without hitting a pickled fisherman.

There were other experts around also. Two of them, very fat ones, came and sat at my table. I waved them away. They waved back. Fat Budgerigario whores. Grinning all over their pumpkin faces. The two fattest whores I ever seen. Man, they were seismic. When they laughed the whole bar shook.

'Beat it,' I said politely.

The experts laughed and one snapped banana fingers at the waiter. They ordered champagne. They ordered caviare. They ordered toothpicks. I told the waiter to order them away. The waiter shook his head.

'They are lovely señoritas,' he said.

'Okay,' I said. 'But I tell thee that I shall never come to thy joint again.'

'But, señor, that would be terrible. This is a clean, well-lighted place.'

'Then tell these lights of the world to light out.'

The waiter hissed at the fat girls, who got up, jabbering angrily. One leaned over and stubbed her cigarette on my forehead.

'I tell thee, amigo, I do not like it,' I told the waiter. 'Now bring me a bottle of Scottish wikkee. Unopened. With the label clearly apparent.'

'Sí, sí,' the waiter said sadly. 'But the señoritas. We have lovely señoritas.'

'Milk,' I said. 'I clean my teeth in the milk of thy lovely señoritas.'

'They *are* clean, truly.'

'Go, get wikkee.'

'Sí.'

Another expert came over. She was slim, with a Mongolian face, a fringe, and nothing beneath her well-cut dress except flesh. She reminded me of someone I had known somewhere. Someone I had known well, perhaps even married. A bitch. A rich bitch, maybe. But this one was poor. You could tell easily how poor she was. These are things you can always tell.

'You like-a me?' she asked, settling in a chair.

'No.'

'Good. I like-a you too.'

'Go away. I tell thee thou art not my type.'

'Good, good. You buy me champagne?'

'No.'

The girl snapped her fingers. 'Pedro, champagne.'

The waiter came over, grinning. Champagne in one hand. Whisky in the other.

I shrugged, and the waiter poured champagne for the girl. I opened my bottle. We drank.

'You like-a wikkee?' the girl said.

'Sí.'

'I like-a you.'

'Thou art a cheap expert,' I said.

'That is nice. Thou art nice. What is thy name?'

'Zanuck,' I said. 'Darryl F. Zanuck.'

'I am Manolita. You may call me Manoli. I like-a thee.'

'Manoli, tell me one thing.'

'Sí?'

'Who is the greatest fisherman on this island?'

'Fisherman? Whyfore doest thou wish to know of a fisherman? I wouldst rather talk to thee of amore, of love.'

'Sure, but I want to know.'

'Then I will tell thee. Thou art obviously a sportif. I wouldst not take any flannel pesetas on your not liking the bullfight. You like-a, no?'

'I like-a plenty.'

Manoli clapped her hands. 'I knew. It is a brave festival. My sister mucho bravo. She bullfighter.'

'That is bad,' I said.

'No, good.'

'No, bad. It is bad that a woman should enter the bull plaza and play at man's games. A woman should only play at woman's games.'

'Sí, sí,' Manoli said, squeezing my hand, then pouring champagne. 'Thou hast much wisdom.'

'Now tell me of the fisher,' I said, pouring Scotch.

'Ai, the fisher. It is necessary that you should know of the fisher right away?'

'Sí.'

'Then I tell thee. It is Don Pablo Ruiz Polianski-Smith. He is the chief of all island fishers and he lives on the little island, which we call the Isletta, at the end of the port. He is very proud and sees no one but other fishers.'

'Don Smith. A noble name.'

'He is a mucho fino hombre. Mucho forte. Mucho bambinos.'

The cocks were crowing when I strolled back to the hotel. Strident, angry cocks bred for fighting. Cockfighting is a great sport in the islands. And in the great harbour of Los Tropicos on the central island of the Budgerigars the sound of fighting cocks can be heard all day and all night. That is how it is down there.

I was dozing by the swimpool the following afternoon when the second plane-load arrived. I had telephoned Don Smith and been told he was out fishing. So I decided to laze. All the gang turned up at once. Perdita. Snorts Valentine, the second romantic lead. Rory Punt, Hollywood's starchiest professional Englishman. Connell Connor, the Irish bantam-weight netball champion. King Connell, the poker player. Cedric Donnell, the calypsonian. Jug Ears Magee, Aberdonian character actor. Count Krantz, the Austrian Schuhplattler dancer who plays the cannibal harpooner. Franz Krantz, the other poker player and unit financial hatchet-man. And the usual bunch of lazy mixed-up film kids. In the sunlight Connell Connor looked like a piece of stale bread.

Perdita bit my left ear, but affectionately. Then things began to happen. Perdita produced a bottle of Moët et Chandon, King Connell produced a bottle of Veuve Clicquot, an epileptic waiter with side-burns produced a bucketful of ice, and a gipsy orchestra produced soulful music. We stuck the two bottles in the ice, and I said, 'Hi, kids, have a good trip?' They said they had. With laughter and song. With drinking and cards. King Connell had, as usual, cleaned up a tidy sum at poker, most of which he had thrown into the harbour on landing for the native boys to dive after. You know how film people are with money.

'Love dat water,' Perdita yelled suddenly, and plunged in without stopping to remove her Dior dress and Balenciaga veil. Most of the other kids followed suit, leaving me to watch the champagne cooling. There wasn't much point my going in; I was wearing bathing trunks. Besides, I had sores on my leg where I had been gored by a starlet in Rome.

An English duchess, sitting near me in a bikini, raised her lorgnette and sniffed.

'What riffraff,' she screeched in the kind of over-cultivated voice you usually put out at night with the cat. 'I thought this place was exclusive. I shall take the next boat to Brooklyn.'

'You can't do that, sweetheart,' I snarled from the far corner of my mouth, the near corner being engaged in tearing the tinfoil off a bottle. 'We just hired it to tow our latest whale.'

'Phui,' snorted the duchess, scratching her hairy chest.

It didn't bother me. The sun was shining. The champagne looked good and cool. It was swell just to sit there watching the bottles and seeing Perdita and the rest horsing around in the swimpool.

A flunkey paged Perdita, who slipped out of the water, slipped into a kimono, and slipped off to the phone by the swimpool. A minute or two later she slipped back.

She said: 'They'll be in at four tomorrow.' Turning to me, she said: 'Hows about you opening up the champagne, Slim?'

I did. The cork came out with a satisfactory pop. I passed the glasses round. We drank. We laughed and chattered and drank some more. It was good there by the swimpool, drinking, chatting and laughing. I poured more drink. It was good stuff, wine that sparkled in the afternoon sunlight.

Then we went back into the hotel.

'Have you a minute, Slim?' Perdita asked.

'All the time in the world for you, my love. What is it, child?'

'It's this,' she said as we sat in a wicker settee in the entrance lounge. 'Frankly, John is slightly worried about that last bit of dialogue you wrote for the whale. He thinks you've given it too much to say.'

'Too much! All I did was to knock out a hiccup and write in a couple of burps.'

'Exactly,' Perdita said, wringing out half the swimpool from her skirt. 'John thinks you're overplaying the burps. One should be enough.'

'Two are far more realistic,' I grouched.

'John thinks the opposite. He wants you to exercise more restraint.'

'I've been exercising it without a break, apart from stops at lamp-posts,' I growled.

'Still, you must allow John his say. And I do know his mind pretty well.'

Yeah, sister, I thought, with fishermen.

'I'll think it over,' I gritted.

'That's my baby,' Perdita said happily. 'I knew you'd be reasonable.' She looked at her waterproof watch. 'Say, what time do they start serving dinner around here?'

'Never before nine. Usually any time after ten.'

'Then we've time for a drive. I'd love to see a bit of the island before dat evenin' sun goes down.'

'Okay,' I said. 'Let's go.'

'Just give me time to change my contact lenses,' Perdita said, dashing off and leaving a trail of water behind. Ten minutes later she was back wearing a crinoline and the most gorgeous turban you ever saw outside the chorus of *Kismet*. A bellboy brought me my favourite Norfolk suit, deerstalker hat, tartan socks and green gumboots, and we were ready for the races. It was the champagne really. Such good champagne.

Simpson's fleet of hired cars being lined up outside the hotel, we selected a big Cadillac and in Spanish told the driver, a fat Budgerigario, to take the hill road and go easy over the glaciers. He said no comprende, so we told him again in American and he was off like a bomb, tearing out of the city by way of the cathedral square, the market square, the four square, and all the squares, then past goat stables occupied by the better-class Budgerigarios and over the slag-heap hills and past the cave colonies in the cliff face with women hauling down laundry and the Budgerigario kids playing patsy in the dust. Then the slag-heaps changed to valleys of green vine patches and banana plantations with cactus plants growing along the roadside and black rashes across the fields where the locusts had been. On top of a high peak the driver slowed down and pointed to two white buildings about two miles apart on a nearby hill.

'Sanatorium,' he said, pointing to one and pretending to gasp for air.

The driver then pointed to the other building.

'Locos,' he said, grinning. He twisted his forefinger against the side of his head. He added : 'Busy place. Many dam' film people came here. Make films. Good for trade everywhere.'

'Make a note of the address,' I told Perdita.

'Yeah,' she said. 'I already noted it.'

We drove on. At the top of this peak was a small restaurant from which you could look into a hole, at the bottom of which was a vineyard with a house in the middle.

'Volcan,' the driver said.

I didn't want to scare Perdita but I decided to break the news gently.

'You will have to be brave about this, Wilhelmina,' I said levelly. 'But we're on top of a volcano.'

'Yeah,' Perdita said, equally level. 'Extinct. I read about it in the guide-book.'

The driver pointed to a cactus bush.

'Cacti,' he said. 'You squeeze, they bleed.'

'Cactuses,' I told Perdita. 'Squeeze them and they bleed.'

'Try it,' Perdita said. I could not resist the challenge in her steel-blue eyes.

I squeezed. They bled. That is the kind of cactus you get down there in the Budgerigars.

Perdita shuddered.

'What's wrong?' I asked, but levelly.

'Heap bad symbolism. Plenty, plenty trouble ahead. Cactus reminds Oriental girl of casualties we've had, making this film.'

'Pooh,' I said. 'Three dead. Seventeen injured. That's nothing.'

The girl shrugged. Or was it almost an imperceptible shiver?

'Sorry, Slim. I must be getting chicken.'

'Na, you just need a drink,' I said, putting on a brave face from the selection I carried around in my vest pocket.

We went into the restaurant and ordered Tio Pepe sherries and drank them in the clean air on top of the volcano. It was good, up there on that volcano. Good and clean and wholesome, like moving along the scorched perimeter of a battlefield when the wind is blowing the smells the opposite way. You know how it is on battlefields.

'We must go back, daughter,' I said.

For a moment the girl looked panic-stricken.

'Must we? *Must* we? Can't we stay here for ever? Just the two of us and the Tio Pepe. You telling me about how you toured the bottlefields of Europe and me telling you little white lies. Just us. And baby makes three. *Can't* we?'

I looked at the girl, so soft, so young. And the bullet I got at Austerlitz jumped around in the old wound. And the arrowhead I copped at Agincourt twisted in my thigh. I knew it was time for me to take the rapido over the marshes and join the duckshooters. Or something.

'We must go, daughter,' I said again, trying not to say it roughly. Hell, you know how it is trying to talk after Tio Pepe on the top of a volcano.

We took a different route down, going over dry river-beds with huge boulders with old Budgerigario bums sleeping in the lengthening shadows, past palms and eucalyptus trees, past old women scrubbing and working, moving around out there under the evening sky, inside Latin America, under milk wood, over the odds, round the bend, up the spout, down under, overthere—overthere—overthere—overthere—overthere. Brother, you could feel the mystery there, all right, all right. Up there in those volcanic hills with that girl and that driver, and all those peasants. Down there in those darkling valleys. And then the atmosphere of it all. In one village we saw an old cripple teaching a boy to swing a ragged shirt he was using as a muleta. That was pretty significant. And good and graceful and true. And there were also glimpses of the sea.

Then also the lights of the port, seen from a distance through the dusk.

Then we were driving along the big bay south of the port, the one they call Las Flamenco.

That is where Perdita screamed.

I did not say anything.

Then she screamed again.

But loud and with handles.

Well, you know how it is with a woman screaming. I clipped her. She bit me. I decided to get on with the scenario and stopped clipping her. She screamed again. Okay, go ahead, scream, I thought, but sadly.

Then the girl stopped screaming, and now she began using other voices, other rooms.

'The fishermen,' she said hoarsely. 'Look.'

'Where?'

'There.'

'Where?'

'There.'

It is necessary for me to record everything as it happened, to tell it true and with Tio Pepe but without handles. That is why I told of the volcano and the cactus and the eucalyptus trees and the old women with their washing. That is why I set down that last dialogue. For that is how people talk in times of stress, or when they share a bed and one has taken all the blankets. Or something. And the main purpose of this story is to give it to you plain, unvarnished and true.

'The fishermen,' Perdita said again, hoarse as an old crow. I stiffened.

'The what?' I said, stalling. This needed careful handling. I would have preferred to have worked this out with my back against the wall in Harry's Bar, not the one in Paris, France, but the one in Venice, Rome.

'The fishermen,' Perdita croaked. 'Look.'

I looked. Yeah, they were fishermen, all right, all right. Fishermen in drunken sleep up against their boats. Scores of them, with nets and tackle. Stinking and dreaming. Dreaming and stinking.

'Step on it, driver,' Perdita shouted. 'The Hotel Casa Mump, rapido.'

'Sí, I step on it rapido,' the driver leered, heading back for the place for the locos.

'No, you dope,' Perdita yelled. 'The hotel, pronto.'

Somehow, we got to the hotel where the production office was. Me softly cursing the fishermen. Knowing they meant trouble, big trouble just then.

It was not so good just then down there in the Budgerigars. Not good at all. Not with all them fishermen around.

．　　．　　．　　．　　．

We took the lift up to the production office on the fifth floor. Or the lift took us. This was in the Casa Mump, and we pushed through the balsa wood partitions and ran smack into this dialogue.

'You're fired.'

'Fine, so I'm fired. So you pay me off and send me home. Fine, I wanna to go home, anyway. I gotta goil in Newark that would make your eyes fall out their sockets.'

'Not so fast. You stay where you are. You been asked to get a couple of smugglers' yachts and, by Goldwyn, you gonna get them.'

'But what with? We run out of money.'

'Hell, what's money. You get the yachts and shadup about money.'

This was Nick La Rodd, the production manager, speaking to his Chinese assistant, Chang.

Seeing us, Nick said, 'Hi, bums, grab yourselves a fistful of Big Berthas and let's have a gabfeast. I'm lonely.'

We said hi, helped ourselves to green cheroots, spat drunkenly into the cuspidor, stashed our six-shooters on the desk, hitched our pink horses to the hitching rack, offered the sheriff a chaw of baccy, and (coming down to earth) sang out :

'What's cooking, pardner?'

La Rodd scratched the back of his bald head with a stockinged foot and (leering at Perdita) said :

'Goulash, the way momma made it back in the old country. Apart from that everything is going fine. We owe money all over the island, and all we got to pay with is flannel pesetas.'

A lush blonde secretary was at that very moment squatting in a corner of the office, making like she was cutting peseta shapes from a huge piece of flannel. But the going was against her. Her eyes were red-rimmed from hours of concentrated cutting (or something) and still there weren't enough pesetas.

That moment I hated La Rodd. Hell, the guy was running a sweatshop in his own office. Back on the coast we operate them in basements, like decent folk.

Just then Kevin o' the Bog rushed in.

'Gug-gug got it,' he yelled. 'A gunboat. A real gug-gug-gug-gug-gunboat. Local admiral has given it to us for the duration provided we feed the cuck-cuck-crew. And I been gug-given a hundred rifles.'

'Good man, Kevin,' La Rodd said, obviously moved. 'I knew I could rely on you. But why the rifles?'

'Shu-shu-shu-shoot shu-shu-shu-sharks,' Kevin said, dancing out of the room.

La Rodd said, 'Okay, Sadie, you can quit cutting flannel for a while. There's a mug of water and a stale biscuit in that trash bin behind you. Get stuck in and build up your strength for the next session.'

'Thank you, Mr. La Rodd,' the blonde said, curtseying gratefully. 'Your worship will never regret the kindness you have shown Bridget the ould applewoman on this blessed day.' (Ya, and I also wrassled with Mister Perelman. How ya making out, Sam? I'll light a candle to *you* the very next time I'm in Galway Bay.)

'Don't give it another thought,' La Rodd said, but magnanimously.

Then Perdita said:

'Lissen, fellas. We gotta move fast. This is a crisis.'

'Ain't everything a crisis?' La Rodd said wearily.

'But you heard what I said. This is a top-priority crisis. We gotta do something about them fishermen.'

La Rodd said: 'Yeah, but *wut*?'

'Guess the only solution is to put them on the payroll,' the girl said.

Enlightenment spread across La Rodd's Breughel-like features.

'I see you're with me, Liberace,' Perdita snapped.

La Rodd shook himself like a dog with fleas.

'Ya, sump'n's gotta give. But not *that*, surely?'

'Lissen, meathead, we gotta put these guys out of action. Get them out of sight before the boss arrives. And how do we do the vanishing trick? By putting them on the payroll and dressing them up as peasants or jockeys or baseball players or something. No, not like any of them. Like bankers, maybe. Or tax inspectors. We could give them Esperanto lessons or teach them how to bake cherry cake. *Anything* to disguise their real occupation. Are you with me, buster?'

La Rodd cried like a little child.

'But there are *hundreds* of them,' he wailed.

'I don't care if there are *thousands*,' Perdita yelled. 'We gotta do it. You know what Johnnie is like about fishing. You know what a pushover he is for any guy with tackle and a tall story. If he sees these characters, you might as well stuff the whale with pig-iron, sink it in the sea, and send the actors home. Because all he'd want to do is to push off with the fishermen and fish.'

La Rodd gulped, but hard.

'Yeah,' he said, all choked up. 'Sadie, quit guzzling your food and get back to work. We'll need a lot of pesetas for this operation.'

He grabbed the telephone.

'Have my car outside in five minutes,' he barked, like a frail Thurber dog. 'First stop, the port. I gotta see some fishermen. Yeah, flathead, fishermen. I'm hongry.'

The strain had been too much. Perdita fainted. I blacked out. Darkness sang in my eye sockets. We drove back to our hotel and, without saying a word, shot to the bar and swallowed a dozen large shots.

Gee, kid, that's cinema.

Vital.

Dynamic.

Crazy as hell.

You should have seen them fishermen down there that night when the news got around. Did the joint start jumping? You could hear them tom-toms beating all over the island. With gold-plated handles.

Oh, those fishermen. Those cute, goddam fishermen.

CHAPTER TWO

The Island

Around five the next afternoon Ernie Sanderson shagged into my room, Suzy Q'd over to my desk, and thumped me on the shoulders. Ernie was Simpson's chief hustler and the unit's peripatetic court jester.

'Having fun, Slim?'

I looked up from my writing; I was having difficulty with those burps. Spacing and timing problems. And then there was the question of artistic restraint.

'Thank God you've arrived.'

'Why, what's the matter?'

'I'm dying of boredom! This place is a flop-house for retired zombies.'

'We'll soon cure that. Where's the bar?'

'I'll show you.'

We went to the bar and Ernie instructed a Castilian idiot boy in the making of a Bloody Mary. There was no vodka, so we made it with gin. The boy made a botch of it and the tomato juice bobbed about like a blood clot on top of the gin. Ernie was too happy to complain.

'Boy, did we have a time in Madrid!' Ernie said. 'You know Chicote's? You seen his library of wines and liqueurs? Rows upon rows, on shelves. Boy, oh boy, you could spend hours in that library, just reading labels. Then John fought a young bull. The crazy bastard went into the ring, took a cape and a sword, and got to work. The bull rushed at him at the speed of an express train. John just stood there and did a few passes with the cape and stopped the bull an inch from his feet. The bull rushed again, and John did the same thing. Boy, did he enjoy himself. You would have thought he'd been doing it for years. By the time he'd made several passes naturales everyone was yelling ole! Boy, was that an occasion!'

'Where was Pinch?'

'Behind the barera.'

'Where were you?'

'Behind Pinch. I know it was only a little bull, but it moved like a cannon ball.'

'What else did you do in Madrid?'

Ernie gulped his Bloody Mary.

'Met bullfighters. Boy, do you know who we met? The guy that broke that story about shaving the bull's horns, remember?'

'Yes.'

'Our first day in Madrid there was a big reception for John and Greg. Later we met this bullfighter. John asked him why he had not been to the reception. He said he had but was too shy to push himself forward. Shy! He once fought six bulls in one afternoon. That was for a big charity fight. Since it was for charity, without fees, none of the other bullfighters could find the time to show up. This bullfighter, who was organising the match, blew his top. Said he would fight all the bulls himself. He did, too. *And* lived.'

'What did John have to say about that?'

'He asked the guy if he slept well on the night after the fight. The answer was yes, magnifico. John said: And the night before? No sleep at all, the bullfighter said.'

'Have another Bloody Mary,' I said. 'To the bullfighter.'

'I'll drink to that guy any time,' Ernie said.

The Dublin sportsman, who had joined us for a drink,

said : 'Did you ask him what his cojones were like after he'd fought six bulls?'

'He wasn't touched,' Ernie said. 'He fought with great skill. I'm sure they're intact. The guy has five fine kids.'

'Did Pinch just stand by while Simpson fought the bull?' I asked.

'Oh, he came into the ring once and slapped the little bull on the ass. Then he stepped back behind the barera again.'

'At least he's game.'

'Oh, he's game,' the Dubliner said.

'What else did you do in Madrid?' I asked again.

'Oh boy, you should have seen the dancers. We saw some Flamenco dancers that were out of this world. Boy, they danced for hours. It was terrific. Then we went to Toledo and saw the El Grecos.'

'What were they like?'

'You better ask John. He was bowled over. There were thirteen paintings in that room. You know the place, inside the house where El Greco died? The joint hasn't changed for centuries. The paintings are there on the walls just as if they was waiting for him to come back and put a few extra strokes to them. Boy, you couldn't get Simpson out of that room for an hour. He just gazed and gazed at the goddam pictures without saying a word. Get him to tell you about it.'

'I will. Where is he now?'

'Sleeping. He'll come straight to this bar when he's wakened. Boy, those El Grecos.'

We drank some more Bloody Mary. After a while, I said, 'God, I wish I'd gone to Madrid with you and John.'

'Never mind. We'll have a lot of laughs down here.'

'Yeah, but I would like to have been with you when you saw the Grecos at Toledo.'

'God, they were good,' Ernie said.

'There aren't any Grecos down here, though.'

'No, I guess not. But what are the women like?'

'Uninhibited.'

'Really? Well, that's swell.'

'Another Bloody Mary?'

Ernie looked at his watch.

'No, I've cables to send off. We're dining with Simpson as soon as he wakes.'

'Then better not let him wake too soon,' I said. 'They don't begin serving dinner before nine. And that's considered early.'

'Is that so? Well, see you later.'

Simpson had not appeared when Ernie returned to the bar. Ernie sat down and we talked for a while about circuses and about lion tamers. A blonde on a high stool against the bar was playing a guitar. A Latin type stood beside her, holding her drink and listening as she brushed her fingers lightly over the guitar strings. We started talking about lions and tigers.

'Who was that guy, who made the lions do anything he wanted?' Ernie said, snapping his fingers.

A familiar voice said: 'Clyde Beatty, kid. Hello, Slim, having fun?'

Simpson loomed over us, grinning. He wore a brown corduroy suit and moccasin footgear with golden foxheads. A red choker hung loose around his neck, cowboy fashion.

'Hello, John,' I said. 'Let me get you a drink!'

Simpson sat at our table. Perdita joined us.

'Yes, sir,' Simpson said with a happy grin. 'Clyde Beatty. He sure knows how to handle cats.'

We talked a while more about circuses, then I said:

'I hear you had a wonderful time in Madrid.'

'Simply great, Slim. What is that you're drinking?'

'They're supposed to be Bloody Marys.'

'I'll try one.'

We got into the dining-room around ten. The place was

packed and we sat at a long table, reasonably clear of the orchestra. The blonde and the Latin had joined us, and Pinch and Perdita completed the party. I sat next to Simpson and we talked about horses and Ireland. Then I heard Ernie telling the Latin about the Flamenco dancers in Madrid.

'They are out of this world,' he said. 'John said Goltz would have loved them. I guess Goltz would have put them under contract immediately.'

Goltz is just about the biggest producer in Hollywood.

'Not without me he wouldn't,' the Latin said. 'I check on all that for him.'

'Goltz would have snapped them up without consulting you,' I said.

The blonde grinned.

'Tell me about the island, Slim,' Simpson said soothingly. 'Have you explored it yet?'

'I been to the top of a volcano. There's a vineyard in the crater.'

'Is there really, kid? You don't say.'

'You can get some damn fine sherry at the little shack overlooking the crater.'

'Tell me about Los Tropicos, Slim,' Simpson said. 'What are the whorehouses like?'

The blonde giggled. The Latin looked startled.

'What's that you said, Mr. Simpson?' the Latin asked.

'I asked, what are the whorehouses like?' Simpson repeated, leaning forward and smiling courteously. He turned to me inquiringly.

'So far as I can tell, they're pretty good,' I said. 'There's a simpatico Negro in one of the clip joints who looks after everyone, as a sort of dragoman. He likes the clients and the girls equally. He told me about one place that seems to be tops. It's called the Casa Maria.'

'Ah *ha*?' Simpson considered the information. 'The Casa
Maria, ha? We must make our devotions there sometime,
Slim.'

'You bet,' I said.

The orchestra started playing the song from *Montmartre*,
one of Simpson's most successful films.

I said :

'I wish I had gone along with you to see the El Grecos at
Toledo.'

'You'd have loved them, Slim. They were great. Simply
great.'

'I've seen reproductions, of course.'

'There was a feel—about that room—that's quite—indes-
cribable,' Simpson said, spacing the phrases. 'The way he got
the faces of these apostles, by Gard! We also went to the
church where they have El Greco's painting of a funeral,
you know the one?'

'Sure.'

'You remember the bishops? Proud as hell. Arrogant
bastards. Gard, the way he caught those bishops.' Simpson
chuckled. 'Why, the man painted a *sacrilege*.'

El Greco seemed very clear to me as he said that.

After supper, we stood on the patio smoking, watching the
black palm silhouettes, not speaking. I thought about the
dummy whale that was being put together in the harbour and
this reminded me of Heine's words : 'Everything bears within
itself an impulse to strive after a higher degree of divinity,
and that is the great I am of progress throughout all Nature!'
I thought of Simpson's determination to get his film done his
way, and felt good and high and progressive.

Turning to the Indonesian girl, Simpson said : 'Will you
book me a call to Los Angeles for seven tomorrow, Perdita?'
He gave a number. When the girl was gone he said quietly :
'How's the fishing going, kid?'

'It needs a day or two to set up,' I lied quickly. 'I'm seeing one of the top guys tonight.'

'Well, hustle it, kid. Good night.'

He walked briskly into the hotel.

* * * * *

Perdita and some of the mob piled into a car with me and we drove to the port. The streets were almost deserted. The houses looked poor and quiet. Many people were already asleep. We found a place called the Angry Coconut. Our party had barely stepped into the place before we were surrounded by girls. Girls in silk blouses. Girls with clownish lipstick. Girls who winked and leered like Dietrich in *The Blue Angel*. And a small Moorish half-caste with large dark eyes and marvellous eyelashes, aged about eighteen, who had a remote, indrawn kind of dignity. Perdita made the whores feel at ease by admiring their bracelets and dresses and buying them drinks and telling them about the latest designs from Paris. Ernie and I stayed at the bar, but I kept seeing the Moorish girl. Perdita danced with an actor. Then I danced with Perdita. I got the band to play 'April in Portugal' and Perdita and I danced. But it wasn't quite right for us, and as soon as the band stopped we hurried back to the bar. Then the Moorish girl and I were sitting together on high stools against the bar, drinking whisky. She drank it quickly, clipping me as fast as she could. A nice Irish girl serving at the bar, Karen, interpreted for us in basic clipjoint.

'She's a nice girl,' Karen said of the Moor. 'Very clean. Her name is Raquel.'

'We sit at table?' Raquel asked after a while. I nodded and she clapped her hands proudly and summoned a waiter who looked exactly like Stephen Spender.

'Table for two,' Raquel commanded. 'Dos.'

The waiter led us to a table near the dance floor.

'Champagne?' Raquel said.

'Whisky,' I told Spender.

'Whisky?' Spender looked puzzled.

'Sí, dos whisky.'

The waiter made a disgusted face and left.

'Try that again and I'll throw thee into the orchestra,' I told Raquel gently.

Raquel smiled a smile that would have melted the snows of Kilimanjaro.

'I like-a you,' she said. 'Let us dance.'

We danced and immediately Raquel got to work on behalf of the orchestra.

'You like that they play something for us?'

'No.'

'Special, for me?'

'No.'

Raquel shrugged, and we danced and we sat and we danced and we sat and then we went back to the bar. When I told her I was looking for Don Smith, Raquel said she would take me to see him that very night. She explained that she could not leave before three. I said, hell, that would be too late, surely. But she said no, and leave it to her, and now let us have that champagne.

We went to the same table and I ordered champagne. Spender smiled largely. Raquel smiled largely. We were very happy.

'I like-a you,' Raquel said.

'I like-a you.'

'Mucho.'

'Sí, mucho.'

'Mucho, mucho, mucho,' Raquel said.

'Let's dance,' I said.

The orchestra was in bad shape.

'Tell the orchestra to play something for you,' I said.

Raquel looked very happy.

'You like-a "Besse-Me"?'

'Mucho,' I said.

Raquel romped over to the orchestra like a small girl at a party, dragging me along with her. She spoke a few excited words and the orchestra leader also began to look happy. A minute later they were blaring out 'Besse-Me Mucho', particularly the trumpeter, who followed us around the floor as we danced. Raquel really danced wonderfully, happily, and when it was all over and I gave the orchestra a few pesetas her happiness was a joy to watch. You know how it is with whores.

A Norwegian sailor came to our table and asked Raquel to dance. She pretended not to understand.

'Scat,' I said.

'I was dancing with her earlier,' the Norwegian said.

'Then you should have taken better care of her,' I said.

'I saw this one first.'

'Scat,' I said again, showing teeth.

The sailor went, and I took Raquel and we danced, and then it was four and everyone began to leave. Perdita and the mob had left long ago.

'Now I take you to meet Don Smeet,' Raquel said.

We said good night to Karen and took a taxi to a native restaurant, with Moors and Arabs and poor Budgerigarios eating. Raquel clapped her hands and ordered from the fat proprietor. I asked for a bottle of good red wine, and we sat and drank the wine happily whilst waiting for our food. When it arrived—a mountainous yellow rice paella with shiny red pimentos and squid and octopus and bits of lobster —we fought into it with forks and fingers, enjoying each mouthful. Two sad thin guitar players with flat sad eyes and long unhappy fingers came from a far corner, where they had been playing softly, and stood by our table, staring mournfully at Raquel.

'You want that they play?' she asked.

'Of course,' I said.

Raquel nodded curtly, and without any change of expression the thin brothers of the guitar drew up two chairs and began coaxing and caressing their instruments, tuning, cocking their ears close to the vibrations of the strings. Then they began to play, softly, with great restraint, and Raquel held my arm and we listened to the guitarists' playing. Sometimes I would pour them a slop of wine and they would sip a little, mutter to one another through the vibrations of their strings, and go on playing.

'Tell them to play with more excitement,' I told Raquel.

She spoke to them in Spanish. The brothers looked flatly at me; then, very slowly, at their strings. They made more vibrations, sounds as fierce and sharp as the wind through the palms outside. Raquel sat close to me, holding my arm, and we listened to the new wild vibrations. The brothers were miles and centuries away from us, in a black bright world of inspired vibrations, and the café was still and everyone was listening. When the brothers stopped it was like the tearing away from love. People began slowly to drift away. Then the door opened and a blue-jowled giant lurched in. Seeing me, he came over and stood by the table, swaying like an oak in a storm. His breath was so vinous and heavy that it would have taken ten men to lift it and carry it out.

'Hey, you der,' the giant growled, 'you get outta here, white trash. Dis is my table.'

'Right now it's mine,' I drawled.

'Ja, iss dot so? Yumping yimminy, I teach you to keep your nose clean.' And before I had time to wipe my nose the ape-man had picked up a heavy table and crashed it down over my ears.

I woke on the pavement. Raquel was holding a bottle of fundador in one hand and waving back a crowd of curious

Budgerigarios with the other. I let some of that liquor trickle down the desert highway of my throat.

'Let's get out of here,' I croaked.

'Sí,' Raquel said. 'A taxi is waiting round the corner. Can you walk?'

I could, although every step I took felt like being pelted with wet sandbags.

In the taxi I said: 'Who was that big baboon that hit me?' Raquel looked sad.

'That was the man you were looking for. Don Pablo Ruiz Polianski-Smith. And he say he no stoppa go out fishing like the others. You come-a my house?'

'No,' I said, but tersely. 'Tell the driver to go to my hotel, rapido.'

'Sí,' Raquel said unhappily. 'Rapido.'

CHAPTER THREE

The Squall

I SLUMPED INTO my cot and slept for two hours. Waking, I heard Cedric Donnell's rich rum-stained voice singing an old slave lament. With the arrival of the second unit there had been a reshuffle of rooms. Kevin asked if I would share the self-contained little suite that made up rooms one and two at the end of the ground-floor corridor. Cedric was in room one. Kevin assured me that it was fu-fu-fu-fairly quiet at that end. This was an important factor with me. Our row of rooms, on garden level, was fast becoming known as Cell Block 11. So far there had been no riots, but there were times when it was hard to concentrate on writing with only a wall between you and characters like the ones you are apt to find on a John Simpson location. And I wanted to concentrate on getting that dialogue right.

'Cedric likes to sing, though,' Kevin had added doubtfully.

'That won't bother me,' I told him. 'I'm a pushover for calypsos in the bath.'

I was soon glad that I had moved. Cedric was fun from the start; and he is a splendid singer.

Now, on waking, I lifted the house phone and ordered my usual breakfast of mashed bananas and rum. By the time I had got through this, and the first cigar of the day, Cedric had gone off to work. I went to the bathroom and took a long, healing shower. The water drumming down on the holes in

my head made me feel like a boy again, like that time I fell
off a cliff when I was trying to peek into a gull's nest.

I put on a pair of heather mixture plus-fours, sandals, a
check shirt and coonskin hat and sauntered into the hotel
foyer just in time to join Simpson and Perdita as they were
setting out for the port. They were filming in the bay on the
other side of the harbour, and we were all very excited about
making a start on this new location. So much so that Simpson
could not keep off the subject of my special assignment.

'Have you managed to get in touch with that—guy—I
was telling you about, Slim?' he asked, puffing a cigar-smoke
screen between us and Perdita as we drove up to the jetty.

'Yeah,' I said. 'I did contact him.'

'How did it go, kid?'

'We didn't get much of a chance to sort things out, yet. But
I aim to see him again.'

'Who's this you're talking about?' Perdita asked sharply.

'Nobody important, honey,' Simpson said smoothly. 'Just
a guy Slim knows who wants to make me a tropical suit for
when I go on safari in India.'

Perdita looked grim but did not say anything.

'I think *Animal Farm* is brilliant satire,' Simpson said
chattily. 'As good as anything since Swift.'

'George was a great fan of Swift,' I said. 'Not when he was
actually writing, of course.'

'Of course,' Simpson said seriously. 'Then he was a fan of
George Orwell.'

I nodded. After all, Paderewski once played the piano.
The car drew up at the end of the jetty and a launch took us
out to one of the tugs.

The wind was fresh, tearing at handfuls of sea like a delin-
quent child on a marijuana jag in a sheep pen. Though we
were still in the harbour, the tug was rolling viciously.

Now, if you should ever plan to visit the Budgerigars there

is something you should know : You can't trust the Budgerigar sun. Especially if your business is with the sea. The sun may be laughing its head off in a sky as blue as a girl's dress, yet the sly swell and the undertow of tides can be upsetting as a mid-Atlantic storm. And whenever the sun ducks into a cloudbank, your boat goes off on a cosmic drunk. So when Simpson stepped into a rowboat, one of the small whaleboats used in the film, it was quite a hazardous manœuvre.

Rory Punt was to be photographed at sea in this boat, heading towards the whale. Already aboard with him were two stuntmen rowing, Pia Viertel, the continuity girl, Ozzie Harris, the chief cameraman, with two camera assistants. The assistants were squatting on a small metal platform fixed to the stern of the boat. The camera was under a square glass waterproofed case. The cameramen were *not* waterproof; whenever the stern of the boat dipped, their backsides plunged into the sea. Now Simpson was also sardined in this crazy cockleshell, and a second later the rowboat bounced away from the side of the tug. I watched them for several minutes as they rowed towards the harbour mouth, the small boat getting smaller and sometimes disappearing altogether behind the waves. Then I went below, where half a dozen stuntmen were lying on the heaving bunks, listening to King Connell talking.

'So he married the frigging girl,' King was saying. 'He's saved up for three years for a down payment on the house, so he marries. Pah, I'm a Simpson man myself. Paddle your own canoe—that's Simpson's philosophy and it's mine, too. Yep, John Simpson is a very lonely man and so is John King Connell. That's the way it is with all artists. Basically, we're a lonely breed. And we don't give a goddam for anyone !'

'Put a sock in it, will you ?' a stuntman pleaded.

'Yeah, give your ego a rest,' another said.

Turning to me, Connell said, 'Hey, cocker—how much do you pay in the whorehouses?'

'Two-fifty pesetas,' I said, teasing him.

Connell's face turned blue. 'You hear that, fellers?' he shouted. 'A blackleg. The legitimate price is seventy-five pesetas and *no* tips.'

'But I only use the best whorehouses, Connell.'

'Ah, go bake a cake.'

'I think I'll go back on deck for a breath of fresh, wholesome air,' I said coldly.

'We could use some of it down here,' one of the stuntmen growled sympathetically.

'Why not help yourself to a lungful?' I suggested generously. 'It's free, and it clears the mind wonderfully.'

'We're worn out, brother,' a stuntman moaned.

'*And* deafened,' another said, looking at Connell.

'You should try my whorehouse,' I said gently. 'The pimp there wakes you with a cup of coffee and a biscuit!'

'Two-fifty pesetas,' Connell said disgustedly. 'I could buy me a whole block of bagnios for that kind of money.'

I climbed up the swaying ladder to the deck and found that we had moved to the harbour entrance and were rolling on the confluence of sheltered water and open sea. The wind was stronger, and ahead of us lay Simpson's flagship, the *Fishbite*, rolling and spinning like a stick in a whirlpool.

Our tug heaved and lunged in the green sea and the land tilted and kept slipping out of sight. In the distance you could see the cockleshell rowboat battling up against the incoming waves like a leaf in a flooded gutter. The unfortunate cameramen trailed behind, waist-deep in water. The sun was still shining, between cloudbanks, but the sea was getting rougher each minute. The actors were huddled in a corner, shivering.

'They're crazy to try and shoot anything in that sea,' Snorts Valentine said.

Cedric, Connell, Connor and Jug Ears looked grim. They remembered the gales in the North Sea, when Snorts broke a leg, and Punt injured his spine jumping into pitching boats.

'We really should have some boat drill before tackling this stuff,' Jug Ears said fussily.

Shortly after this, the small boat straggled back to the tug. A message was sent to the *Fishbite* to return to port, and Simpson went on the bridge and talked earnestly to the skipper. A few moments later the tug headed for the open sea. I joined Pinch against the swaying starboard rail near the stern of the tug. The world's biggest romantic box-office success was reading Proust.

'Choppy enough for you?' I asked.

Clouds had moved across the sun and the coastline had turned grey and drizzly.

'You get used to it,' Pinch said, grinning through the old-fashioned beard he had grown for his part as skipper of the whaling ship. Unlike the other actors, he seemed to be enjoying himself.

'This is pretty tame after the North Sea, what?' I said.

'It suits me. I love ships.'

We watched the sea for a minute.

'John has been telling me about Toledo,' I said.

'It was quite an experience.' The actor stared into the sea, watching the waves affectionately.

The tug was in open water now, rolling on a great swell that hid the coast most of the time.

'Yes, quite an experience,' Pinch repeated. 'It's a surprising place. After all, you've seen paintings of it and there it is, clinging to the rocks exactly as you knew it would be. Yet when you actually *walk* along those hot narrow streets, and stretch out your hands and touch the old walls of the houses on either side of you—when you actually *feel* all those centuries of sun trapped inside the stones—boy, it gets you. You

4—TCK

can almost see El Greco and Cervantes walking ahead of you. God, what a place !'

'Madrid must have been fun also,' I said.

'It was great,' Pinch said, his giant body swaying easily with the roll of the tug. 'One of the wonderful things about being—' he balked at the word—'a film star, is the number of fine people you meet whom you wouldn't otherwise run into. This bullfighter. God, what a guy. We went to his house and saw his collection of souvenirs and photographs. John was in raptures. He asked him to sign one of the photos. The guy was delighted. He signed one for me as well. I wanted one, but I would never have dreamed of asking. That's where John scores; he'll always go that one step farther.'

Waves were rushing over the decks, the shore was far away, and the sea was racing round in huge dizzying circles. The tug seemed to bend like a rubber toy under the pressure of the waves. Then a big wave smacked over Pinch and me, soaking us.

'We'll have to move from here,' Pinch said.

We staggered over to a wooden cabin amidships and clung on. Actors and stuntmen were helping the crew lash bits of the ship together. Pia Viertel, a solid Britannia in a wind-cheater, was sitting calmly on a wooden table.

'You certainly have fun on these locations,' I said, joining her.

Pia grinned. 'I suppose that is why they have me along. I'm supposed to be tough.'

Pia had been with Simpson since his first big commercial hit, *The Jungle Trader*.

I should have remained by the cabin, for, suddenly, under our joint weight, the table collapsed. We landed squarely on the deck where the water was slopping around the stern. A stuntman threw the broken bits of table overboard and we lurched over to the cabin. Just in time. For now a great wave lifted a whale rowboat two yards above where we had been sitting, and dashed one end over the side. It trailed along in the sea whilst crew and stuntmen struggled to rehook it, working waist-high in water whenever the stern dipped under the waves. They struggled to right the boat but it continued to trail over the side. Whenever the stern of the tug dipped sideways and scooped in more water, the rowboat rose beyond their grasp and swept back towards the deck, missing their faces by inches. Finally, a stuntman pulled a knife from his belt and cut the rope, and a big wave caught the boat and carried it out of sight.

'God, this is crazy,' Snorts Valentine said savagely. 'Haven't we taken enough punishment? Why doesn't the crazy bastard turn back? It's impossible to get pictures in this sea.'

Simpson, on the bridge, was trying to get us round the rocky coastline into quieter waters. The harbour lies on one side of the strip joining the main island to La Isletta. On the other side is the Bay of Las Flamenco. Sometimes the water outside the harbour is calmer than in the bay, or the other way, depending on the prevailing wind. Acting on the skipper's advice, Simpson was trying to get us into the calmer waters of Las Flamenco.

But we did not know that then. We clung to bits of ship and watched the water rising around our legs, wondering what Simpson was doing at sea when it was so manifestly impossible to take pictures.

'We're turning,' Cedric said suddenly.

I looked round. We were moving steadily back towards the harbour.

'About time too,' Jug Ears muttered.

'You can say that again,' Snorts snarled.

As if to mock us, the sun came out as we neared the harbour, and the wind dropped. We anchored near the jetty.

Simpson was climbing into a launch when Tom Pegg, a former prizefighter, said :

'There's boxing at the local fight arena tonight, John.'

Simpson's face crinkled into an interested smile.

'There *is*?' he said delightedly. 'A boxing match? We must go to that, Tommy.'

Turning to me, he snarled : 'You're coming too. And bring the fisherman along with you. This kind of weather is too good to miss. So quit stalling around and let's make a start, even if it means working all day and fishing all night. Okay, Perdita, I'm just coming, honey.'

CHAPTER FOUR

The Fight

PINCH, COUNT KRANTZ and I had lunch brought up to us on the bridge as we waited for instructions from Simpson. Over red Budgerigar wine, salad, meat, salami, cheese and tangerines, the Count, an expert horseman, talked at length about Colonel Podhajsky who rides the Lippizans, and about the late General Harry Chamberlain of Fort Bliss, Texas, who headed the Army jumping teams, and about riding over the Andes.

'I wrote to Chamberlain from Vienna,' Krantz said dreamily. 'He wrote back saying, come out. So I went to Texas and rode with him. He was a fine horseman.'

'Where is John?' I asked.

'Asleep,' the Austrian said phlegmatically. 'Or tormenting his friends.'

Pinch said : 'Is it true, that a good salami sausage must have a bit of donkey meat in it?'

The Count scowled through his cannibal's make-up.

'Yes.'

'Have you ever eaten locusts, Count?' I asked.

'Several times. They are very nice fried.'

Pinch had his Proust—it was *Swann's Way,* volume three —beside him.

'You've got some great reading there,' I said, spitting tangerine pips into the oily sea.

'Great.'

'I never got round to reading him,' I said. 'I always think of his writing as one continuous work, and so I keep putting it off until I find time to read the lot.'

'You can start anywhere and still enjoy it,' Pinch said.

'You think so?' I said. 'His being a fruit has also put me off. I felt he couldn't possibly create a complete world, as Balzac did. I felt there would be many gaps.'

'You just don't want to read Proust,' Pinch said, grinning.

'That must be it,' I said. You know how it is making the literary chitchat with actors.

We had still heard nothing from Simpson after we had eaten, so Pinch decided to finish for the day. I drove back to the hotel with him. There was no sign of Simpson. Pinch removed his make-up, and we went to the pool and lay on towels and looked at the women in bikinis and talked. Three bronzed, muscular bath attendants, each one the image of Brando, were doing stunts in the water. They were showing off like puppies for the women in bikinis.

'Proust would have gone for those boys in a big way,' I said.

Pinch pulled a wry face. After a while he plunged into the water. He swam splendidly, far better than any of the Brandos, who watched with open respect as, quite unconsciously, the actor outswam them. Then I dived in and kicked around and swam underwater, but I came out before the sores on my leg got too soft. Then Pinch got bored with swimming and we rested on our towels in the sun and Pinch told me how he had first started swimming as a kid of three at Monterey. That was before his Broadway début, as Lear. As we talked I had fun watching the women in bikinis watching Pinch with starved eyes while their fat husbands and boy friends slept.

Shortly before sundown I returned to my room and put on

a gaberdine suit, red shirt, goloshes and fedora hat, and went
to the bar, where I joined Snorts Valentine and Bert Plumb,
the make-up director, for a Scotch and soda. They were still
sore about the morning.

'Joking apart, we should never have gone out in that
weather,' Snorts said.

'It was madness,' Bert agreed. 'Sheer madness.'

'As if we hadn't had more than a gutful. He could have
finished the goddam picture in a tank, with rubber actors.'

'I fail to see the sense of it at all,' Bert said.

Snorts said : 'I don't think it will add a thing to the picture.
This passion for realism can be overdone. Judas priest, it isn't
even *box*-office.'

Bert said : 'You're right. Who are the people who go to the
movies? Women and kids. What woman or kid will want to
see a movie about a bearded guy chasing a goddam whale?
It's hardly sporting. Whales are lovely, helpless, harmless
things. It's cruel the way guys sneak up on them and stick
harpoons in their backs. It's mean and dirty. And, you're
right, it isn't box-office.'

Snorts said : 'We shouldn't have gone out this morning.
Jesus God, that was plain crazy.'

I listened a while longer, then joined Simpson. Around
eight o'clock we set out for the boxing. We stopped off on the
way to watch the pelota games. There were five of us :
Simpson, Perdita, Pinch and Connell Connor. Perdita was
wearing a gold and shell-pink sari. Simpson explained the
game to us.

'They play it a lot in Mexico,' he said.

'What are the balls made of?' Perdita asked.

'Horse-hide,' Simpson said. 'They're hard. Very hard.'

Simpson beamed and added : 'It's a hard ball. Whatever it
hits, it breaks. If it hits your arm, it breaks your arm. If it hits
your head, it breaks your head.'

The thought made him very happy and his thin long body shook with secret mirth. We had a drink at the bar of the pelota hall before going in to watch the games. The usual crowd of women lined up, staring at Pinch with naked bedroom eyes.

Simpson turned to me and said: 'When is the fisherman coming?'

I said: 'He couldn't make it. He's out fishing.'

Simpson said: 'Kid, if you're stringing me along I'll beat your brains out.'

He turned and smiled at a Budgerigar fan, and signed an autograph book.

The pelota was dull. The players wore white shirts and pants and played behind a wire cage. They knocked the balls backwards and forwards against the walls, using long hooked baskets strapped to their arms. They looked like cricketers.

There were two teams: red and blue. The official matchmaker refused to take any bets on the favourites, the reds. So I placed twenty-five pesetas on the blue team. Simpson bet Pinch a thousand pesetas that the reds would win. The blues lost and Pinch handed Simpson a thousand-peseta note. It became even more boring, so we moved on to the fight arena.

.   .   .   .   .

This was much more fun. We arrived a few minutes before the fights began. It was a fine place, with rough wooden benches rising to the roof and a small, fourteen-foot ring and bright arc lamps. The crowd might have come straight from Central Casting. There were fat Latin faces, lean Latin faces, faces with gold teeth, and faces with narrow 'Cisco Kid moustachios. And the noise they made was the noise a fight crowd makes any place in the world.

Our seats were by the ringside. When the crowd saw Pinch

there was a sudden hush, followed by excited hand-clapping. But the crowd soon got back to being a fight crowd, shouting and arguing and shadow boxing and getting good and mad. It really was a good fight crowd, considering they were mostly Budgerigarios.

Pinch being there continued to send waves of excitement through the crowd. You could feel it from the way people kept looking across whenever they caught themselves in some exhibitionistic performance. Pinch gave an edge to their jokes, their hand-waving, their arguments. A boy in militiaman's uniform started a drunken fight with two doorkeepers and was bounced, staring wildly at Pinch as he was hurtled through the exit. Two opposing packs, led by cheer-leaders wearing their white shirts loose over their pants, began yelling like maniacs. Even before the fights started the packs were howling. But they would break off self-consciously whenever they remembered that Pinch was there, and giggle apologetically.

The first two fights were dull. The fighters were lightweights, poor underfed island kids fighting for pesetas. They fought pluckily, but badly. I don't think they had ever heard of, or seen, a straight left in their lives; and they fought jerkily, using queer little hooks and uppercuts that rarely connected. The third fight was between a conceited-looking fair-haired boy in pink satin pants, and a thin kid. As with all the fights that night, there was much preliminary limbering up and sham jabbing at shadows. Their seconds took a long time to fix the gloves, then there was more strutting around and pulling at invisible chest-expanders. Only after much consideration did they move towards each other after the bell tinkled. The conceited kid was a complete ham, winking at a girl, waving at his cheer pack, looking with a melodramatic sneer at the thin kid, and nodding with exaggerated confidence whenever his seconds whispered to him. Most of the house was rooting for him, though.

Simpson and Pinch were having thousand-peseta bets on each fight. First Simpson would pick a boy, then it would be Pinch's turn. Simpson obviously disliked the cocky kid, but it was his turn to pick a fighter and he placed his money on him. The thin boy fought badly from the start. Then, in the second round, he lay down in the ring and *cried*. The cocky kid had tapped him lightly on the head, a blow that could not have hurt a baby. But the thin boy had had enough. He lay down on the canvas like an anæmic baby and cried and cried. The cocky kid kept dancing around, blowing through his nostrils, waving his fists. But the thin kid refused to move. He lay there for a long time, ignoring everyone, his knees drawn up like a fœtus. Then he crawled slowly through the ropes and wandered in a daze to the dressing-rooms, still crying. The crowd did not take it out of him. They applauded the cocky kid, but there was no excitement or admiration in their applause.

Simpson was disgusted.

'He quit,' he said in astonishment. 'He just quit.'

He looked stunned.

After a while he said; 'He was just a bum. Just a lousy little bum,' and, shaking off the memory, began to discuss the betting on the next fight with Pinch.

The next two fights were also dull, but Simpson watched them keenly. My attention wandered. To Perdita's Slav-Oriental-Irish features. To Connell Connor's bashed-in face. ('Yes,' Simpson had once said, 'Connell got his wrinkles honestly.') To Pinch's shrewd eyes surrounded by the absurd beard. To the gentle Budgerigario faces, soft and corrupt, but momentarily savage whenever something happened in the ring. Then I settled back, prepared to yawn my way through the main bout.

This was between a noted champion from Spain and the best fighter in the Budgerigars, a youngster from the mountain town of Peror. There were no programmes and I do not have their names, but I disliked the champ as soon as he showed up in the ring with the red and yellow Spanish national colours draped round his middle like a ribbon under an Easter egg. He swaggered in a good eight minutes before his opponent, grinning like a mandrill and flashing his eyes conceitedly over a squat nose and thin stupid moustache. One of the seconds brought him a chair and he sat there grinning, letting the adulation of the crowd wash over him like a foam bath. Fighters like that always make me want to climb into the ring and wipe the silly grins off their ugly mugs.

It was Pinch's turn to initiate the betting. Including his pelota losses, he was six thousand pesetas down, and he studied the champ carefully.

Simpson said : 'Let's raise the stakes to ten thousand, shall we, Greg?'

'Sure,' Pinch said. 'Anything you say.'

They waited for the boy from Peror to appear. He entered at last, a stocky peasant with huge ox eyes and a welt-flattened nose. He was not quite such a ham as the Spanish champion, but he did his share of bowing to various parts of the arena. Both fighters did a big act with the gloves, weighing them, peering inside them, fussing like old maids about the way they were laced. When the bell tinkled the champ reluctantly removed his sash, and the local boy stepped uneasily forward.

'I back the champ,' Pinch said.

'Okay,' Simpson said. 'Fine.'

Twenty seconds after the bell went the Spaniard charged in and smacked the Budgerigario hard round the ears. He followed with half a dozen quick jabs at the heart, carried the rest of the round with ease. There was nothing faked about the punishment and pain he inflicted on the Budgerigario, and at the end of the round the champ swaggered to his corner, rolling confidently on his heels like a sailor on shore leave. The Budgerigario moved to his corner in a daze and accepted the worried ministrations of his seconds with doglike gratitude. By the middle of the second round the fight was as good as over. The Budgerigario's legs sagged and his face would not have looked out of place in a slaughter-house.

Then, from out of his bloody agony, his peasant eyes rolled towards Simpson and were caught and held there. In that instant before going down for what seemed like being the last time, the Budgerigario turned with shame towards us. Perhaps he was looking for Pinch, but it was Simpson's eyes he caught. I don't know what Simpson did to the kid, but, sitting close to him, I saw a positive message of eyes flash between him and the fighter. It didn't galvanise the Budgerigario. He did not instantly snap into powerful action, or make a spectacular recovery, as they do in hack boxing stories. *But he didn't go down.* His legs sagged and the Spaniard continued to beat him unmercifully, yet somehow he stayed that round.

No one else had noticed what had happened—certainly not the champ, whose back was to Simpson at the time. And it didn't particularly do the Budgerigario kid any good, merely exposing him to a great deal of unpleasant punishment. But through the remaining four rounds the kid somehow found the strength to stay on his feet. The Spaniard, a vain and bewildered man, continued to hit and hit hard. Sometimes the Budgerigario would look through a curtain of blood to see if Simpson was still watching, and Simpson always was. The director's motionless brown eyes continued to hold the boy, encouraging him to fight to the limits of his strength and endurance. And as the fight went on, you could see the Budgerigario visibly growing in stature.

By the end of the fifth round, the local boy was just a red mess of flesh and agony. Yet he continued to fight back, even occasionally landing a blow on his opponent. The audience was as bewildered as the champ; it was a new experience. They began to roar for the Budgerigario. Pinch, who stood to lose all his bets if the Budgerigario won, was yelling for him as enthusiastically as anyone. Simpson alone remained silent and tense, watching the boy with unswerving eyes. Then the champ actually began to *take* punishment. His early strategy, of rushing the fight and taking it to his opponent, had exhausted him. The Budgerigario found an opening, and moved in. The champ fought back, and both boxers now sought to force a decision. The crowd went wild. When, just before the end of the fifth round, the referee asked the Budgerigario if he wanted to quit, and the boy shook his head, it seemed as if the arena would collapse under the strain. The bell brought a merciful respite.

I looked around. Perdita looked pale and shaken. Pinch and Connell were grimly silent. Simpson continued to stare at the Budgerigario, who was being sponged by his seconds like a helpless baby.

When the fighters tottered towards each other for the final round, everyone in the arena realised that an unusual battle was being fought out in that ring. Simpson leaned forward in his seat, a brown cigarette hanging unlit from his lower lip. For the rest of the round the boxers fought in savage slow motion. It was a parody of fighting, yet without subterfuge or sham heroics; truth had been skinned down to the bone. When the bell finally released them from their slow, macabre saraband of pain neither fighter knew what was happening. They were gently led to their corners. There was a hush throughout the arena while the judges computed the points. Then the referee went to the champ's corner, steered him to the centre of the ring, and slowly raised his right arm. The mob yelled and whistled, neither for nor against the decision, but because they had seen a real fight.

People began to move to the exits and we rose, trying to get out before the fans got to Pinch. As we pushed forward, I saw the Budgerigario's raw face swivel round like a bladder

on a stick, the peasant eyes searching for Simpson. Simpson
waited until the boxer caught sight of him, then raised his
thumb. For an instant the dumb peasant face became serene.
Then his seconds cut across our view. We never saw him
again.

.   .   .   .   .

We got Pinch into the car, but the crowd quickly surrounded us and we moved forward like mutes at a funeral.
We sat very quietly in the car, thinking about the fight. Then
we reached the sea-front and began to pick up speed.

'That was quite a fight,' I said as we bowled towards the
hotel.

Simpson looked ahead, silent.

'You should have seen the Dempsey-Firpo fight,' he said
at last. 'I was a kid at the time. Gard, what a fight that was.
They kept getting knocked down. And they just kept getting
up again. Yes, it was a great fight.'

'They were a pack of bums tonight,' Pinch said.

Simpson said: 'Ya, they were bums, but they gave it all
they got.'

'Oh, yes, they exerted themselves,' Pinch said.

'They sure did,' Simpson said. After a pause he said: 'But
you're right, Greg. They were a complete pack of bums.'

We drew up at the hotel, and Pinch went up to his suite.
Simpson looked hard at me but did not say anything. He
went to his rooms. I went to the reception desk and bought
some postcards and newspapers. Other people who had been
to fights came into the foyer. Snorts Valentine was sitting in
a wicker chair, talking to Pia Viertel.

'Judas priest,' he was saying, 'we should never have gone
out this morning. Not in that sea. At least three people could
have been killed when that goddam boat came off its hooks.'

'It *was* rather mad, Snorts,' Pia said, her big pop eyes round and adoring.

'Hi, Slim,' Snorts said. 'How was the boxing?'

'Lousy,' I said. 'They were just a pack of bums.'

'Judas priest, what can you expect from a bunch of Budgerigarios?'

'What indeed?'

'I don't like boxing,' Pia said primly.

'I know what,' Snorts said. 'Let's all go out and beat up someone. Let's beat up some English, down at the port. I heard a new boatload sailed in this evening.'

I said good night quickly and went to my room. I read the papers. I wrote a few postcards. I went to bed. Tomorrow I would sort out that baboon of a fisherman. With handles.

CHAPTER FIVE

Fever

BUT MOST OF the next day, a Sunday, I spent in my room nursing an attack of the local dysentery known throughout the archipelago simply as the Budgerigars. Other names for it are the Tourist's Trot and the Guitar Twostep. Everyone who goes to the islands gets it, if only in a light dose. Old hands down there say you get periodic bouts of it, even if you have lived there for a lifetime. During our stay there no one in the unit quite escaped it, though the consistent whisky-drinkers were less affected than the half-measure men or near-teetotaller. The best way to keep it down is to avoid putting ice into your drinks. Cold beer is also a good stabiliser, particularly the Tropical brewed on the island. If you must have water, then order a bottle of the Fuente Ideal, or aqua mineral natural, as good a bottled water as can be found anywhere outside Paris. Plain water is poison, in the Budgerigars as anywhere else.

Through staying in bed I at least got on to better reading terms with Kipling, a writer I had been avoiding for years. It is always good to feel your way back to a really fine writer. I had long regarded Kipling as a pretentious and tedious Jingoist; even Eliot's enthusiastic championship of his work failed to excite me. But the first story I read, *The Man Who Would Be King*, made me realise how wrong I had been to bracket him with Proust or Scott or Simenon, writers I have put aside as possible comforters of an old age I cannot truly hope to reach. I read warily, taking the story in short snorts, the way you drink raw whisky. After reading a page or so I would put the book aside and let the story swill round my mind like liquor seeping into the bloodstream. A week later I was still trying to finish reading the story, but I got enough of it on that first day in bed with the Guitar Twostep to know that I had been wrong about Kipling. It is a fine story; a fine Simpson story, at that. I liked its harshnesses, and cruelties, and crazy cockeyed courage ending in untidy death.

I also read tourist pamphlets on the Budgerigar Archipelago written in smiling guide-book prose. Reading them, you could see the writers sucking at their authors' pipes as they steered you through phoney palms, treacherous sunshine, and iced gin, smack into an attack of the Twostep. I been beat up and holed in so many places that I am beginning to look like an old sieve, but them trots are just about the most debilitating things that could happen to any man.

Ernie looked in around two in the afternoon, and grinned when he saw me huddled under the bedding.

'How's the boy? Something serious, I hope.'

'I'm dying.'

Ernie screwed an imaginary monocle into one eye.

'Good show, old man. Any last wishes?'

'Yes, shut the door behind you as you go out.'

'Message understood. Over.'

'What's happening today, amigo?'

'I'm joining Simpson and Ozzie Harris in the car for a quick trip round the island. They're looking for alternative location sites. They're very upset about yesterday.'

'I'll come with you,' I said, rising.

'Don't bother, kid. Simpson will probably sleep through the drive. He's tired and very cross!'

'I think I should go along.'

'Just stay where you are and die quietly, in comfort, without bothering anyone,' Ernie said. He was about to leave when I called him back.

'Ernie,' I said. 'I got something on my mind.'

'Sing it, boy, sing it.'

'John phoned me from Madrid and asked me to fix up a fishing trip.'

Ernie did not even blink.

'Yeah, he told me. He's looking forward to it no end.'

'That's just it. Perdita has signed up all the fishermen and put them out of action, with one exception. This is a big hood called Pablo Ruiz Polianski-Smith. And the only time I saw him, he crowned me with a restaurant table.'

Ernie whistled low.

'Boy, are you in a jam.'

I winced.

'Simpson will screw you up for sure if he finds out that you're crossing him,' Ernie said.

'I'm not crossing him—yet.'

'You haven't told him what's happened, though.'

'No,' I said.

Ernie scratched the anthropoid relic he calls his head, and said :

'But the whole thing is impractical. Perdita can't stop the fishermen from fishing for all the time we are here. Hell, we'd all starve.'

'I hadn't thought of that,' I said.

'Never mind, kid. Leave it to Ernie. He'll think of something.'

'You better,' I said. 'Or Simpson will put us all in front of a firing squad.'

Ernie shuddered, and left.

.   .   .   .   .

I spent the rest of the afternoon dozing and nursing my dysentery and reading Kipling and tourist pamphlets and having nightmares about fish eating humans and whales that only fed on dialogue writers. When Ernie returned I was half asleep, the room was almost dark, the crickets were chirping softly, and the palms and cacti beyond the patio were becoming silhouettes. The sea was snarling quietly in the distance; my leg wounds were throbbing; the Twostep was kicking up a rumpus, and Ernie had a black eye.

'What's cooking?' I asked feebly.

'Nothing much. A Kraut photographer has flown in from Paris to do a picture story.'

'What news of the fishermen?' I asked impatiently.

'They're threatening to start a revolution,' Ernie said nastily. 'How's about getting up and coming to my room for a nice strong Bacardi rum. It will help you face up to what I have to tell you.'

'Be with you right away,' I said, leaping up.

Ernie poured a rum.

'Brace yourself, kid,' he said.

'Go on, tell me the worst.'

'Simpson found out about the fishermen coming on the payroll. Perdita broke down and spilled the whole story this morning.'

'Jesus! What happened, kid?'

'Simpson fired the lot. Struck them off the payroll and sentenced Perdita to ten years in the galleys. Now the fishermen are up in arms and threatening to sue the company for breach of contract. Don't ever talk to me about simple fishermen, my boy. These babies have had other film locations down here, and the way they do a deal would make any Hollywood agent blush for shame. Meanwhile, they refuse to take Simpson on any kind of fishing trip what-so-ever. Look what happened to me when I tried to talk turkey.'

Ernie's eye was rapidly shutting up shop.

I gulped rum and stuck out my glass for more.

'So what's the score now?'

'The score,' Ernie said heavily, 'the score is that you gotta go out and find this Don Pablo wassname and bring him back alive. Simpson wants to meet him.'

'Why, will he play ball?'

'That's for you to find out, kid. He sounds like a pretty independent kind of guy to me.'

Ernie raised his glass.

'Happy days,' he said gloomily.

I did not say anything. You know how it is when you got the Twostep and a heap of other trouble besides.

The Bacardi gave me sufficient energy to face eating in the dining-room. I sat on my own at a table and, having ordered boiled fish and white wine, settled back to listen to Cedric singing 'Silent Night' up with the band. Simpson was sharing a table with a strange blonde. Perdita sat at the table next to mine with Snorts Valentine, Pia Viertel, and a deeply sun-tanned crop-haired stranger in a brown suit. Simpson watched Cedric with a thoughtful expression. No one was saying much to anyone.

Apart from our party, the rest of the hotel guests seemed also to have gone sour. The starched matrons, the sad million-aires, the bored honeymooners, the crushed hired companions, were listening to Cedric, enthralled, but unhappy. Dreaming of home. Dreaming of falling stocks. Dreaming of a white Christmas. When Cedric switched to 'Ol' Man River' even the waiters seemed to suffer more than usual, going miserably on their rounds and putting dishes and bottles on the wrong tables at half the usual speed.

Snorts leaned over and, tapping me on the arm, introduced me to the brown stranger, who turned out to be the Kraut photographer. This was a Kraut with charm. He smiled a lot, directing his eyes at one person at a time and turning his mouth down in a long Germanic smirk, the way Conrad Veidt used to in the thirties. Most of the time he was directing his charm at Pia, and after ten minutes of the treatment she succumbed and asked the Kraut to dance with her. He accepted like something out of an old Ruritanian weepie, and they waltzed away on heavy feet.

Shortly after the Kraut started dancing, Simpson vanished. Someone asked: 'Where's John?'

'He's gone to bed,' Snorts said flatly. 'He's terribly tired.'

Bed, I thought, but tragically, and never called me brother!

This was a black day all right, all right. The band switched from a slow waltz to a fast one, a change of tempo which drove Pia and the Kraut back to the table, puffing.

'Finish,' the Kraut said. 'The plane journey has tired me out.'

Tired, tired, tired, I thought.

Simpson tired, Kraut tired, everyone tired. We wear ourselves out filling in the blank spaces on cinema screens or in the pages of newspapers or the glossy magazines, and people flick the pages and yawn at the screen and that is all.

'Why do we do it?' I asked the wine bottle.

'For money,' the bottle replied.

'Is that the only reason?' I asked the bottle.

'The only one that I know of,' the bottle said.

'The hell with you,' I told the bottle.

The bottle shrugged. It was a two-thirds empty bottle of white Budgerigar wine.

The Kraut leaned over towards me and began to talk about Bob Capa.

'He het courage,' the Kraut said. 'Det voss his great gift. He voss fearless.'

'He was fearless in bed,' I said.

I knew all about Bob's courage and fearlessness, and I did

not want to talk about it. Not there. Not with the Kraut. Not with the fish not biting and everyone cross and tired and the goddam fishermen up in arms.

'Why not get the orchestra to play "Gloomy Sunday"?' I said to Perdita, but viciously.

Back in my room, the Twostep started up again. I slept badly that night.

.   .   .   .   .

Daylight was glowing outside, beyond the french doorway that opened on to the patio, and I was testing my reflexes for wounds and dysentery when I heard Kevin's voice stuttering in anger into his telephone.

'Nur-nur-nur-nur *no*. I want Don Smith, not room service.'

I turned in the bed, groaning.

'No, you idiot. Smith, Smith. Señor Smeet. Don Pablo Ruiz Polianski-Smeet. *No*, I have already had my breakfast. No, I do not want another breakfast. Get me Señor Smeet, por favor.'

So Simpson was putting others on to the trail. I had failed him badly.

I got through to room service and ordered breakfast and went to the bathroom to shave. Cedric had preceded me, for he is an early riser, and my socks blotted up the puddles from his shower. (Even when a writer's heart is breaking he must retain his eye for small details, see things at a remove.)

It was another sunny morning outside. The sameness of the days on the island was beginning to affect one's normal sense of time. Everything seemed off-beat. Somewhere in the world it was snowing. Somewhere perhaps a Russian was saying no, or a Broadway starlet was saying yes, or a Los Angeles virgin was saying maybe, or a Spanish waiter was saying mañana, but whatever they were saying, or wherever they were saying it, nothing mattered much to us on that island. Time was adrift, and our anxieties were centred around getting location shots at sea, building a dummy whale, and, so far as I was concerned, fixing up a fishing trip. I put on my best sponge trousers, silk hat, and morning coat and went out in search of Don Smith. On the way to the Isletta I stopped off in a café where a crowd of stuntmen were discussing the latest news of the whale.

'They say the bloody thing will weigh a hundred and twenty tons by the time they've distributed all the ballast,' one was saying.

'Yeah, and it will sink the moment it touches the water,' another said.

'There's a curse on this picture,' yet another said. 'Nothing works out right, you know that as well as I do.'

'Hear me, brother, it will sink as sure as yeggs is yeggs.'

'It won't be ready in time.'

'It'll be ready, kid. They're working day and night in the shipyard. These local craftsmen are terrific. They'll work like blacks for peanuts.'

'Yeah, but can we find even enough peanuts to pay them with?'

'I hear that they've run out of Vermiculite.'

'What in hell's name is Vermiculite?'

'The stuff they mix with the rubber to make the whale's skin.'

'Have you seen it lately? The son of a bitch is really taking shape.'

'If you ask me it's a better whale than the one we lost off Heligoland.'

'It's a damnsight better than any whale I've ever seen, real or dummy.'

'It's a goddam beaut.'

'It's an eighty-two-foot miracle.'

'Eighty-six.'

'Eighty-two. What will you bet me?'

'A hundred pesetas, flannel.'

'It's a deal.'

'To hell with the size. All I know is that it will be a miracle if it's ready on time.'

'Yeah, and if it floats when it hits the water it will be another miracle.'

'It will float, kid.'

'I wouldn't like to bet on it.'

'I'll risk a hundred pesetas.'

'That's a deal. Flannel, of course.'

On the Isletta I was told that Don Pablo had left on a long fishing trip along the African coast. He would not be back for several days. I decided to break the news to Simpson, but, as usual, he had heard it already. He did not seem to hold it against me. In any case, he was busy setting up an elaborate shot, involving six whaling rowboats, that promised to kill, maim or injure at least a dozen actors in one glorious go. He was concentrating so hard on this that, for a while, he did not care what happened about the fishermen. I had to stand by for possible whale noises, and for a while I was reprieved. But I wasn't such a fool as to think it was a long-term reprieve. That kind of happy ending only happens in Grimms' fairy tales.

.   .   .   .   .

I think I have already indicated that the sea, down there in the Budgerigars, is as misleading as the writing in those tourist pamphlets.

Seeing it from the hotel terrace as you breakfasted in the early sunlight, it would look flat and languid and half asleep.

The sun would shine through the palms and the breakers on the shore would look warm and soft. Even riding out to the location sites in small launches was pleasant. After all,

what is eternity to six potatoes? And what are six potatoes to
eternity? But as soon as you settled on one of the tugs, or with
the actors standing by for camera calls on the *Fishbite*, the
wind would veer round and the sea would rise and roll like a
bride. There was a sly underwater swell, a dark under-the-
surface drive of currents eddying out of the harbour and
drumming into each other like telegraph wires in a gale. Then
the sea would seem to be spinning round like a great, silent
carrousel, and you would long for the ships to move instead
of remaining anchored in that dizzying central swell.

It was always a relief when the flotilla moved on to another
site, or when you switched from a tug to a launch, or the
reverse, for that was movement. Most of the time, though,
we just stayed put in the tethered boats while elaborate shots
were set up and actors and stuntmen in tiny whale boats were
towed into position. And far out over the blue water you
would see the local fishermen, going off towards Africa, mind-
ing their own business. They had boycotted us altogether, and
Simpson looked black whenever he saw the fishing fleets.

Apart from the day-to-day tedium of waiting, the actors
were also beginning to show signs of exhaustion. The strain
of the past months of filming at sea, and in the studios, had
been great. Now this final phase was wearing away their
reserve. There was a tendency to carp and bicker. The least
sign of tactlessness would touch off emotional squibs.

Actors and stuntmen not required for camera takes would
lounge on the rolling decks, sometimes for days, waiting for
a call to work. They passed their time by talking, reading,
playing cards or chess, or in catching up with their sleep.
Sleep was at a premium at Los Tropicos, everyone staying up
late without levelling things up with a long afternoon siesta.
Those not actively at work would try to sleep in snatches on
the boats. But there were many disturbances, and this added
to the general snappishness.

Simpson spent two nights a week playing poker. This was quite a school; if Hitchcock had been around he would have wanted to put it on film. One night I decided to risk my string of racehorses and sit in for an hour or two.

Simpson sat at the head of the long table in the drawing-room of his suite, with his back against the open french windows. The sea throbbed on the beach, the palms moved dryly in the tropical darkness. The excitement of the game ran through Simpson's lean nervous frame like an electric storm. He wore pyjamas and a blue silk dressing gown, and his lank hair cascaded down both sides of his face, like Irving's when he played Matthias in *The Bells*.

'Have a ceegar, Slim,' he said, looking up from his cards as I entered. Perdita, squatting cross-legged on the floor by the liquor cabinet, pointed a finger at the bottles and looked inquiringly at me. Silently framing the word 'Scotch' I squeezed in beside Pinch and Snorts Valentine

The other players were Rory Punt, Count Krantz, Franz Krantz, Ernie Sanderson, and, of course, King Connell.

I am not a good poker player; my experiences on racetracks are enough to warn me off card games. But I don't mind occasionally risking a thousand or two, especially if you are playing for wooden nickels, bouncy cheques or flannel pesetas.

There are moments when Simpson's face catches something of the sardonic expression of Bogart, especially when his lips stretch back and show his fangs in a parody of Bogie's most characteristic snarl. That night he snarled a lot, and held his cards as if his fingers were dissected nerves. There was something of Captain Queeg in the way he shifted about in his chair, moving his little brown eyes from player to player, drawing spasmodically at his Corona-Corona.

The slightest interruption threw him. Punt had booked a telephone call through to Santa Barbara, and there were incoming calls from Paris and Madrid for Pinch. In the usual

Budgerigar way, the switchboard was making a production of the Santa Barbara call, asking for Punt every ten minutes until in desperation the actor cancelled the call altogether. All calls were taken in Simpson's bedroom, and whenever Pinch or Punt left the room Simpson would look up crossly and show great impatience, tapping the table with his fingers, squirming in his chair, refusing to join in the small talk until everyone was seated again.

Pinch, wearing horn-rimmed glasses and a grey check shirt open at the neck, was the calmest player. The white streak that the make-up department had stained into his thick black hair, to go with his skipper's scar, shone in the lamplight like a patch of snow on a thawing mountainside.

Punt, immaculate in a dark suit, with a red carnation in his lapel, chain smoked. The way he ejected each cigarette stub from his holder and wavered as he pushed the next one into the tube was not the action of a wholly relaxed man.

Snorts Valentine was inclined to let his attention wander; to Perdita, or to the liquor cabinet, or to a mosquito buzzing in the lamplight.

King Connell broke all the rules. He fidgeted, groaned when he wanted to indicate that he had a bad hand, asked fatuous questions, muttered to himself, drank steadily and shuffled the cards clumsily. Sometimes he would check on points with the other players, or discuss the day's shooting, or prattle in a highly coloured biographical vein.

'So help me, I'll be ruined before the night's out,' King roared suddenly.

'What the hell are you moaning about?' Snorts said. 'You're playing with winnings.'

'I'll be down to my last cent if things go on this way.'

'Judas priest, do you expect to win all the time?'

'No, Snorts, but you know how it is. Well, Christ, you know. Now, where were we?'

A minute or so later King started again.

'Hey, Slim, fix me a drink, will you, boy? Oh, Perdita's over there. Sorry; sorry, everyone, I didn't see Perdita. Thought she'd gone out to powder her nose. Well, you know how it is with women. Okay, okay. No, I'll have a beer. Tropical. After all, we're in the tropics. Hah? Heh, heh, heh. Well, more or less. Sorry, everyone. Judas, I nearly broke my back falling out that boat this afternoon. God, does my back hurt.'

'Play cards, Connell,' Simpson snarled. 'Play cards.'

'Sorry, John.'

And a minute later :

'Ace nine,' Connell roared. 'Five pounds.'

'Judas priest,' Snorts said.

King said : 'Cut 'em, Greg.'

Pinch cut the cards.

Snorts said : 'Will you quit moaning, now that you've won again, King?'

'I ain't moaning. All right, so I just won a hundred quid. It takes some getting used to, to win, I mean.'

'Just try to get used to it, Connell,' Pinch said wearily. 'That's what I would like to do in this game, get used to winning.'

King said : 'You're not doing too badly, me old dear.'

'All right, darling,' Pinch said tersely. 'Let's all start calling each other names. We're all friends here.'

'I don't know why everyone picks on me always,' King said in a hurt voice.

'Play cards, Connell,' Simpson snapped. 'Play cards.'

'Sorry, John.'

'Stop being sorry and play cards.'

'Okay.'

Simpson kept the scores on a sheet of paper weighted down by a glass ash-tray. Perdita sat on the floor, yawning, looking tired. From time to time the card players would toss cigarettes across the table. Simpson stubbed his cigar butt and started chain smoking, burning out cigarettes faster than Punt. Towards two o'clock we decided to finish the game for the night. There was silence as Simpson totted up the scores. The upshot was that I lost enough flannel pesetas to have kept me in cigars and fundador for the rest of my natural life.

'Never mind, Slim,' Simpson grinned as I was going out. 'Cheer up, kid. We'll be going on a fishing trip soon. Fishing, off the African coast.' And after a pause, 'That *is* so—isn't it, kid?'

.   .   .   .   .

Despite the late nights, Simpson always managed to wake in a bright mood. I got into a routine of going to his room about eight for a morning conference. Perdita would come down from her room and start taking the day's memos and correspondence and sorting out the work for the secretaries generally. Simpson would sit up in bed with a breakfast tray on his knees and amuse us with anecdotes or impersonations of punchies, rummies, or mere movie people he knew. He would always listen delightedly to any outrageous adventures or scrapes which might have occurred overnight.

'King Connell broke a Chinese vase in the reception room of the Casa Maria,' I began on the morning after the poker, and immediately a wide, interested grin started to spread over Simpson's leathery face.

'You don't say, Slim. How did it happen, kid?'

And I told a shameful anecdote I'd just got from Ernie, embroidering it whenever I felt that it wasn't spicy enough. And Perdita smiled and shook her head indulgently and said :

'Judas key, it was bad enough having to face the morning with the Boss to deal with. But with the two of you, oh, Judas key.'

He very rarely talked whale talk. As often as not the conversation would be about ourselves. Simpson has a flair for drawing information from you. When he switches on his attention and asks you about your work, or your love of life, or how you shot the cat in Rio, or what you did in the war, you just tell him. I think that is why he can get so much more from actors or technicians than most other directors; he really gets to know them. And then he will lead them into the craziest situations and then confront them with a flash of truth that illuminates whatever they are doing. And because Simpson knows as much, and sometimes more, about acting than most actors, he is able to command his team for as long as it suits him to do so. The good ones learn to recognise him as one of the great masters of film art. The lousy ones just don't know what is hitting them.

That morning after the poker, after tussling for hours with the script, I joined Perdita in the dining-room for lunch. We sat at a table near the band. The rest were at sea, smashing up rowboats, but Perdita was handling inter-continental phone calls.

'Where's Ernie?' I asked, remembering that Ernie Sanderson had also decided to work ashore that day.

'At the airways office, arranging about a passage from Madrid for his twins. He's been able to get them down that far, and now he's trying to get them on the next flight to Los Tropicos.'

'He'll do it,' I said.

'I wouldn't bet on it,' Perdita said. 'There's a big Christmas rush on all forms of transportation.'

'Are the girls alone?'

'No, their mother is travelling with them.'

'Is that so? Well, I hope he makes it.'

'I sure do too,' Perdita said. 'Gee, he's crazy about those twins.'

I couldn't get it at the time, a guy so crazy about his kids.

But I had not met the twins then, so how was I to know what was in store for all of us?

.   .   .   .   .

That evening, seeing the unit doctor on the hotel terrace, I asked him if he could fix me up with a pill or something to check the dysentery, which was still bothering me spasmodically.

'I've a taxi waiting to take me back to my hotel,' he said. 'Hop in right away and I'll fix you up.'

We drove to the Hotel Casa Mump and took a lift up to Doc's room, where he immediately began to tear the tinfoil from an unopened bottle of Scotch.

'Rinse those two glasses out, please,' he said, but professionally. 'No, not under the tap. Pour some of this mineral water into them, then swill them out over the wash basin. That's right.'

Doc next produced a bottle of white tablets and an envelope.

'Now, you take four of these tablets right away. Here, I'll crush them for you.'

He placed a sheet of hotel notepaper on the small writing table, dropped four tablets on the paper, then getting a grip round the neck of the bottle, used it as a pestle to crush the tablets into a soft powder. Then he slipped the powder into one of the glasses and half filled both glasses with Scotch.

Raising his glass, he said : 'Down in one.'

We gulped our whisky.

'Now, before you go off to bed there's something I have to say to you, me boy. You are responsible for fixing up a fishing trip for the Boss, right? Well, kiddo, if you don't do something about it soon I won't be responsible for what he does to you. It may seem to you that he doesn't mind having his plans upset, but I know different. He's livid. And remember that he learnt to shoot in the Mexican cavalry and that this is a lawless part of the world. He's dead set on this fishing trip, so don't let him down. I'm telling you as a friend.'

I finished the Scotch quickly.

'Sure, Doc,' I said. 'Good night—and, thanks for the pills.'

I rejoined Ernie at our hotel and we took the cab down to the port.

. . . . .

'That's a swell doctor we have with us,' I told Ernie as we drove along by the bay.

'One of the best,' Ernie said. 'Just the guy for this unit.'

I agreed.

'But, Ernie, is he right in the noddle?'

'Who, Doc? He's as sane as we are.'

I did not find that particularly reassuring.

'No, but he said Simpson will probably shoot me if I don't fix up that fishing trip.'

Ernie said : 'Well?'

I said : 'Has he shot many people?'

'Dozens,' Ernie said, putting his feet up on the flap seats.

I did not say anything.

Ernie said : 'Cheer up, kid. All you got to do is do what the gentleman says. When is this Don whatsit coming back?'

'Any day now.'

'Well, then, what are you worrying about? He's probably a reasonable guy. You and he will probably get along like brothers.'

I thought of Cain and Abel and winced.

'Yeah,' I said. 'It will be all right.'

'Sure it will.' Ernie gazed serenely at the moonlit sea. 'And then my twins are coming down. Boy, wait till you meet them. They'll cheer you up. I might even get them to help you with the fishing arrangements.'

'Thanks, Ernie. You're a real pal.'

'Think nothing of it, old man,' Ernie said as the taxi drew up outside a high-class clip joint.

.   .   .   .   .

The doctor's pills worked like a charm and early the following morning I took a dip in the pool. Two young Spaniards were plunging in and out of the green water, crossing themselves every time they dived from the side of the pool. They were fine swimmers, but they never forgot to make the sign of the cross whenever they dived. When they saw me they looked startled and, picking up their towels, ran out of the pool muttering and crossing themselves. As they passed near me I heard one muttering fearfully, and I caught a name. The name was Don Pablo Ruiz Polianski-Smith.

.   .   .   .   .

I did not stay long in the pool because the sores on my leg kept getting softer the longer I remained in the water. I didn't want to get chicken, inside *or* out.

Driving with Simpson to Las Flamenco later that morning I told him that a Norwegian skipper had sighted an albino whale fifteen miles north of the island.

'Yeah, I know,' Simpson said, but inevitably. 'Of course,' he added thoughtfully, 'it *might* be the whale we lost off Heligoland.'

'Could be,' I said, refraining from pointing out that his had been a dummy whale. You know how it is with film directors.

'Most of the whales in these seas keep a good twenty miles south of this island,' Simpson went on dreamily. 'Still, I've got one of the Air Force generals interested. He's sent a helicopter out looking for it.'

'Hope they find it,' I said.

So help me, right then I meant it.

6—TCK

'Yeah,' Simpson said. 'That would be swell. Perdita, did you send that cable to the President?'

'It went yesterday, John.'

'Did you tell him that it was all right by me if he ran again?'

'Yep.'

'Fine, fine.'

Simpson boarded the tug and began to set up whaleboat shots with Ozzie Harris. I joined Kevin in a rowboat that was going to meet the *Fishbite* half-way round La Isletta. Kevin had an urgent message for the skipper to keep sober for a customs inspection. We bumped over the reef and plunged into a choppy sea, the sun bright above us. Behind us the mountains rose up clean and wet in the rinsed morning light. Far away to the west, a pile of clouds rose round a hidden volcano. Some four miles from the port we sighted the *Fishbite,* rolling like a drunkard over the fresh green sea. We tied our rowboat to the stern, tugging our two monkey-like boatmen behind us to the anchorage a quarter-mile offshore from Las Flamenco.

There were two girls aboard. A blonde Swede called Britta, and a Spanish opera singer whose name I forget. Britta, who had come to the Budgerigars to recover from a nervous breakdown, was organising the meals aboard the *Fishbite,* the crew being too perpetually drunk to do any catering.

Simpson came aboard the *Fishbite* for lunch. We ate in the state-room below, rocking from side to side, with the food and plates and glasses sliding backwards and forwards and tangerines rolling into our laps. It was good, feeling that boat roll down there in that choppy bay.

'We'll have to distribute the ballast amidships,' the skipper muttered. He was in a complete drunken stupor.

'No amount of ballast will right this tub,' Simpson said with a Bogart snarl.

The opera singer had been seasick on the trip round the Isletta.

'I thought when you invited me here that I would see filming,' she told Simpson reproachfully. 'Instead I have seen nothing, only high seas. I have been often on private yachts, but never anything like this.'

The director grinned falsely.

'It doesn't bother you, does it, John?' I asked.

'Never been seasick in my life, kid,' Simpson said happily.

The opera singer curled her lip. Then she uncurled it again and began to talk about Monteverde and Bizet and Stravinsky. Turning to me she said :

'Do you know Carl Ebert?'

'I watched him rehearse *Don Giovanni* at Edinburgh,' I said.

'What do you think of him, Slim?' Simpson asked interestedly.

'He's a maestro,' I said. 'The real thing.'

'Yeah, that's what he is, kid. A maestro.'

'When I work for him I have an attack of soul,' the opera singer said defensively.

'Say, that's good,' Simpson said, winking. 'An attack of soul.'

'Yes, is it not?' the opera singer said greenly. By now she was a very sick chick, that warbler.

Simpson now switched his lethal attention to Pia Viertel.

'The most inefficient continuity girl in the business,' he said affably. 'Do you want that in writing, Pia?'

'Why don't you pick on someone else, for a change?' Pia said, also affably. 'If I had known you were going to be like this I wouldn't have come here in the first place.'

'I didn't want you to come,' Simpson said silkily.

'Then why didn't you stop me? You're the boss.'

'I thought you'd take the hint. You must have known I didn't want you.'

'Flattery will get you nowhere,' Pia said sturdily.

I said: 'Have you had news of your Irish hunters lately, John?'

Simpson beamed happily.

'Sure. My wife takes them over the jumps every day.'

'I hunted in Italy earlier this year,' I said. 'With the Milan Blazers. Do you know that, there, a hunt servant hits the fox on the head with a mallet before letting him limp off into the woods?'

Simpson looked horrified.

'No,' he said. 'I can't believe it.'

'It's true. I wrote an article about it. Got hundreds of letters from indignant readers.'

'I should just think you did,' Simpson said indignantly.

'They keep the fox in a hutch——'

'No!'

'Yes. Then they bash it on the head with a mallet, and then a bunch of Italians in full hunting kit trot after it. They actually dress up and wear silk hats and red coats for the sport.'

'That's terrible, Slim,' Simpson said, shocked. 'Simply terrible.'

'It's true,' I said. Now Simpson was looking sick, but it wasn't because of the rocking of the boat.

'In Ireland they'll follow the fox till they drop,' Simpson said, brightening. 'I've seen men with broken necks and broken ribs following the hunt from a car. They'll leave their ploughing, unharness the plough-horse, and grab a handful of mane and give chase.'

The opera singer said: 'I suppose hunting is to Ireland what the bullfight is to Spain.'

'Dominguin is coming to Ireland for the hunting,' Simpson said, his mind far away.

'No!' The opera singer looked astonished.

'Yes. I've invited him, and he will stay at my home and hunt.'

'Wonderful,' the opera singer said.

'He'd better bring fishing tackle along, too,' I murmured into my wine goblet.

'Shall we go up on deck?' Simpson said, looking sharply at me.

.   .   .   .   .

After lunch I leaned on the rails of the *Fishbite* and talked to the opera singer.

'John Simpson is a great character, is he not?' the girl said. 'He shows a rare appreciation of Spain.'

'He loves Spain,' I said. 'I think he may do a bullfight film there some time.'

'That would be splendid,' the girl said. 'I believe if he worked in Spain he would catch the mysticism without making it ridiculous; and catch the happiness without making it vulgar.'

Simpson joined us, watching from the rails as Ozzie Harris and his crew worked out set-ups. Pinch was dozing in a lifeboat, his little Proust book lying folded face downwards near his inert fingers.

Looking at Pinch, the opera singer said: 'Last night in the hotel, a young married woman stared and stared at Gregory for a long time. Then she went up to a woman friend and I heard her say, "I swear, he does *nothing* to me".'

As the opera singer said 'I swear' she made a fierce gesture with her forefinger, sweeping her hand down from the tip of her head to her navel. Simpson shook with laughter.

'God, that's funny,' he chuckled. 'Come on, let's wake Greg and tell him.'

We shook the actor, who sat up blinking amiably.

'Go on, kid,' Simpson said. 'Tell what the married woman said last night. Do it with the gesture.'

The opera singer repeated her story, throwing in the gesture with a fine operatic flourish.

Pinch grinned.

'Now say it in Spanish,' Simpson said eagerly. 'Say it exactly the way the married woman said it.'

The opera singer said her piece, in Spanish this time.

'God, that's funny,' Simpson spluttered. 'Don't you think it's funny, Greg?'

'Screamingly so,' Pinch said, smiling. 'Guess that will make her a faithful wife for ever.'

'Okay, kids,' Simpson said, forgetting the joke. 'We're all set to go.'

That was how we had lunch that day. One of the good days when no one was hurt very much.

.   .   .   .   .

The crew went into action for the afternoon's shooting.

'You can throw meat, Slim,' Simpson said as our launch steered over to a tug on which half a dozen Spanish seamen were cutting up hunks of raw meat into tiny slices. Two basketfuls of meat together with a large sack of bread rolls were lowered down to us, and we set off across the bay to attract seagulls by throwing meat and bread across the course of the whaleboats. Within half an hour we had collected a hundred gulls, and, keeping out of camera range, we hurled the meat and bread into the choppy water.

'Bird bait,' our Spanish boatman said with a contemptuous glance at the loaves and meat. 'You get fish bait. Mucho good fishing between here and Africa. You should fish with us.'

I became suddenly alert.

'That would be mucho fino,' I said cautiously. 'I tell Señor Simpson. Perhaps we go fishing.'

'Good, you tell Señor Simpson soon. This way we fish for birds, no good. Malo.'

'Sí,' I said. 'But birds good for film.'

'You, Señor Simpson, me; we prefer real fishing to bird fishing for film, no? Señor Simpson mucho fino hombre. He, you, should stay with us two-three year and fish for real fish and forget film, no?'

'Good idea, amigo. You, me tell Señor Simpson pronto. Maybe he burn all film and settle here and fish.'

The fisherman nudged his companion and laughed, showing three yellow teeth.

'Burn film, that good. Señor Simpson too find hombre to play always with film. He big fisherman with us. You, me, all of us.'

'Sí,' I said. 'Pass more meat, por favor.'

'Ah, the meat,' sighed the fisherman. 'You all loco.'

The other fisherman said: 'Much tuna off Africa. You know the Rio de Oro?'

'The Golden River,' the other fisherman said. 'You know it?'

'No. I regret that I do not know it.'

'Ah, there is a place for fish. Big giant tuna. Plenty other fish, too. We must go, you, me, Señor Simpson.'

'Yes, we must. Now turn the boat towards land, for we are in the way of the cameras.'

'Ah, the cameras,' the fisherman said contemptuously. He spat into the moving-up-and-down sea. 'Cameras malo for hombres like Señor Simpson. He much happier fishing sea for tuna than throwing meat to gulls. That is no sport for a man.'

'It must be done, amigo,' I said gently.

The fisherman shrugged and turned the boat away from the cameras. As we moved in towards the reef, I said:

'How come thou invitest Señor Simpson now. Is there not still a boycott?'

'Ai,' the fisherman said mysteriously. 'Ai.'

'What meanest thou with ai?'

'Ai,' one fisher said. 'It means that we have much sadness. Me, my amigo, we given dispensation to work as rowers but not as fishers. We fear.'

'Ai,' said the other fisher. 'We fear.'

'What fearest thou?'

'We fear that we may be boycotted by the other brothers of the fish when you leave.'

'Ai, we fear the boycott.'

'Then let us think of making peace,' I said. 'Gatherest thou thy other amigos of the fish and suggest methods of reconciliation. Tell them of the true Señor Simpson who is sad about the fishing. We can all be amigos again.'

'Truly?' the first fisher said.

'Truly,' I said.

'Ai,' the other fisher said. 'It is good so.'

'Good,' I said. 'Good, good.'

'Good,' said the fishers.

.   .   .   .   .

The rest of the afternoon's shooting was concentrated on Pinch. It is a shot of the Whale Captain urging his whaleboat crew to move in closer to the giant white whale threshing angrily in the boiling sea. He has snatched a harpoon from his harpooner and is crazily urging his rowers to get in close for the kill.

'In,' Pinch shouted in a wild, hoarse, strangulated voice. 'In. . . . In. . . . *In*.'

A powerful hose, attached to one of the tugs, was trained on the actor. You know how it is with hoses. As he shouted the water hurtled from the hose and knocked into his face.

On film it looks like giant spoutings from the turbulent whale. The water came out with great force, splashing over Pinch and his crew of stuntmen. Simpson insisted on handling the hose himself.

'In,' Pinch screamed. 'In. . . . In. . . .'

'That's fine, Greg,' Simpson said. 'One more.'

'In,' Pinch shouted desperately, as the water crashed into his face and blocked his shouting. 'In. . . . In . . . glullgl . . .'

'Fine, Greg. Marvellous. One more, kid.'

Once again the drenched Pinch stood in the bow of his crazily rocking little whaleboat on the pitching sea.

'In,' he yelled in an agonised roar. 'In. . . . In. . . .'

And Simpson hosed that noble face with powerful jets of water. Truly, it was like spit trickling off Van der Weyden's Christ.

'In. . . . In. . . . Guggle guggle. . . . In. . . .'

Simpson half turned and raked the camera boat with the water from the hose. It caught Ozzie and Pia unawares and knocked them back, almost landing them in the sea.

'Okay,' Simpson said briskly. 'Turn off the water. That was fine, Greg. Simply fine. Okay, kids. Pass along the whisky. And towels. And blankets. Hurry. Say, Ozzie, what's wrong? Did I catch you with the hose. Here, kid, take this towel and wipe yourself dry. Okay, everyone. That was fine, just fine. We'll have a good night's bowling tonight, hey, fellers?'

. . . . .

Half an hour later we were in the launches heading back for Las Flamenco. The houses here run right into the sea, with balconies hanging over the water and women and children among the washing waving at the incoming boats. The beach was packed with brown, laughing Budgerigarios waiting for a glimpse of Pinch and the other bearded loco actors who were becoming familiar landmarks in the bars and clip joints of the port. And when our launch crunched on to the sandy beach and Pinch stepped out, a wet, heroic giant from the sea, the gentle Budgerigarios began to clap softly with the fingers of the right hand striking the palms of the left, liquid applause from people who were beginning to love the locos in their midst. And most of all they loved Cedric Donnell, the huge, bearded hero in bronze from the sea, who sang for them, who had taken the trouble to pick up their native tunes and sing them back to them under the wide evening sky, daubed with sunset.

They were awed and thrilled by Pinch; they were awed by Simpson; but they loved Cedric.

That night, after the meat throwings and the drenchings, as on most nights, Cedric's rich, noble voice soared over the still water on the safe side of the reef and melodies rose from his throat like a cloud of nightingales, scattering their music gently into the hearts of the meek and courteous Budgerigarios.

And with the sun behind them, and to the sound of Cedric's noble singing, Pinch and Simpson strode across the sand and through the liquid applause of the Budgerigarios and stepped into the great automobile waiting at the terminus of the port and drove away to the showers and Scotches and phoney crackpot luxury of the grand hotel behind the floodlit palms.

And as they hurried through the corridors, past awed chambermaids and bellboys, to their suites, Cedric would stroll behind them, slowly, grandly, his slave bangles and charms clattering melodiously as he stopped to exchange greeting with the barber, the manicurist, the porter, the girl who sold Paris fashions from behind a glass case, the barman, the bellboys, the chambermaids. Then he would come into our small suite and wait patiently while I showered, refusing to spin a coin for first turn. He would sit on his bed in a white bathrobe, quietly storing up new strength to give out in song and gesture, a living embodiment of human love and gentleness. That is how I saw Cedric Donnell during our time together down there in them Budgerigarios, and if you want to read that as a tribute to a great living entertainer it's okay by this chick.

By seven, everyone was ready for the bowling. This was Simpson's sad alternative to poker, since there was no fishing. It was a long, brightly lit double bowling alley. The balls were of different weights and sizes, with holes to hook your fingers in, and you might have been in any Mid Western bowling alley when Simpson, Pinch, Snorts and Ernie Sanderson were playing.

Simpson, impressive in a blue shirt and with red suspenders buttoned to his long fawn twill slacks, would hold the ball to his lips, balancing it on his fingers, then quickly spring forward with a lithe, jungle movement, and smash the ball straight into the middle pin. He was constantly making strikes, but he was in good company with Pinch, Snorts and Ernie.

Word having got round among the island señoritas that Pinch was bowling, the side of the alley was a blaze of young girls with red dresses and white mantillas and expensive hair-dos raptly watching Grigorio hurling the bowls down like a god out of their Greek mythology books. Yeah, they actually read them down there, didn't you know?

They were genteelly educated, these high-class island chicks with their brothers and maiden aunts hovering as chaperones, among the palms between the swimpool and the hotel. But the players were so immersed in the game that they barely noticed the young and fragrant talent watching the play with wet virgin lips. Had they known, they might have moderated their language, though I doubt it.

On the occasion when Simpson knocked down all but one pin, he jumped up and down in anger.

'Judas priest,' he yelled. 'I did the same thing in nineteen thirty-four.'

'Back in Hecate County?' Dublin asked.

'Yeah,' Simpson growled. 'My mother gave me bloody hell.'

Then Pinch bowled.

'You got a winner there, Greg,' Simpson cried prematurely.

'I've had bigger wins,' Pinch growled as his bowl knocked down only four pins.

'God! Hell! Judas!' Snorts Valentine yelled. 'That was real bad luck, Greg. Judas priest!'

A bright boy with dialogue, Snorts. Such range. Such invention.

After the bowling there was still poker. Just a small school. Those who did not play dispersed into the night, that long tropical night of stars and palms and guitars and willowy blondes and dark island girls, and drinking and talk and island wines and paellas and walks by the crashing sea, with and without handles.

At dinner I asked Cedric Donnell what he intended to do when the film was completed. He had narrowly missed being spliced by a harpoon that afternoon.

'Have me two weeks bedrest in a nursing home,' he said huskily.

Simpson was setting the pace at a fast clip now. Working all day, playing all night, he kept us all on the jump But he was very sad inside, hurt by the business of the fishermen. And much of it was my fault. And when a guy does that to a guy he respects and likes, with or without whale dialogue, then, kid, it's time that guy did something other than just lounge around the bistros and clip joints, moping.

But what to do; do what?

CHAPTER SIX

Felizes Navidad

THE ARRIVAL OF greetings cards showing stage coaches stuck in snowdrifts and skaters and snowmen and frosted holly and old people sipping wine by log fires reminded us (as we kicked around the pool and drank wine and ate cold chicken on the *Fishbite,* or strolled through the sun-warm markets of the port, or drove slowly along dusty roads, past palms and camels and handles in the sunset) that Christmas was almost upon us. A few came through to me : a witty one from Peter Ustinov, a couple from friends in jail.

Some English kids sang carols outside the hotel. Christmas lurked in the palms, biblically.

I really knew it was Christmas when we all went to a party in the Itranian Vice-Consul's home. These Itranians favour everything British. There are times when you would almost think they were British, by gad. Simpson joined Cedric and a couple of stuntmen in a corner, and was happily downing Scotch-on-the-rocks when he was captured by a pink young Englishman, who spent the next half-hour assuring the director that he should make a film of the *Iliad.*

'The *Iliad,* mind you, sir. Not the *Odyssey.* The *Iliad,* you see, is a great tragedy. The *Odyssey* is rubbish, a mere novel.'

Simpson gave a gangster leer.

'Yeah, they already made a picture of the *Odyssey,* kid,' he said. 'They done a brilliant job of it, too. They got Ulysses to take a knock on the head and tell the story in a series of flashbacks. He was suffering from amnesia, see? Ain't that cute?'

'Terrible, terrible,' the pink boy said. 'Now you, sir, in my considered opinion, are the only person in the world who could translate Homer into cinematic language.'

I thought: Two more drinks and he'll be pulling out a synopsis of the screenplay.

The Tourist Twostep was still bothering me spasmodically, and I was down to drinking Cinzano and soda. Such a drink, and now this boy was squeaking his nauseating guff! I went to an alcove cluttered with Christmas cards, books and plaster casts of Winston Churchill, and took down several volumes of a set of *Punch* anthologies. Putting aside *Mr. Punch Afloat, Mr. Punch's Cockney Humour, Mr. Punch's Railway Book,* I settled in an easy chair with *Mr. Punch With Rod and Gun.*

Then Cedric began to sing.

I replaced the books and left the alcove to get a better view of Cedric, who was standing half-way up the stairs in the large entrance hall, gripping the banisters with both hands and singing easily, in full command of his audience.

'And now, friends,' Cedric said, 'I want to give you a negro version of Genesis. This is Christmas-time, and I want you all to know how some of us coloured folk interpret the first chapters of the Holy Book.'

Clearing his throat, Cedric began:

'God said, "Ah'm lonely, Ah'm lonely, Ah'm gonna make me a world ..."'

And I thought: Yeah, that's how it is when a picture begins. I'm lonely, a guy says, so I'll make me a celluloid world. . . . It's a way of fighting loneliness, shedding your ties and responsibilities and influences with each film, carrying over perhaps a few fragments of companionship into the next production, but never really establishing a binding relationship. That is the way I was beginning to think down there in the Budgerigars. Dostoyevsky, there's a hole in your samovar.

Since coming to the islands I had seen Simpson the character, Simpson the clown, Simpson the raconteur, Simpson the good friend who made everything seem gay and brilliant. I had seen the successful film director, the celebrity. But there were other things to record. There was the running fight Simpson had had with his backers, about the financing of his picture. Then the executives positively hating Simpson, delighted when he left on location. There was his determination to get things right, fighting all along the line. And then the bad luck, losing whales, actors, valuable technicians. It had been quite a trail, and now the only thing Simpson had set his mind on doing, apart from getting his film done, was bitched up for him.

Oh, those fishermen. Those crazy, crazy, crazy fishermen.

Hell, and now the team was falling apart. Simpson's pace was making them all sag at the knees. Mind, no one had turned a hose in *my* face. No one had told *me* to jump into a rough sea and cling on to a slippery barrel for two hours while the cameras were slowly grinding and the wind blew at your wet clothes. No one had ordered *me* to jump from a yard-arm, or rick my back, or smash my ankle leaping in and out of little boats on high seas. All I had to do was provide an occasional hiccup for the whale. But it made me feel bad to see the way everyone was breaking up, hating the location, hating the job, hating Simpson.

The job had been too much for some of them. This was not just a film location; it was a marathon. For some, that is. I had seen the same set-up at times during the war, in some of the rougher newspaper offices—the more successful studios. This was comparatively tame.

Then I reminded myself that it was Christmas, and I drove down alone to the port, to the Angry Coconut.

·   ·   ·   ·   ·

The moment I went into the Coconut two things happened. The band played 'April in Portugal', and Raquel ran over and kissed me on both cheeks. That's how it is when you bum around with film people; other people give you the star treatment. I've seen too many punks crack up under it to be impressed, but it can be dangerous, brother. Ask Joe. Ask Sean. Ask Scott, if you ever find yourself in his neighbourhood.

Karen said : 'Hello, stranger.'

'Hello yourself,' I said. 'I've been sick. Malo.'

'You malo?' Raquel said, pushing away from me.

'Sí.'

Raquel went over to Karen, and stared at me with a horrified expression.

'What's wrong wit' you?' Karen asked.

'The usual trouble. Tourist Twostep.'

Karen laughed and turned to Raquel and spoke quickly in Spanish. Raquel's face unclouded.

'Comprende, oui, oui,' she said.

Karen said : 'She misunderstood. When you said malo she thought you had caught a disease from one of the señoritas in another bar.'

'Tell her she's crazy,' I said roughly. To Raquel I said : 'You much loco.'

Raquel looked contrite.

'Sorry,' she said. 'I very sorry.'

'So you should be,' I said. 'Now tell her, Karen, that I have come here to think. I want to sit quietly at a table, and think. I have no desire to speak roughly, but she must not provoke me. She is welcome to my champagne, but she must not interrupt my thinking.'

Again Karen spoke in rapid Spanish, and again Raquel nodded seriously and said she understood.

So I went with Raquel to a table away from the band, and Spender came over and took my order. I sat back in my chair and thought about Simpson and the way people didn't understand him.

'I should have known,' I told Raquel.

'Sí,' Raquel said, nodding.

'How dumb canst thou get? Some of them hate his guts.'

'Sí,' Raquel said. 'Here, I pour champagne.'

'I should have known,' I said again. 'I should have known that most people are allergic to geniuses. Thou following me?'

'No comprende.'

'No, but thou wouldst if I put it in thy language. Now, calling Simpson a genius won't get us anywhere. So let us call him screwball. That is a good, round word.'

'Here, more champagne.'

'Gracias. It is good for my illness. Me no longer malo.'

'Malo?' Raquel looked uneasy again.

'No, no malo.' I groped for a reassuring word. 'Salubre.'

Raquel nodded happily. 'Ah, salubre. Bueno.'

'Let's call a conference,' I said. 'Let's have Spender at this table and hold a conference.'

'Santos? You want Santos?' Raquel raised her hands proudly above her head and clapped. Another waiter rushed up and she told him to fetch Santos.

'Santos,' I said, when Spender arrived. 'Amigo. Sit down. Drink with us.'

Spender sat down in his white jacket and passed me a cigarette.

'You, me, friends,' Spender said.

'Si.'

'More champagne?' Raquel said. 'Champagne for Santos?'

'Sí.'

Raquel clapped again and the other waiter came over and she ordered champagne for Spender.

'Sec,' I said.

'Sí, señor,' the waiter said. 'Comprende.'

'Now, Santos, we are in conference. Comprende?'

'Sí, comprende. What do you want to know?'

'Nothing. All you have to do is listen to me and nod occasionally and say yes and no. That makes it a conference, understand?'

Spender nodded.

'Listen, amigo. Simpson is a screwball, comprende? He puts people's backs up, comprende? But he doesn't stop to wonder if he upsets people or not, so long as he does things his way. With or without flannel pesetas. That is wrong according to the herd morality, comprende? According to the herd, you must pretend to believe in liberty, equality and fraternity. We must all pull together, comprende? We must toe the line and be regular fellers. We must also be on the square. Now this attitude is phoney, comprende? Thy herd hero doesn't give a damn, really. But he pretends to, even when he hates his neighbours' guts. This, of course, dries up his humanity. He gets into such a rut of phoney solicitude and goodwill that he's tongue-tied if he tries to speak honestly, or face a true situation, or perform an unrehearsed action. So the people who have learnt to live without putting up a phoney social front, who talk straight and see clearly, are sniped at by those who prefer the hack stuff and the social deceit. Most of them would deny that they are phoney, but that doesn't make their hatred of screwballs any less vicious or hurtful. Comprende?'

'Sí,' Spender said. 'You, me, friends. We drink to that.'

I raised my glass.

'Amigos.'

Raquel said: 'You buy me packet of American cigarettes?'

'Sí,' I said. 'You get them.'

Raquel clapped her hands.

Spender said: 'You got bambinos?'

I spread out three fingers.

Santos turned to Raquel and grinned as he said: 'Sleem, tres bambinos.' To me he said: 'Me, three also. All boys.'

'Amigo,' I said profoundly, without the aid of handles.

Raquel said: 'You happy with your wife?'

'Sí, I said. 'Mucho.'

Raquel beamed. Santos said: 'You, my brother.'

I did not reply to that.

Raquel said; 'Santos he say he your brother. If Santos say that he take care of you for life. He take care of me often. When no men dance with me, boss give me no money. Then Santos take me to his home and his wife give me food and drink. Santos mucho fino hombre.'

'Sí,' I said.

'We brothers,' Santos said, looking squarely at me.

'Yes,' I said sadly. 'Brothers.'

Santos went off to attend to some seamen and their girls, and Raquel asked if I would like to dance now.

'Not yet,' I said. 'I wish to think some more.'

'Sí, very sorry. Raquel no interrupt your thinking again.'

But I did not think much more, though I tried to think aloud for a bit.

I said: 'A very wise man called Thornton Wilder once told me that our lives are a struggle between two elements, the Life Force and the Repressive Force. He was goddam right.'

'You have clever amigos,' Raquel said.

'Not many. Most of my amigos are considered foolish, or screwballs, or drunkards.'

'Try not to think so much. It only makes you unhappy.'

'Okay, I no think any more. Tell me about yourself.'

'Me? My mama and papa from Andalusia. We live in small village near Sevilla. Mama, Papa die. Me quite alone. Go work South of France for few months. Become hostess. Travel. Come here. If mama, papa no die, me no be here. That is all. Comprende?'

'Yes, I understand. How old are you?'

'Eighteen.'

'A good age. Let us dance now.'

'You finished thinking? Bueno, we dance.'

The orchestra started playing 'Besse Me Mucho', the trumpeter getting down from the stand and following us round the room.

'Dancing much better than thinking,' I told Raquel.

'Mucho, mucho. I like-a you best when you dance.'

An hour later Santos came to our table.

'You very sad,' he told me. 'I see, I know. You mucho trabajo with Señor Simpson.'

'I'm not sad, Santos.'

'Sí, you listen to your friend, your brother. I tell thee something. I hear that some of the fishermen are sad for the troubles that have happened. I myself go speak to many in the fish market tomorrow. I think soon Don Pablo Ruiz come back tomorrow. I try do things about the fishers for you and Señor Simpson.'

Raquel looked at Santos, then said: 'He go sleep. He know we help. Now he can get rest. I send you message at hotel as soon as I have news.'

'Okay,' I said heavily; 'I'll go.' I was very, very tired.

As I got into the taxi, Santos said: 'You no pay driver. Me pay. Me pay already. You no pay one peseta. Flannel or any kind. Remember, I send message of the fishers soon.'

The taxi drove off before I could thank him. Hell, how do you thank a guy like that?

. . . . .

The next day Ernie's twins arrived. Ernie introduced them to me as I was lying on a towel by the pool. Two little girls aged about twelve. Dressed in frilly frocks. Very demure. Curtseying as they were presented.

'This is Doll.'

'How do you do, Mister Slim.'

'Dill.'

'How do you do, Mister Slim.'

'But they speak with an English accent, Ernie,' I said.

'Sure they do,' Ernie said. 'They've been to an English convent for the best part of four years.'

'Well, I won't hold that against them,' I said, smiling like a Dutch uncle. 'I think they are two very attractive little girls.'

'Thank you, Mister Slim.' Curtsey.

'Thank you, Mister Slim.' Curtsey.

Jointly: 'May we go back to our room and change into swimsuits, Daddy? Please, Daddy, let us swim; please, please, Daddy. We're dying to swim. Oh, don't say no, Daddy.'

'Okay,' Ernie said. 'Check with your mother first, though.'

'Oh, thank you, Daddy. Goodbye for now, Mister Slim.'

'Thank you, Daddy. Goodbye, Mister Slim. I hope we meet again soon.'

They ran away, shrieking and giggling.

'What attractive kids, Ernie.'

Ernie smiled like a beat-up Mona Lisa. I should have drawn a few conclusions from that smile. I should have gone into purdah and never seen the twins again. Or I should have been really constructive, and cabled Charles Addams to drop everything and move in with a dozen thick sketching blocks and a crate of aspirin tablets.

.   .   .   .   .

That night, I had one or two liveners with Ernie Sanderson and the twins before going up to Simpson's suite. Ernie was wearing a bullfight shirt he had had sent from Madrid after Simpson had fought the little bull. The shirts were frilly and beautifully cut, hell to iron, but magnificent. I stuck my nose in my tumbler of Scotch and pulled faces at the twins. Then I went up to see Simpson, feeling very ordinary in a Russian blouse with a gold collar and red cuffs. I wasn't sure that it went with my kilt.

Simpson was sitting in an easy chair with a pile of gifts on a small side table and a big Scotch in his hand. Perdita was playing hostess to Pia and Kevin. Simpson was telling a funny story about a blacksmith and his mate who both stammered.

'Holding up the horseshoe, the blacksmith says, su-su-su-su-su-su-su-su-su-su-strike it wur-wur-wur-wur-wur-wur-wur-wurl it's hor-hor-hor-hor-hor-hor-hor-hot. And the other guy says, Tu-tu-tu-tu-tu-tu-tu-tu-too lur-lur-lur-late. It's cur-cur-cur-cur-cur-cur-cold ug-ug-again.'

Kevin laughed, a loud manic bark.

'Bur-bur-bur-bur-bur-bur-bur-bluddy funny,' he gasped.

'Ya, I thought you'd appreciate that one, Kevin,' Simpson said.

'Blur-blur-blur—oh, Jesus Christ!'

We all laughed.

I gave Simpson a pair of whale-shaped cuff-links, wrapped up in a bit of coloured gift paper.

The room filled up with people. I nursed a tumbler of Scotch and thumbed through Pinch's present to Simpson: a history of the bullfight. Luis, a Spanish production man, started talking about Christmas in Spain.

'It is a family fiesta tonight,' he said, 'not the real fiesta. That is on the sixth, the fiesta of the three kings.'

'We look like having plenty fiesta, what with New Year as well,' I said. 'But it's not much of a family occasion for most of us cats.'

Luis grinned.

'Mucho fiesta,' he said. 'You wait, you see plenty.'

He glanced at the bullfight book, and I made a horn gesture with my fingers against my forehead.

'One of the generals here has promised to import a little bull from Spain for a special bullfight,' I said.

Luis pulled a face.

'Bulls do not travel well from the mainland,' he said. 'The sea upsets them. Even little bulls are no good. It is a bad time for the bullfights. They are not what they used to be.'

'But you still have fine matadors.'

Luis shrugged.

'Ten, fourteen, maybe. We have Chicuelo II and Chamaco, but no one to approach Manolette or the Belmontes, father and son. There was Litri, but he made a fortune of twenty million pesetas and retired while the going was good.'

'What about the boys who have revived fighting on horse-back?'

'There is really only one. That is Perallta. He performs well on the horse. It is well to have revived the mounted fight, for it is the true beginning of the toreo. The kings used to fight bulls on horseback in the Plaza Mayor, in Madrid, five, six hundred years ago. The nobles continued the sport, and then came the professionals. It was the professionals who first fought the bull on foot. Now the professionals have become lazy and stylised. There was Dominguin, but we all know what happened to him. American women, pah. They are bad for the toreo; bad, bad, bad.'

'You may be right,' I said; 'but nothing will kill the toreo. I hope to be in Spain in May, for the season.'

'You must travel,' Luis said, his eyes lighting up. 'Do not stick to Madrid. Follow the fairs. Keep on the move.'

'That is my intention.'

'You will be there in May, truly?'

'As truly as can be. Unless my work takes me out of Europe altogether.'

'There can be no work sufficiently important to prevent you from following the fairs.'

'Then the toreo is *not* finito?' I said, grinning.

Luis smiled.

'Perhaps not, but one has to be critical. The professionals would become hopelessly lazy if we failed to be critical.'

'I may go to Mexico instead,' I said, teasing him.

'That would be a tragedy,' Luis said solemnly. 'The bulls in Mexico are not brave. They are lousy. The bulls that pass the test of the bravuda in Mexico we would have for meat in Spain.'

The Spanish opera singer, who had come in a few minutes earlier, turned to Simpson and said : 'If the general finds us a little bull, will you fight it ?'

Simpson smiled wearily.

'No, honey,' he said, 'my bullfighting days are over.'

There were other excitements that evening. Pinch's girl, Virginia, had arrived from Paris in the same aircraft as the twins, and she and Pinch joined Simpson's table for dinner. Others there were Rory Punt, Jug Ears, Snorts Valentine, Pia Viertel, Perdita and the Kraut. I sat between Simpson and Perdita. I had gone to my room to change after seeing Simpson dressed, and Simpson and I were wearing tuxedos, red fezes and snakeskin sandals.

'For the hotel, Juan,' I had said, arriving dolled up.

'For the hotel, Slim,' Simpson agreed, pulling a sour face at his own formal jacket.

Some concession; some hotel.

It was just a big, expensive dump.

Ernie and the twins were sitting at the next table with the Kraut, who was telling how, in Africa, he had shot at a boar from an aircraft with a point thirty-eight Smith and Wesson, and how someone with him had almost wrecked the aircraft trying to get into range. It took a long time telling.

'Why in hell didn't you land the kite and kill the boar with your hands?' I asked, after the story had gone on for twenty minutes. 'You could have thrown a rock at it.'

'You try lenting an aircraft in a canyon,' the Kraut said.

'Easy, I land aircraft in canyons regularly when I'm boar hunting.'

'Ach, nudds.'

I turned to Simpson.

'It's not sporting, is it, John?'

'What's that, Slim?'

'It's not sporting killing boar from aircraft. Especially with a point thirty-eight Smith and Wesson.'

'No, Slim. Not at all sporting. Who has been doing such things?'

'Old Krautie.'

'Shame on you, kid. Shame on you. Perdita, doesn't that old guy in a paper hat at the table behind you look sad?'

'Poor old thing,' Perdita said. 'All alone on Christmas Eve. Shall I ask him to come and join us?'

'Not yet,' Simpson said. 'Keep an eye on him, though.'

He was a fat old millionaire holding a glass of Spanish champagne up to the light, squinting at it and talking happily to himself under a funny paper hat.

The hotel was full of such oddballs. Members of the British aristocracy with their keepers. A couple of old dears from Connecticut whom we called Arsenic and Old Lace, they must have been eighty apiece, and who spent the time between courses dancing old-fashioned valetas irrespective of whether the band was knocking out jive, waltzes or sambas. A beautiful Spanish infanta, aged about twenty-four, who never went anywhere without two tough black-clad women keeping a tight grip on her arm. Sometimes this chick would start laughing to herself, and singing wild Spanish songs, until the women led her off. There were even more spectacular weirdies around, but these are the ones I remember with the most affection.

'Has Greg told you about the El Grecos?' I asked Virginia.

'He has,' Virginia said, smiling.

I had liked her immediately. She once studied art at the

Louvre school, next door to where they keep the Mona Lisa. For my money they can keep the Mona Lisa.

'Judas gold, those El Grecos,' Simpson said. 'Don't get us on that subject again, Slim.'

'You could finance a war with those pictures,' Pinch said moodily.

'I must go and see them,' Snorts said. 'I really must. God!'

Simpson was so engrossed in drawing a little sketch on the table-cloth he barely noticed when his guests began to file out. They had arranged to attend Midnight Mass, down-town at the cathedral.

'Going to Midnight Mass, John?' I asked.

'There's no hurry.'

So we remained at the table, sketching, throwing coloured streamers at other people and trying on the paper hats the waiters kept bringing round.

'It's not my religion,' Simpson said after a while; 'but I've been to Midnight Mass. The trouble is trying to avoid getting involved in a fight with the bums and rummies who hang around the entrances.'

'Let's skip it,' I said.

Simpson went on sketching on the table-cloth. Perdita started wrapping streamers all round the old screwball millionaire. I doodled dialogue on the menu.

'Is there any sport you're not good at, John?' I asked, half a bottle later.

'Sure, ski-ing. Every time I ski I fall on my ass.'

'Let's go ski-ing sometime.'

'Sure, kid, sure. That's a date.'

He looked very sad. I thought of the fishing we could have had, and felt very sad also.

'Let's ask the old screwball to join us,' Perdita said.

'Sure,' Simpson said, fetching up a cobwebby grin from the cellar of his emotions.

But when she called him over, the old man was unable to move from his chair. He tried, but he couldn't stand up. His lower lip jutted out like a baby's and I thought he was going to cry. But Perdita went over to him, and comforted him, and soon he was grinning again and making long speeches into his champagne glass.

Then Simpson looked sad again and I couldn't bear to see his sadness any more. So I went to a table, where an English girl with the French name of Jeanne had been sitting quietly all night with her parents and small brother, and I asked her to dance. The next two hours or so I spent dancing with Jeanne and drinking her father's champagne and smoking his cigars.

'What do you do in the film?' Jeanne's father asked me.

'I've been called in to write additional dialogue,' I said. 'For the whale.'

Jeanne's father laughed and slapped me on the back. Turning to Jeanne's mother, he said: 'Didn't I tell you, darling? They're all crazy in the film business.'

'Everyone's crazy,' I said. 'Mind if I dance with Jeanne again?'

'No, dear boy. Enjoy yourself.'

It was fun dancing with Jeanne. It helped me to forget about Simpson's great sadness, and my being so much the cause of it.

I went to bed around four. There had been no message from either Santos or the fishers.

.　　.　　.　　.　　.

The next day everyone had a day off because it was Christmas. It was the only free day we had throughout our stay in the Budgerigars. Shooting at sea went on, even on Sundays.

Waking around nine, I went to the Sandersons' rooms,

where I found the family unwrapping presents. The twins' mother, Jigs, handed me a box of dates.

'Oo, Mister Slim, do stop and have breakfast with us,' a twin said.

'Oo, yes, Mister Slim, you must stop and have breakfast with us,' the other twin said.

I turned and looked at Ernie.

'How's about we open a bottle of anisette?' Ernie said. 'It's a gentle drink.'

'Wonderful idea,' I said, settling down on his bed.

Ernie half filled three tumblers with the liqueur and I settled down to wait for the breakfast. Of course, ordering my breakfast in the Sanderson suite threw room service into a thorough tizzy. The Sandersons had finished breakfast and I was finishing my third half-tumbler of anisette before my fried eggs, orange juice, rum and coffee were wheeled in by a perplexed Andalusian moron. He was even more perplexed when the twins began dancing around him, stuffing sweets into his pocket as he solemnly juggled my breakfast tray from his trolley on to my lap. I gave the orange juice to the twins to fight over, swallowed the rum, and had a fourth helping of anisette. It was a merry breakfast.

'Say, Slim, coming along to the football match?' Ernie said.

'Not if you want to keep the peace,' I said. 'Used to play village football on Christmas mornings as a boy. Always wound up throwing the ref in the duck-pond.'

'Goodie, goodie,' the twins chorused. 'Then you can come swimming with us.'

'Mister Slim—er, Slim, do you mind if we just call you Slim, it's so much nicer?' a twin said.

'Yes, Slim, darling, do you mind if we don't call you Mister Slim and call you Slim. It's *much* nicer.'

'Sure,' I said. 'Much nicer. But don't expect me to call you anything but twin, irrespective of which one I'm talking to, because I never manage to sort out twins, except my wife. She is a twin.'

'Oo, are you married, Slim. Oo.'

'Oo, Slim, I didn't think you were married.'

'Oo, Slim, I was hoping you'd propose to one of us.'

'Or both of us. Boys sometimes do, you know. They propose to one and then the other. It's awfully funny. Oo, Slim, isn't it sad you're married.'

'Are you very unhappy, Slim?'

'Does your wife thoroughly misunderstand you, Slim?'

'Most wives do, don't they, Dill?'

'They all do, Doll. When we marry we shall thoroughly misunderstand our husbands, won't we, Doll?'

'Oo, yes, and then they'll beat us.'

'Do you beat your wife, Slim?'

Ernie yelled: 'Will you two beat the hell out of here for half an hour and let Slim finish his breakfast in peace?'

'We like it here with Slim, don't we, Dill? We'd rather be here than anywhere in the world.'

'Oo, Daddy, don't be cruel and send us away. We couldn't bear it, could we, Doll?'

'No, we'd be heartbroken, Daddy, really we would. Don't let him send us away, Slim. We wouldn't know what to do with ourselves till Slim took us to the pool.'

Jigs said: 'Have you forgotten Kevin? I can hear him singing in the next room down. Didn't you promise to help him to shave last night?'

The twin I learnt to recognise as Dill leapt from the bed and dashed through the open french windows, yelling: 'Oo, oo, oo, oo, Kevin. I almost forgot you. You haven't started shaving yet, have you? Oo, you beast, you're half-way through. You are mean. Still, I forgive you.'

Her voice trailed away and the twin who I learnt to recognise as Doll snuggled up to me and said: 'Well, *I* won't desert

Slim. I don't care if he *is* married. I still love him, and I shall look after him while we are here.'

'That's fine,' I said. 'How would you like to be my wine-bearer?'

'Oo, I would love that, Slim. Can I really be your wine-bearer? Can I start now? Can I pour you some more anisette right away? Hurry, drink that up. Pass me the bottle, Daddy.'

'Hey, take it easy,' Ernie yelled. 'It's not ten yet.'

'Don't worry, Daddy,' Doll said. 'Slim can take it. I saw the way he was knocking back the drinks last night.'

'Well, go easy,' Ernie growled. 'And save some for your old dad.'

Jigs yelled: 'Steady there, Doll. Gosh, it's pouring over the top. Pour some of it back.'

'No, Mummy. You must let me do this my way. *I'm* Slim's wine-bearer, aren't I, Slim?'

'You are, sweetheart.'

'There you are, Mummy. You see, Slim understands me. I think he loves me. Do you, Slim? *Do* you love me?'

'Just keep on bearing the wine, sweetheart, and we won't quarrel.'

'Oh, Mummy, I'm so happy. Will you come to our wedding, Daddy?'

'Oh, for Christ's sake,' Ernie said, putting his tie on. 'I've got to get down to that goddam football match. Don't let them drown you in that pool, Slim.'

'He won't drown,' Doll said smugly. 'He's got *me* to look after him now. Don't worry, Slim. You'll never feel lonely again. Isn't it wonderful?'

'Wonderful,' I said, gulping down the anisette between mouthfuls of lukewarm fried egg.

Fortunately, the twins soon found other friends by the pool and I had a quiet morning writing and sipping gin and Cinzano and watching the swimmers. Then we drove down to Las Flamenco where Ernie had reserved a table for lunch : Simpson, Pinch, Perdita, Virginia, Snorts, Ernie and me.

The restaurant, close by the seashore, was almost empty. A slow-witted head waiter ambled over and showed us to a table near the window. Some island urchins squatted by the half-open window and began to hiss for us to throw them pesetas. A cop chased them away.

The service in the restaurant was painfully slow.

'God,' Snorts groaned, 'it's as bad as the hotel.'

'We must hustle them up,' Simpson said irritably. 'We must be at the football ground by three-thirty.'

We were going to watch a football match from the Governor's box, and Pinch had agreed to kick off.

The first course was shrimps. Big, fat shrimps. But taste-less. They came a plateful at a time, at five-minute intervals. We talked about Hollywood, whales, horses and Farouk.

Then Snorts said : 'God, you should of been to that Mass they held in the cathedral last night. Christ, the spectacle, the drama. They kept up all the old customs. They laid down a greasy carpet for the old priest and then he didn't use it. Ten minutes later the goddam carpet was taken away again. God, you should have seen that line-up of priests. It sure was a Mass.'

The last helping of shrimps had only just arrived and the next course was not nearly ready. Simpson slapped the table with his hands and said : 'We can't wait a moment longer. Come on, let's go.'

He rose and walked out to the car. So we paid for the shrimps and went to the football arena. Pinch being with us generated the usual excitement. It was like being at the fight arena; a sort of remote-control reaction shot through the crowd like an electric wave. And within seconds everyone in the place was chanting :

.   'Grigorio Pinch, Grigorio Pinch.'

And :

'Viva Grigorio.'

And then the slow, liquid clapping in the sunshine.

Pinch stood up and waved, and that calmed the crowd for a while. We bowed to the Governor and his party in chairs just behind us, and settled in our seats. It was a wide, green soccer pitch. The stands were almost packed out. It was sunny. We felt good.

Pinch turned to me and said : 'How the hell do you kick a soccer ball, Slim? With your toe, or with the side of your foot?'

'The side of your foot,' I said. 'But don't worry about it. Just kick it naturally. You'll do it splendidly, anyway.'

'I'm not so sure,' the actor grunted.

But when the teams were lined up and an escort of island beauty queens came to lead him on the pitch, he looked easy and confident, He went up to the ball, eyed the pitch, then slammed the ball almost into the goalmouth. The crowd loved it, and roared approval. It really was a splendid kick.

Both teams played to kill, and several players were knocked out and carried off on stretchers. One may have been killed, I forget. During the interval an acrobat did handstands on top of two chairs piled on three tables. Ernie kept passing up chilled bottles of La Tropical beer with Felizes Navidad printed across the label. It was a splendid game. We gambled on the teams. Pinch did well out of the game all round. Everyone was happy as we drove back to the hotel in the Cadillac. You know how it is with Cadillacs.

At the reception desk I was told that Santos had phoned and would phone again after midnight.

The Christmas party started with drinks on the patio at seven. When I strolled in around seven-thirty the party was well under way. King Connell was showing everyone his new bible : a pack of playing cards in a transparent wrapper

Simpson had given him as a Christmas present. Count Krantz, looking like a blown-up Von Stroheim, was advising Simpson on what hunting guns to buy in Austria. Rory Punt and Jug Ears were talking about the latest cricket scores from Australia. Dublin was talking shrilly about Palestrina. Cedric Donnell was holding himself in, clearing his throat every few minutes, ready to burst into song. We went into the banqueting room. Ernie had placed me between Doll and a bearded, sad-eyed stunt-man called Reg Atilla. Doll, very prim, coy almost, did not forget her duty as wine-bearer and my glass was never short of the good local wine.

It was quite a banquet; caviare, bananas, rum.

King Connell, facing me across the table, had been watching Doll's ministrations with deep interest. He suddenly pointed a stubby finger at me.

'You think you can drink?' he sneered, tossing a chicken bone over his shoulder. 'There's only one man at this table who can drink, and that's John King Connell.'

Egged on by Doll and the sad Atilla I found myself challenging Connell to a drinking bout.

Reg wrote the following contract on a menu : 'King Connell v. Slim Hammer. 1. Drink for Drink for 1 day. 2. 500 pts plus cost of Drink for both. King, Brandy. Slim, Whisky. Both uncorked. Both to start at 11 a.m. Adjudication—The first contestant to become unconscious. (Signed) John King Connell. Slim Hammer.

I added a clause : If one or other of the Contestants becomes excessively obnoxious, or objectionable, the decision will go to the opponent.

I figured that it would be easy, after an hour or two of solid drinking, to throw insults at Connell and bring out the worst in him.

There was a clearing of plates and then a sand-artist known as Bennie Smiles, uncrowned King of the Zambezi River,

8—TCK

called for silence. People began to make speeches; you know how it is at banquets. I did not listen too carefully, but I heard Pinch propose a toast to 'the man who has dragged us half-way through God's green acres and across the world'. Then Simpson rose and announced that he was going into the fight business and that he was going to put on a boxing bout at the local fight arena. With the co-operation of the island's boxing promoters, he assured us, he was going to raise funds for Budgerigar charities. Ever since he had been to the fights on the previous Saturday, Simpson went on, he had been brooding about something. This was it. A unit boxing contest. Himself a former lightweight champion of the State of California, he intended to referee the fight. Two of the toughest stuntmen were to fight alternate rounds with Tommy Pegg, a born killer. Pinch, Snorts and Punt were to act as seconds. Dublin, a former Irish Universities amateur, was to act as timekeeper.

Perdita looked pale, and there was a loud groan when Simpson announced that tickets would cost one hundred pesetas apiece. And no flannel substitutes accepted.

The director then spoke of the approaching end of making the film.

He said :

'A picture is made and we go our separate ways. It will have a frame round it and our job will be over.' He was obviously moved by what he was saying : 'This has been a long voyage.' He paused, then said : 'I think very highly of every-one here tonight.'

And sat down. There was a silence, then applause.

Then the Vice-Consul rose and said :

'You are nourishing the island; not only because we have taken a real liking to you, but because the island will have reason to remember you all.' (You can say that again, I thought. With orchids.)

The speeches over, a troupe of island dancers and singers skipped in, slapping tambourines and guitars. They played several dashing Budgerigario melodies, and then the Vice-Consul got in amongst them and sang 'The Virgin of Fundador' and 'The Seguidilla', a fierce song involving much hand-clapping and fierce stamping of the feet. Then there was a request for Simpson to sing.

Looking happily cockeyed, the director stood up and obliged with 'I met a Venezuelan with a basket on her head'.

Then Cedric sang 'Ol' Man River'.

And King Connell sang 'I fell in love with Mary from the Dairy'.

And someone got up and said :

'Ladies and gentlemen, I have been asked to announce that we'll all sing the theme song of the Casa Maria.'

And everyone joined in singing 'Night and Day'.

At this point the banquet began to fall apart. The revellers rose and stood round the pianist roaring songs and arguing in little groups. Several fights started. Hotel guests, in Dior creations and tails, peeked in fearfully as they hurried past the banqueting room.

I sat for a while on the steps leading to our room, talking to Simpson.

'How you making out with your writing, kid?'

'Fine,' I said. 'Couldn't be better. The words are just singing out.'

Simpson stared ahead in silence. Then he said :

'I'll tell you a story about Papa Hemingway, kid. Once when I was down at his place he was talking very much along the same lines. Everything was fine. The words were singing. There was no greater feeling in the world, he said, than anchoring your words firmly on paper. Some months later I saw him in New York and we went some place, the ballet or an art gallery, and it bored us to hell. It was a bad ballet or a bad collection of pictures. I don't remember which, it was that bad. So we beat it. As we left, Papa groaned out loud and said : "Jesus, that was terrible. *I'd rather write.*" '

I spat gloomily.

Ernie joined us on the stairs, and then other people came. 'God, what a mob,' Ernie said.

The singing by the piano was very loud.

We sat on the stairs for a long time.

Then I wandered out of the hotel and went down to the beach. There was no moon. I didn't think any beautiful thoughts. I did not think about anything. It was good to feel the night wind and hear waves instead of voices; to be there not thinking anything. Then I returned.

Back in the hotel a dozen stuntmen and technicians were carrying the piano, and the piano stool with the pianist still on it, out the banqueting room, through the foyer, then upstairs towards the bar. All the time they carefully kept the pianist balanced on his stool, close up to the keyboard. The pianist remained perched on his stool, pounding out jazz, as he was carried through the hotel along with his piano to the bar.

'Where do you think the manager is?' I asked Ernie.

'Locked away in his room, I guess,' Ernie said, yawning.

He was probably right, at that.

The party had moved over to the American bar. Nick La Rodd, with his jacket turned inside out, was going round forcing everyone else to do the same. Some timid souls fled. The rest did as Nick asked, apart from a solid-looking doctor from Texas who puffed out his cheeks angrily and clutched his tuxedo defensively.

'Rip it off him,' someone yelled, but the doctor dug his heels in and the inside-out brigade moved on. The boys were chicken, really, when it came to roughing-up Texans.

Simpson reappeared, a thin, drooping figure in the middle

of a long conga chain. He looked tired and cockeyed and I don't think he was really enjoying himself any more, but the other conga dancers had fetched him from his bedroom just as he was about to undress and he was doing his best to keep everyone happy.

A page called me to the reception desk. I was wanted on the telephone.

I picked up a receiver.

'Señor Sleem?'

'Sí.'

'He is here. He is willing to see you.'

'The big fisher?'

'Sí, but do not say it now. When you come I take you to private room.'

'I'll be there in twenty minutes, amigo.'

'Good. You my brother; we fix.'

I took a studio car to the Angry Coconut and pushed in through the crowd, spotting several members of the unit being happily clipped. Raquel gave me a big hello, but Santos caught my arm and steered me rapidly into a back room. I clenched my fists when I saw the big baboon sitting in the corner, a simple, reflex reaction. But the big guy was slobbering happily over a wine bottle and he waved in what seemed a friendly way.

'Thou, me, amigos,' Don Pablo said. 'Thou white trash, me no care. Viva General Grant. Viva Barbara Hutton. Viva all fishermen. Here, you sit down. Drink from my wine bowl. Hey, drink. Rapido.'

I drank.

'I tell thee, also rapido, for I have much to do,' the fisherman continued. 'Island fishermen, they sad. They hear that the great, sportif huntsman director Simpson is truly a fisherman. They also hear that he did not understand what had been done about the fishers before he arrived on the island. Now I, Don Pablo Ruiz Polianski-Smith, personally invite the big white hunter to fish with me. We go, on the first day of the New Year. As a gift and token of our respect. We fishermen are proud. We ask no payment, nor do we ask that any of our fishermen go back on the payroll. We have our own stock of flannel, and we do not wish to encourage inflation. So tell your big white hunter to be ready for the chasing of the big fish on the first day of the year. Leave it to Psmith. Now sit down, drink from wine bowl of fisherman.'

'I thank thee, but——'

'Drink. Rapido.'

I drank, rapido.

'Now go,' the fisher said. 'Go, dance with your señorita. I see her there, waiting. I bless thee and have told the headman at the bar not to milk thy camels too severely. We drink, to fish. The big fisherman drinks to the big white hunter. We go fish together. And remember about the camels. We clip thee not. Farewell, my blessing season this in thee.'

'Gracias,' I said, but truly. 'Mucho gracias. Felizes Navidad.'

'Felizes Navidad,' the fisher said, bending down to his wine bowl. 'Long live Teddy Roosevelt. Up the Dodgers. Viva Lilian Gish.'

I returned to the dance room, where Santos and Raquel were waiting with champagne, with handles.

It was dawn when I got back to the hotel. Due to the Christmas overflow in the hotel, the Kraut was sleeping in the spare bed in my room. The french doors were wide open, the sun was beginning to light up the palms and cactus bushes in the garden. I felt good, seeing the dawn and knowing that I was the last to go to bed and that soon we would go fishing. I felt *so* good I did not even mind having the Kraut's cameras and lens cases cluttering up my desk. Mercifully he was not snoring. I was not feeling all that good.

I picked up a note from my pillow. I read: 'Beware, if you are unfaithful I will have you shot and thrown to the dogs.' It was written in a smudgy, little girl's script. Dear Doll, I thought. I must be careful not to break any young hearts in this madhouse world. Then I sank heavily into bed.

The pillow felt cool and starched and clean against my cheek, and sleep came quickly. For a while I did not dream, not even of fish; no, not even of flannel fish with handles. But then harsh, sunshot pictures began to float like fins, briefly seen, to my surface mind. . . .

CHAPTER SEVEN

Dream Sequence: Of Bulls and Guitars

THE LANGUAGE OF the bullfight is one of specialised words. Hemingway's glossary at the end of *Death in the Afternoon* gives it comprehensively, from abanico to zapatillas. In between, you have a wide range of jolting, onomatopoetically exciting vocabulary : caballoo, capa or capote (for the cape used in bullfighting); or defenderse, desigual, pica, novedad, mamarracho, or ligereza. If you are new to bullfighting, such words will seem esoteric and flash. If you have followed the fairs they will sound as commonplace as an old love-word, and the most consistent image they form upon the inner eye is that of a tattered and once-gaudy carpet slipper lined with razors. But there is one word that even people who are barely on the edge of aficion will use with respect, and sparingly : recibir.

Hemingway tells us that this is the most difficult, dangerous and emotional way to kill bulls; even he has only seen it executed completely three times in almost three hundred bull-fights. It is the killing of the bull from in front, awaiting his charge with sword without moving the feet once the charge has started; with the muleta low in the left hand and the sword in the right hand, right forearm across the chest pointing towards the bull, and as he comes in and takes the muleta, putting the sword in with the right hand and swinging him out with the muleta in the left as in a pase de pecho, not moving the feet until the sword has gone in. It is the perfect kill.

Now in this dream I saw Simpson wearing a bullfight outfit and standing up to a succession of angry bulls. There were brave small bulls, large cowardly bulls, and clumsy bumping bulls. The funny thing about all these bulls is that each one had a human face, and each face belonged to members of the unit. Punt. Perdita. Pia. Pinch. Some others. And some bulls were fresco, or cynical, some were flogo, or weak, and some were abano, or cowardly and refusing to charge. Others were very, very brave. But Simpson killed them all.

Only one bull was completely frank in his charges, noble and perfect in all his movements. It wore the face of Pinch. To switch to the terminology of show jumping, one could not fault this one.

I became interested and the unaccountable sound of guitars in my ears irritated me, for I wished only to concentrate on the outcome of this rare fight. Simpson was preparing for the great moment of perfect communion with the bull, the finest recibir of all time, and then the guitar noises woke me and I was surrounded by a crowd of hophead Budgerigar musicians and singers. But this was also in dream experience.

Still in sleep, I tried to send my vision back to the sunlit bullring, to where the kill was about to take place, but the guitarists pushed their jangling strings close to my ears and I fell back into an existence which was all sound. Someone held a glass of vino Rioja against my lips, a thick, full-bodied wine, and I sank away from the guitar strings and lost myself in a kaleidoscope of Spanish skirts, many colours cart-wheeling in fierce Flamenco patterns. Then the dream snapped.

Nick: 'You're a pretentious bastard.'

Slim: 'I know. But how would *you* handle this material?'

Nick: 'I'd stuff it. I would avoid writing it.'

Slim: 'That's the trouble with so many of you. You've become so goddam smart you choke on true words and write only the things you feel sure are most likely to impress the smart set, whatever that is. You know how a flashy bullfighter resorts to the method of *adorno*, of useless or flowery theatricality performed to show his domination over the bull. You would have me do that.'

Nick : 'You can do what you damned well please. I am not writing this book.'

Slim : 'Then remain quiet and stop trying to distract me. We are barely half-way through and there is much more to tell.'

Nick : 'About the fishers? I like it when it deals with the fishers.'

Slim : 'Yes, there will be more about fishers. And also more about Simpson and his kill. Bear with me about this matter of *recibir*.'

Nick : 'Okay, get on with it. Here, have a drink.'

Slim : 'Not just now, thanks. There is much work ahead.'

Nick : 'Check. Lights, cameras—*roll* 'em !'

CHAPTER EIGHT

'I Like it when my Sleep go to Feet'

'THEY'RE GOING TO kill Connell Connor.'

The twins' voices tore me from a dream of standing naked in a cinema queue. By the sun it was nearing ten o'clock. The Kraut had left without disturbing me. I had had a good three hours' sleep.

The twins were absentmindedly pulling feathers out of a cockatoo and chattering on the long stone veranda beyond my french doors. A low wall separated my section of veranda from the bit that ran past the Sandersons' suite and on to Kevin o' the Bog's room at the end. I slipped on a bathrobe, tripped over a chair, and went out and watched the twins. They had released the bird, and were now throwing Christmas cake to the wild budgerigars that flew among the sunlit tropical plants and flowers in the garden beyond the veranda.

'Oo, Slim, good morning. They're going to kill Connell.'

'Good morning, Slim. Yes, it's true. They're going to kill him, really they are.'

'At sea.'

'Yes, they're going to *drown* him.'

'How do you know?'

'I heard Kevin talking about it on the phone before he shaved.'

There was a commotion nearby. Hearing a shriek, the twins dashed off. A few seconds later Doll rushed back.

'Oo, Slim, Slim, come quick. Connell thinks he's a bull-fighter. He's in the corridor fighting Cadenzia.'

Cadenzia was one of the chambermaids on our floor, a fat, jolly Budgerigario in her thirties.

I turned back into my room, went through the hall, and opened the door. The twins were perfectly right. Connell, fierce as a fighting cock, was ducking and dancing around Cadenzia on his tiptoes. He held a broom in one hand and a duster in the other, prodding with the broom and making sketchy reboleras with the duster. Dropping the broom and grasping the duster with both hands, he parodied a few veronicas. Then picking up the broom again, he attempted to stick it into her neck. Connell was very serious about it.

Cadenzia fought back breathlessly, half laughing, half scared. Sometimes she put her fists up to her forehead and stuck out her forefingers to simulate horns with which to butt and ram Connell. But the wiry Irishman kept leaping out of her way, tickling her with the broom-end as she lumbered past him. His cheeks mauve, his little eyes hot and angry, he pranced round her and jabbed with the broom.

He was partly dressed in the old-fashioned seaman's costume he wore for the film.

The twins clung to me.

'Oo, he's really in a rage, isn't he, Slim?'

'He looks fierce enough,' I said. 'But don't be scared, he is without salsa.'

'What is that, Slim?'

'Sauce,' I explained. 'He lacks the salsa torera. He is fighting a bull of straw and knows it.'

'I know why he is doing it,' Dill said.

'Bet you don't,' Doll said.

'I do, too. It's because he knows they're going to kill him at sea today and he doesn't like the idea at all. Poor Connell.'

'You're right,' Doll said thoughtfully. 'Poor Connell. Of course. That's why he's drunk.'

'He's not drunk,' Dill said. 'He's only scared.'

'He's drunk, too. He must be drunk.'

'Why?'

'He asked me to marry him.'

'Then he *is* drunk,' Dill said. 'I've never had a sober proposal yet.' She giggled.

'What is it now?' Doll said crossly.

'I was just trying to picture you married to Connell.'

'I would reform him.'

Cadenzia had manœuvred Connell into a corner.

'Go on, Cadenzia,' Dill yelled. 'Kill him.'

'Oo, Slim, stop them. They'll slaughter each other.'

Then Kevin arrived, looking very stern. Connell's dreams of glory in the bullring faded at the sight of the second assistant director. Cadenzia gave a scared asthmatic cough and fled with her broom and duster to her cubby-hole. I went back to my quarters and took a shower. By the time I was shaved and dressed Connell had been safely coaxed away to his drowning scene. I decided to work by the swimpool. The twins joined me there.

'Isn't Mister Simpson cruel?' Doll said. 'He must have known that poor Connell would be in bad shape on Boxing Day. Yet he fixed his drowning scene for today.'

'It's being kind really,' Dill said. 'I know how these things are done.'

She drew a finger across her throat.

'Poor Connell,' Doll said. 'We'll miss him. Will you swim with us, Slim?'

I dropped a writing pad and the Kipling book on the grass and spread a towel out.

'Not now,' I said. 'I've just had breakfast.'

'Never mind, you won't sink,' Dill said scornfully.

'We'll rescue you if you do,' Doll said. 'You need never be afraid of sinking when we are with you, Slim darling. We'd rescue you and give you artificial respiration.'

'And brandy,' Dill said.

'I would fetch you an enormous bottle from the bar.'

'All the same, I'm not going in yet.'

'Meanie,' Dill said.

'Don't be so inconsiderate,' Doll said. 'Slim has every right to do whatever he pleases. Here, let me spread out your towel.'

Doll picked up the bath towel and crumpled it into a heap.

'There, make yourself comfortable. Shall I fetch you a drink?'

'Not just now. Ask again in an hour from now. Now beat it, twins.'

'All right, Slim.' Doll hesitated. 'Do you think they'll really kill Connell?'

'Who knows?' I said, ruffling through my notes. 'I could think of worse things.'

'Oo, you are horrid.'

'Stop chattering and come and swim, Doll.'

'All right. Goodbye for now, Slim. Let me know if you hear what's happened to Connell.'

I got through a lot of work and swam a little. At lunch Ernie talked about the arrangements for the boxing match. He had found a local printer to do the fight announcements. The posters were printed in English and Spanish. The Spanish versions spelled all the actors' names wrong. This had had to be altered quickly. You know how actors are about their names. But they still hadn't got Snorts Valentine right. I pointed this out to him as he passed our table. Snorts took one look at the proofs and said :

'Judas faces, these goddam Spaniards. What kind of people are they? You'd think they'd get a guy's name right. God.'

And he picked up a waiter and threw him through a window. Hell, the waiter wasn't even a printer.

After lunch, Ernie and I sat in the patio, drinking coffee. The fight was still boiling over in his mind.

'John has taken Terrible Tom completely under his wing. You know how?' Ernie asked. 'He keeps going over to Tommy with fresh instructions, each one cancelling out the other. John is very serious about it, and Tom listens carefully and nods and then goes off to a quiet corner and tries to piece it all together. The other actors are getting quite jealous. They think Tommy's getting a bigger part in the film. All the time John is acting like he's punchy, slurring his words and glazing his eyes till they look like contact lenses. You want to watch him the next time he talks to Tom. What a performer. Stanislavsky couldn't teach that guy a thing, not a thing. It's getting so that Tom is beginning to believe he really is a punchy.'

I worked in my room till five. Then I boxed for half an hour at the gymnasium, down-town. It was funny boxing with Budgerigarios. They were punks, most of them. Then I changed into a white Spanish shirt, thick black tie, lightweight gaberdine suit, sandals, rainbow socks and clapped a Cordobés hat on my head. Doll pushed in as I was knotting the tie, her big dark eyes troubled.

'I'm terribly worried about Connell, Slim. I think Mister Simpson really has killed him. He didn't come back from location.'

'Don't worry,' I said. 'He's probably drinking in a bar somewhere.'

'No, I've asked. He definitely didn't come back on any of the boats. Everyone else is ashore, but no one has seen Connell.'

'Okay. Let's go to Mister Simpson's suite and find out what he has done with Connell.'

We ran into Kevin on the way up.

'Perhaps he can help us,' Doll said.

'Wur-wuts bothering you two lu-love birds?'

'Oo, Kevin, we think Connell has been killed. Do *you* know what's happened?'

Kevin looked sly.

'Hurvent a clue,' he said vaguely. 'He wus ur-ur-ur-ursleep on the *Fishbite* most of the day. Apurt from wur-when we needed him for shur-shur-shur-shur-shur-shots after larunch.' To me, he said : 'Yur should have seen it, old boy. Don't think Connell really knew wur-wur-wur-what wus happening to him. That drowning scene should look blur-blur-blur—very good on the scur-reen. After he'd been dur-dur-dunked several times he didn't look human. Maybe we *did* drown him. Could *be*.'

'We'll have to organise a search party,' Doll said firmly. 'We must get the local admiral to drag the harbour for Connell's body.'

'Bur-better check with John,' Kevin said hastily. 'Must get a shower. Goodbye.'

'Hello, kids, have a Scotch,' Simpson said amiably when we entered his suite. 'Will you have something to drink, Doll?'

'No, thank you, Mr. Simpson,' Doll said severely. 'What have you done to Connell?'

Simpson looked startled.

'Why, has anything happened to Connell? What is all this about, Slim?'

'Doll is worried, John,' I said, pouring whisky. 'She thinks you've killed Connell.'

'She does, huh? Well, let me see.' Simpson rummaged around the room, as if searching for something. He tapped the table with his fingers. 'Connell, Connell. He's missing, hah?'

'Yes, he certainly *is*, Mister Simpson,' Doll said sternly. 'And it's no use trying to fool me. I know you drowned him.

It's not the first time you've thrown actors to the sharks.'

Simpson looked hurt.

'Now, Doll——'

The telephone rang. It was a call from London.

I said: 'Come on, Doll. Let's see if someone else knows anything. Rory Punt is a lawyer. He might help.'

'Oo, Mr. Punt is such a terribly nice man. I'm sure he'll help.' The child scowled at Simpson.

I swallowed my whisky and left the director talking into the phone. We couldn't find Rory and then Ernie turned up and told Doll to do some little chore with her mother.

'But Mister Simpson has drowned Connell,' she protested.

'Never mind about that now,' Ernie said. 'Run along to your mother.'

I borrowed the latest copy of *Time* from Ernie and went to a corner of the bar and read. There was a report of Simpson's fight with the little bull in Madrid in the Names Make News section. Suddenly I looked up from the magazine and saw Connell stalking towards Simpson's suite, a gaunt, tattered little figure shaking his fists and dripping like a terrier washed up on the seashore.

Seeing Kevin, I called to him and pointed to the drenched Dubliner.

'Hey, what gives?' I asked.

'Gug-God only knows. Lurooks like he's come straight out of the sea.'

We peeped into the door. The little Irishman was trembling with rage. Simpson towered over him, shaking with laughter.

'Cur-come on,' Kevin said. 'Let's leave them to it.'

'What do you think happened?' I asked as we moved off.

'Huvn't a clue. Still, Connell looks pretty much the same as usual.'

'Yeah. Maybe he just had a shower and forgot to take his clothes off.'

'That's exactly what did happen,' Kevin said quietly. 'Come on, let's go to the bowling alley.'

'Sure.'

We didn't mention Connell again. You know how it is with half-drowned actors.

.   .   .   .

At the bowling alley we heard of other disasters.

The Kraut had fallen into the sea and ruined a new camera.

A sailor had smashed an arm while lowering a boat.

Eight more people had got the Tourist Twostep.

Someone had thrown King Connell's bible overboard. King had clung to the rails, real tears running into his beard, yelling goodbye to each of his cards as they fluttered away across the water.

Dill joined us, complaining of a headache.

Then Simpson made one of his quietly dramatic appearances. He was wearing a sombrero, the slippers with foxheads on them, and a Spanish cloak. My head was also aching, from a boxing blow across the temples. So I told Dill to ask her mother for an aspirin. Overhearing this, Simpson put Dill on his knee, and said : 'Go easy on the aspirins, kid.'

'Why, Mister Simpson?'

'If ever you get to Mexico, you'd know why. Have you never heard about Pancho Villa's aspirin?'

The child shook her head.

'Well, one of Pancho's generals showed up with a hangover after a heavy night and told his leader that he had a headache. "You have?" Pancho said. The other guy nodded. "Okay," Pancho said. "Then you better take an aspirin, kid." "Thanks," the general said, "where is it?" Pancho raised his gun and said, "Here, kid, here!" And he shot the guy; shot him dead.'

'At what distance?' I asked.

'Two yards,' Simpson said, scowling at me. 'They never waste bullets in Mexico.'

'Do you still want that aspirin, Slim?' Dill asked.

I looked at Simpson, and shrugged.

'No,' I said, 'skip it.' To Simpson I said: 'In the Mexican Army, didn't they used to save ammunition at executions by killing several men with one bullet?'

'Sure,' Simpson said, brightening. 'Yeah, it was like that still when I was in the cavalry. Whenever there was an execution, the officer in charge of the firing squad would stack up three guys in line, one behind the other, and have one bullet go through the lot of them. Then he'd pick up the three cigarettes these guys had been smoking and hand them to the next three victims. Very economical.'

The director was happy again.

Doll said, 'In Mexico they used to bury people up to the neck in sand and then have men on horses ride over them and smash their heads in like eggs.'

'Sure, kid,' Simpson beamed. 'Sure.'

Dill said: 'I think I'm going to be sick.'

Simpson went off happily and joined the skittles players. King Connell, on the prowl for a poker school, nudged me.

'John's one of the cleanest bowlers I ever seen,' King said. 'Watch that action. Hell, Rodin could have made something out of the way John slams that ball at the middle pin.'

'Yeah,' I said, accepting a chaw of tobacco from the poker player.

King sighed.

'Judas priest, I could use a woman,' he said.

'Why don't you move in over there?' I said. 'I've never seen so many popsies.'

Half of the island's female population must have turned out to watch Pinch playing in the bowling alley.

'You want to leave them alone, brother,' King advised.

'Unless you want a knife in your back. They're watched over like——'

'Hell, they're just punk Budgerigarios,' I said, sipping my third Alexandria, a brandy-based cocktail.

King shook his head and chewed his curly beard. Tobacco juice ran through the hairs.

I said : 'You've gone chicken.'

King spat and said : 'I'm not chicken. It's just that I got a pain in the gut.'

'You got the Tourist's Twostep,' I said.

'Who, me?' King looked indignant. 'I just got gut-ache worrying about John. Look, I see this film as a crisis in our lives, in *all* our lives. But mostly I see it as a crisis in John's life. Hear me, for twenty-five years he's been planning this. Now it's almost over. Unless something terrible happens, we'll wind up soon and disperse. And what do I see? Brother, I see a very lonely man.'

'You see that? You *really* see that, King?'

'Yeah. I see a lonely man. A very lonely man.'

'But there'll be other locations,' I said. 'New crowds, new artistic problems, new scenes, new actors——'

'So what? Hear me, John Simpson is one of the loneliest men on earth. And this film has made him lonelier than ever. I know—I know what human loneliness is, believe me.'

'You're a goddam profound hombre,' I said.

'You're telling me I am.'

'And you goddam stink,' I said.

'Milk,' King said. 'Your mother's and your sisters' milk. You couldn't even fix up a fishing trip.'

'I can and I have,' I said.

'I'll believe it when I see it,' King said, and he spat.

'Ah, forget it and have a drink.'

'Yeah, okay. I might as well keep in training for our contest.'

'You haven't a chance, punk.'

King spat again. Good yellow tobacco juice.

'I'll murder you when the time comes,' he said.

'I wouldn't be so sure, son.'

'I never been surer of anything in my life.'

I got drinks and the Kraut joined us. I told him to cover the fight for a picture magazine.

'It hess possibilities,' Kraut said cautiously. 'I vill take my cameras vizz me and see if it is verse vile.'

'Worth while,' Ernie exploded, joining us. 'Judas Iscariot, with Pinch as a second and Simpson refereeing, the whole world will think it worth a gander.'

'Veevait and see, no?'

'No,' I said. 'I've got to cable right away if we are to do it.'

The Kraut sighed.

'Okay, vee do it.'

I got Ernie a drink and we watched the bowlers.

After a while, the Kraut said: 'Nuzzing is heppening here. All I get is pictures of Chon Simpson directing a film.'

'Isn't that what you came down for?' Ernie said.

'It is not enough. Ver iss der vale?'

'You'll get your whale,' Ernie said. 'You'll get all the whale you want.'

'But ver is der vale *now*? Vy isn't it ready? Chon Simpson neffer hess anything ready on time. He does not seem to care vezzer he hess a vale or not. Vy is det?'

'Simpson cares very much,' Ernie told the Kraut. 'But he doesn't believe in yelling around for things.'

'Vy not? Det is chust vot he should do.'

'He is busy with other things.'

'Such ess?'

'Such as photographing clouds, and birds, and Greg.'

'Nussing but bird ent clouds ent small boats. I cannot choost photograph ectors in small boats all the time.'

'What's the hurry?'

'I vish to go soon to Efrica. Photograph Morocco.'

'I'll see Simpson about it right away,' Ernie snarled. 'I'll get him to hustle his film through so you can go take pictures in Morocco.'

The Kraut was not convinced.

'But he iss not hustling anysings,' he said. 'All this afternoon he play cards on board the *Fishbite* and talk about fishing teckle. You call det being a great director? Uzzer directors trow me off the set when I em arount. But he play poker wiss people who cannot afford to lose, ent giff me bick hello. He hess much more money than most people here, yet he play high stakes poker instet of getting on wiss making film. He's nod a great director.'

'You should worry, so long as you get pictures.'

'Anodder thing. A great director would not be chealous of his star.'

Ernie bunched his fists together.

'So now you're telling me that Simpson is jealous of Pinch?' he said.

'I em,' the Kraut said. 'Diss evening ven we step ashore the crowds rush the police cordon and mob Grek. For five minutes he stents on the beach signing autographs. The fens ignore Chon Simpson. So after five minutes of this he says sneppily, "Come on, Grek, stop signing autographs." '

'Five minutes is a long time,' Ernie said. 'There are such things as incoming calls from London, Calcutta, New York, Hollywood, *and* from his wife in Ireland. He has conferences with Ozzie and the production boys. He spends hours on the telephone fixing things.'

'Ven I saw him he voss nod on the telephone,' the Kraut said darkly. 'He voss drinking whisky.'

'You don't say. What do you make of that, Slim?'

'Guess he was thirsty.'

'But do you sink it voss funny to half drown Connell Connor?'

'Yeah, very funny. After all, Connell knew he wasn't going on a Sunday school sleigh-ride when he signed on for this trip.'

'Ent you really sink det funny? I cannot understent you.'

'Ah, cojones,' Ernie said.

Late church bells ringing in the distance suddenly made me think of Christmas. I didn't want to think of anything, really. I didn't want to think of whales or Krauts or photography or actors or even fishing. Least of all fishing.

Ernie and I joined a crowd round Simpson. The director was talking quietly to Terrible Tom.

'You gotta make it look good, kid,' Simpson was saying, his mouth slipping to one side like a rubber catapult.

'Do I really talk like that, John?' Tommy asked anxiously. 'No, seriously, tell me the truth.'

'You tell him, Ernie,' Simpson said, turning to us.

Ernie stared thoughtfully at Tom.

'He's got the symptoms, John. He's well on the way, all right, all right.'

'Go on, you're kidding,' Tom said.

'I wouldn't kid on a subject like that,' Ernie said seriously. 'I seen too many punches to joke about it. You want to watch yourself kid.'

'Hell, this is terrible,' Tom said.

He went away, shaking his head slowly.

Simpson began singing 'On the Bays of Mexico.' We joined in on the chorus lines. You know how guys get nostalgic about Mexico.

'When did John first go to Mexico?' King asked as the director moved away.

'It was way back,' Ernie said. 'He was just a kid out of high school. But he was already following the gee-gees, and one day

he had a big win at the track. He went to Mexico to spend his
winnings, and while he was there he went on a three-day bat
and woke up with all his money gone. Well, he'd seen crack
Mexican cavalry displays at the Garden so he decided to enlist
in the cavalry down there. Just like that. For the next three
years he travelled half round the world as a Mexican Army
show jumper.'

'Judas priest,' King said. 'He sure loves animals. Hell, do
you know what he gave his wife for Christmas? He sent her a
Spanish donkey and cart. There's a real thoughtful gift. The
donkey can pull her and the kids all around Ireland.'

'Why the hell don't *you* think up nice Christmas presents
like that?' Ernie's wife said, coming up beside us.

'I nearly gave you a couple of guitarists,' he said.

'Real live ones?' Jigs asked, delighted.

'Yeah,' he said, "live and kicking. They adopted me after I
rashly chucked them a hundred-peseta note shortly after I
arrived. Now they wait outside the hotel till I come out and
then follow me around the streets whenever I go for a walk.
They're very polite, they only play when I ask them to. Getting
a bit bored with them, though. Thought you might like them
as a present.'

'Why not wrap them up in a parcel and send them to me?'
Jigs said.

'Sure,' Ernie said. 'Or perhaps the twins would like them?'

Before Jigs could answer, Ernie said: 'No, I won't give
them to the twins. They'd probably break them. You better
have them.'

'Don't take them, Jigs,' I said. 'This island is lousy with
guitarists. I got two boys who've adopted *me*. You can have
my pair for free.'

Jigs turned on Ernie. 'So you wanted to pass off your old
junk on me. And to think that I was going to fall for that.
Why, you cheap skate——'

'Never mind,' I said hurriedly. 'I'll give you a camel before we go. Would you like a camel?'

'Thanks, old boy,' Jigs said coldly.

I guessed she was wishing Ernie had had the idea first. You know how it is with women.

'You'll fu-find some really fine camels south of the airport,' Kevin said helpfully.

'How do you know?' Jigs asked.

'Wu-waiter told me. Wu-waiter said there's a Moorish camp on a stretch of sand with dozens of camels. Millions, in fact.'

'This I must see,' Jigs said, rushing off to the car park.

.　　.　　.　　.　　.

Kevin, Ernie and I joined Simpson. The bowls game was over and for a while we talked about the fishing trip. I got on to a phone and asked Don Pablo if he could come over. I was surprised and delighted when he said he could.

An hour later, he and some of his fishers were settled in Simpson's suite, drinking the director's Scotch at a rapid clip. Having downed half a tumblerful, one of the fishers said:

'It is the Don, here, who really knows everything about the fishing. He is a rare sportsman. He is as mad as thou art, Señor Simpson. About fishing, that is, ha, ha.'

'Fine,' Simpson said, happy to be with the fishers at last.

The fishermen talked of tides and tackle and fish. Simpson suggested we use the *Fishbite* for the fishing, and asked the fishers to provide nets for the big fish, and also rods, and to prepare baskets of live bait. Although Don Pablo insisted we leave everything to him, there was much discussion of detail. These were not the simple fishers who rowed us each day to and from the location boats, but men of consequence on the island—Don Pablo's picked crew. Now that it was formal and true, everyone was very friendly. With great courtesy, being true Budgerigarios, they wanted Simpson and his friends to enjoy and share the bounty of their native seas.

Don Pablo spoke of the tuna fishing to be found between the volcanic island of Pinzecote and the African coast.

'We should go after the smaller fish,' he said. 'The little fish put up a bigger fight than the big tunny inshore.'

Simpson said : 'Where is the best fishing ground of all?'

They told him, as their humbler brethren had already told me, that it was at the mouth of the Rio de Oro, off Spanish Morocco.

'Could we get there in the *Fishbite*?' Simpson asked. 'Have we the time?'

'No, but thou couldst fly there,' Don Pablo said. 'We could arrange with the General of the Air Force to fly thee there.'

'It is a pity we have to wait till the first day of the New Year,' Simpson said. 'But we must have the right tackle. I will buy whatever thou thinkest we shall need.'

He was like a boy planning a holiday.

'No buy,' Don Pablo insisted. 'We will provide everything.'

'Let us sail to the volcanic island,' one of his fishers said excitedly. 'There you will find good sport. When I came back home from a trip to Libya last year I saw flying fish with two fins like wings. They were like no other flying fish anyone has ever seen. At first I thought, what sort of thing is this? Is it seaweed? Nobody on ship know. Maybe a sort of shark? No. There were *hundreds* of them, I tell thee, leaping about in pairs. Were they mantuas, the blanket fish? I never discovered. Let us go out and look for them. Nobody aboard that ship knew. It is a mystery. These are mysterious waters. Let us go soon and find strange fish.'

'We'll go the first thing in the New Year,' Simpson said, responding to the fisher's enthusiasm.

'We should go close to Africa,' Don Pablo said feverishly. 'That is a hotspot for thee. Do you mind heat, señor?'

'It does not affect me at all,' Simpson said.

'To Africa, then, where the fish live at the bottom of the sea,' Don Pablo shouted. 'They come to the surface when they want to make love. That is the time to catch them, at the height of their love ecstasy. Aie, they taste delicious then. Cooked and eaten in the clean air under a great sun, señor.'

'He is right,' the other fishermen cried.

Don Pablo raised his glass and said: 'When I was a child I used to wade into the sea and catch the octopus with my hands. Other fish I caught by the hand also. You catch them, and break their central nervous system, and they die.'

And one of his fishers said: 'I was fishing off Portoventura and caught a ray weighing forty kilos. It took me twenty minutes to haul him in, he was fighting like anything.'

'Ah,' the others said, 'that is the good sport.'

Simpson said: 'We'll go immediately. Just as soon as we can.'

He would have gone to sea that night if the fishers had agreed to take him.

Don Pablo said happily: 'Yes, we go soon. We shall have much sport.'

Another fisher said: 'We will catch the Old Woman fish. We will bring the Old Woman out of the water and boil it. This thou must eat when fresh, while still on the fishing expedition.'

The other fishers shouted agreement.

Simpson said: 'Why are they called Old Woman fish?'

The fisher who had spoken of the Old Woman said: 'They sleep at the bottom of the sea, just like a woman who is tired and beyond her use. The best way to fish for an Old Woman is to send down a small crab. Just dangle a crab near its mouth and the Old Woman is thine. They are easy fish to catch, but you must eat them quickly.'

One fisherman said: 'I am mad about fish.'

Another placed his hand on Simpson's shoulder, and said: 'It is good to talk to a true fisherman.'

And yet another fisherman said: 'Time is of no account when you fish. I used to play tennis, billiards, golf. But there is nothing so exciting as fishing. That way you become the master of time.'

Don Pablo drank down another tumbler of whisky, and said: 'You, señor, are a true fisher. We shall enjoy ourselves at sea.'

'We must go soon,' Simpson said.

He was very happy, sitting there making plans with the Budgerigario fishermen.

. . . . .

When the fishers were gone, we left Simpson smiling over a bottle of Scotch, and Ernie, Kevin and I went to the dining-room and ordered dinner. It was late and the band was struggling through a number called 'The Virgin of Fundador,' but they cheered up when we sat down and gave us a big collective grin. Kevin got them to play Flamenco music and there was much hand-clapping. The millionaires, their hired companions, and all the other rich crackpots dining there suddenly looked happy and the place brightened up a lot.

I carefully ordered a red wine from Rioja, the Frederic Paternina gran reserve of 1928, which is very good. Half-way through the meal Connell Connor tottered into the dining-room with an island socialite on his arm. We laughed and waved to them. Connell ignored us and sat down and ordered a meal with much waving of the hands and fierce, ineffective consultation of the menu and wine list. Then he rose, bowed, and his woman companion leaped up and they whirled round the dance floor together. We waved to them again, and this time they came over and greeted us. We asked them to join us, but Connell refused, coldly. He was still feeling sore about the drenching he had had earlier that evening. Then the music stopped and he and his partner weaved precariously over to their table. Kevin beckoned the assistant manager.

'You see wu-wu-where Mr. Connor is sitting?'

'Yes, sir.'

'Gug-get six waiters, gug-give each one a bottle of aqua minerale and tell them to place the bottles in front of Mr. Connor, wu-one after the other.'

'Six waiters, sir?'

'Yes, six.'

'Six,' the guy said dazedly. 'Each with a bottle of water.'

'Yes, as su-su-soon as possible.'

'Yes, sir.' The assistant manager went away, shaking his head.

Ernie said: 'That's a dangerous thing you're doing, Kevin. Connell may chuck the lot on the floor.'

'Or at the waiters,' I said.

'Or at us,' Ernie said, fingering his spectacles.

'Lue-ets see what does happen,' Kevin said, sucking contentedly at an asparagus stalk.

A minute later six waiters filed in, each with a tall bottle of water. They carried stopper-openers and began tugging at the metal caps before setting them before Connell. He didn't notice the first two. But he noticed the rest. The waiters trooped solemnly away, leaving Connell staring blankly at the bottles. Slowly he turned his face and looked at us. Several tables separated us from him, but the way Connell glared at us we knew he had guessed what had happened. Moving in slow motion, he grasped one of the bottles by the neck and tottered to his feet. Taking aim, he was about to hurl the bottle at us when his companion clawed his arm. Connell sat down again.

Kevin stretched his lips back over his teeth in a happy, tigerish grin.

'I should have sent tur-twelve waiters with tur-twelve wu-waiters,' he said thoughtfully.

People were watching the little drama now, some a shade uneasy as they saw Connell lurch towards us with a menacing scowl on his smashed-in face. The band stopped playing.

He came up close, and stood glaring at us.

'Hi, Connell,' Kevin said innocently, 'don't forget that you've another early call tomorrow morning.'

Connell glared some more.

'Kevin,' he said thickly, 'I'm not interested. I'm not interested in you, or this film, or anyone here. I don't give a damn about you, or Simpson, or any whale, black or white, live or stuffed. But if you try any more tricks on me I'll kill you. Good night.'

He stalked back to his table.

'Looks as if Connell has decided to give up acting as a career,' Kevin said sadly. 'More wine, everybody?'

The band started up again. The hotel guests resumed their dancing. It was just one little scene, but that is how things were getting to be down there in the Budgerigars. Simpson was stepping up the pace, and some of the boys were beginning to fall apart. It's always that way in a Simpson film.

Having the fishing fixed up at least would make things easier, perhaps.

But perhaps not.

You never know anything for sure when you're working with Simpson.

.   .   .   .   .

'El Greco,' I said, 'was a fruit.'

'I don't care what he was,' Ernie said. 'The guy could paint.'

'He painted with his ass.'

'He's a great artist,' Ernie insisted.

'Yeah, and so is Menuhin. But he's chicken. He refuses to fly.'

We were on the terrace watching the shipping and having breakfast; the morning rum and hot water was working overtime.

Ernie said : 'Brother, you're losing your sense of values. You wouldn't talk that way about him if you had stood in that room and seen those thirteen paintings hanging on the walls. Judas, the walls alone were works of art. A sort of light manila shade and older than Bette Davis. You walk into that room and figure, Judas, it's just another room. But the more you look the more powerful it gets. It's almost as if he's going to walk in with his brushes and put a few more strokes across the canvases.'

'I prefer Velasquez,' I said. 'There's a painting of his in London, done in his early Seville manner. It shows a water-carrier. I'll take you to see it one day.'

'He painted some fine dwarfs,' Ernie admitted.

We finished our drinks. There was half an hour to spare. So we collected Kevin and got into one of the studio cars and drove to a bar in the port. Kevin had a friend there, one of the barmen.

'You listen to this,' Kevin said quietly. The barman had gone to fix our drinks. 'I've been teaching him the days of the week in English. He knows that Domingo is Su-su-su——'

'Sunday,' Ernie said. 'Go on.'

'I'm getting him to memorise the other days. Now you mu-mu-may have noticed that I stammer occasionally.'

We nodded.

'I mur-manage to say most of the days without difficulty, but I sometimes get stuck with words like Su-su-su-su-su-su—— the day after Furiday.'

'Saturday,' Ernie said.

Kevin nodded.

'You can im-agine wu-what happens, can't you?'

'No,' I said. 'What does happen?'

Kevin pointed to the barman.

'Ask him,' he said.

The barman pushed the drinks over. He grinned at Kevin.

'Go on,' Kevin said. 'Ah-ah-ah-ah-ask him.'

I said: 'How are you getting on with your English lessons?'

'Very good,' the barman beamed. 'Señor Kevin teach me plenty.'

'You know the days of the week?'

'Sí, sí.'

'What is Lunes?'

'Monday,' the barman said.

'Martes?'

'Tuesday.'

'Good. Now Miercoles.'

'Wednesday.'

'Jueves?'

'Thursday.'

'Splendid. Now Viernes?'

'Friday.'

'That's great. Now Sabado?'

The barman drew in his breath, twisted his face into an agonised balloon, and roared:

'Su-su-su-su-su-*Rat*urday.'

We all laughed. It was early in the morning, and Christmas week, with lots of early morning drinkers around. Everyone in the bar folded up laughing.

'Huvva dur-rink,' Kevin said happily.

'You stut-stuttering sonofabitch,' Ernie said affectionately.

Then he began chuckling himself. I asked him what the joke was.

Ernie said: 'I was thinking about the time John tried King Connell out with a bit of dialogue as he climbed the rigging of the whaler. You were away doing whale research in the museums at the time. It was King's big moment. But every time King spoke his line he fluffed it. In the end King said: "Hell, John, let's skip it. I'm a sailor, not an actor." John looked sorrowfully at him and said: "That's your trouble, kid. You climb the rigging like an actor and speak your lines like a sailor".'

. . . . .

It was time for the other two to catch the rowboats out to the location. We left the bar. Ernie and Kevin took a boat and I went back to the hotel to work out a couple of whale soliloquies. I was sipping Campari and writing by the swimpool, when a blonde came over and said:

'Hi.'

She was the blonde who had been sitting with Simpson that time Cedric sang 'Holy Night' in the dining-room, when I was sick with the Budgerigars.

'Hi,' I said back.

She said: 'Don't let me interrupt you. I hear you are a writer. I'm writing a book too. My name is Sorrell, Mimi Sorrell. But don't let me interrupt your work.'

'Sit down, Mimi. Being a writer, you must know how we like interruptions. What is your book about? John Simpson? Every other writer I know is writing a book about John Simpson.'

Mimi sniffed.

'Nothing so commonplace,' she said. 'My subject is Leonardo da Vinci.'

'Great,' I said. 'How's it going?'

'I've been working on it for two years now and I'm only a
fraction of the way through with it. It's a tremendous subject.
I've got an office in the church where Leonardo painted, and
I only flew down from Florence for a vacation because my
doctor told me I had been working too hard and must get more
sunshine. Guess you're terribly fond of Italy.'

'I love it,' I said. 'But how did you guess?'

'The Campari. You drink it truly, with respect. You only
get to drink it that way in Italy.'

'And I always thought blondes weren't observant,' I said,
giving her a Cagney leer for luck.

'Don't you know many blondes?'

'You're the first I've met who's writing a study of Leonardo
da Vinci.'

'It's a great subject,' Mimi said.

'The boys in our mob are mostly El Greco fans,' I said.

'Do you always work with the John Simpson unit?'

'No, apart from writing occasional dialogue for the whale,
I'm strictly a freelance.'

In the sunlight by the pool, Mimi looked like something
off a magazine cover, slick, yet with depths. Depths with
handles. Chromium plated.

'That's fine,' she said. 'This way it gives you objectivity. I
presume that when you get round to writing your Simpson
book you will be objective about him?'

'I don't think I'll do one,' I said. 'After all, I happen to
like the guy.'

'That's bad,' Mimi said. 'You should be much more
objective than that.'

'But can't you like a subject and still write about it? Do
you hate Leonardo?'

'No, but he's dead,' Mimi said. 'You know, of course, that
the latest findings have established without a doubt that
Leonardo was a homosexual?'

'Is that a fact?'

'It is. Furthermore, the Mona Lisa was a man.'

'Well, what do you know?'

'I've seen the original letter from Lisa Giacondo's father commissioning Leonardo to sculpt her tomb. His, I mean.'

'How does that make the Mona Lisa a man?'

'It's a long story,' Mimi said. 'I'll explain it to you some time. Right now you're busy.'

'Let me get you a Campari,' I said.

'All right, then.' Mimi settled cosily beside me and we watched the swimmers. The waiter brought two Camparis. Mimi told me of her childhood in California. The usual stuff. How she had married young, been divorced, how she had been travelling around. The usual places, Europe, Cuba, Jamaica, Mexico, Rio. She said how she liked coloured people, and how she thought Cedric was marvellous. ('Those drum rhythms in his voice, gee!') She knew a lot of the hotels I knew, and some of the people I knew, and she urged me to get to know Florence better and write a book there, and look at pictures. She would show me around the place, she said. Mimi was a nice, friendly blonde with a habit of getting to know people.

After a lot more about doctors and Leonardo and Florence she told me about The Slap.

She said: 'I was sitting with a Certain Person the other night at dinner when he began sketching on the table-cloth. No, I won't tell you who This Person was, but he was obviously trying to impress everyone that he was an artist. He started sketching that Spanish opera singer who's staying here. You know the one. She was sitting at the next table and I happened to look over his shoulder and made a few comments. Let's be fair about it, it wasn't a bad sketch. But her eyes were all wrong, and I told him so. "It's her eyes," I said. "They are all wrong." He turned and glared at me and said: "Who the hell are you?" I said: "Just someone who happens to be a student of Leonardo da Vinci." I'd barely finished speaking when he *slapped* me across the face. Smack! Now isn't that a childish, petty thing to do? The Great Artist couldn't bear to be criticised. I'd upset him, rattled him badly.'

'You mean to say you didn't slap him back?' I said.

'Surely you don't expect me to descend to *his* level?' Mimi said, scandalised.

A swarm of flies was sucking at the sores on my leg.

'Shall we swim?' I asked.

'I won't just now,' Mimi said. 'Isn't it strange, I didn't know till the other day that John Simpson was the son of Walter Simpson. I used to know his father quite well. Boy, what a difference! My parents saw a lot of him when he was staying at the Beverley Hills Hotel. I remember him as a quiet, well-mannered, kindly man. I met John's mother, too. She was *very* different to the husband. If you ask me, I'd say John has inherited more of his mother's characteristics than his father's. There's a strong feminine streak in him.'

Writers, I thought. The hell with writers. Can't they get anyone straight? Leonardo, El Greco, Proust—and now Simpson. Writers, I thought again. The hell with writers and the hell with blondes. I got up and crossed to the edge of the pool, the flies tagging along to my leg.

'Don't forget what I told you,' Mimi called after me. 'Try to be objective. And if you want any further observations on your Particular Subject, don't hesitate to ask me.'

'Gee, tanks,' I said coldly.

'Mimi,' I thought, as I dived into the pool, drowning a lot of flies, 'Mimi, your tiny mind is frozen.'

· · · · ·

At lunch with Perdita I said: 'Do you think John has a feminine streak?'

She giggled.

I said: 'Be sensible for a minute. I'm trying to be objective.'

Perdita giggled some more.

'God, you're funny, Slim.'

'Now listen,' I said. 'I'm just a writer trying to get the facts. All writers must have facts. Ask Connell Connor; he's a writer as well as an actor!'

'Stop it, Slim, you're killing me.'

'Do you know,' I went on, 'do you know what Emile Zola did when he wanted to get his facts? He bored holes in the floor above people's apartments and peered through them to watch them during their most intimate moments. Zola was a great writer. Connell is a great writer. I want to be a great writer, too.'

'Eat your rice and drink your wine, Slim, there's a good boy.'

'Have you no respect for writing?' I said. 'I would have you know that I have been talking to a student of Leonardo and it has made me think. Believe me, I have been lazy, and untrue to myself as a writer.'

'Don't kid yourself, brother. *You've* been talking to *Mimi*.'

'Women,' I said, amazed. 'Where did you hear of this?'

'From Mimi, of course. Now eat up.'

'But——'

'I also know about the slap, so quit worrying.'

Later Perdita said: 'Of course, John has got a feminine streak. It's part of his charm. He adores a good gossip. Who doesn't? Judas Jones, just think of the way you and he gossip at breakfast.'

'Oh, Lord,' I said. 'Is that bad?'

'Oh, *brother*.' Perdita started giggling again. 'You know something, Slim? Quit worrying. Only women really understand these things. We've had too many he-men weeping on our shoulders, between smacking us across the chops, to worry about feminine streaks. And just to reassure you, I'll tell you a secret. John's a pretty rugged guy. Now, finish your wine.'

'Mimi said the Mona Lisa was a man.'

Perdita pulled a face like a Dead End Kid.

'Yeah,' she snarled, 'and Shakespeare was a queen. But I still get kicks out of his blank voiss.'

'Shall I compare thee to a summer's day,' I murmured into my goblet.

'Nah, drink up and let's get outa here. I don't know about you, but I gotta lotta woik to do.'

.   .   .   .   .

I worked through the rest of that afternoon. Around seven I called on Simpson. He was having a hair-cut. The unit hairdresser had tucked a hair-cutter's bib around his neck and perched him on a high chair in the centre of the room. She was snipping his hair off at a great rate. Simpson looked up.

'Come in, Slim. You know where to find everything. Help yourself.'

I poured myself a Scotch and settled on a sofa and browsed through the Spanish book on bullfighting. It was a good book to handle, beautifully bound and printed. The illustrations were magnificent. Simpson talked shop to Perdita while the hairdresser snipped his hair off.

There was a knock at the door, and a small American voice said, 'Permisso.'

'Why, *sure*,' Simpson said. 'Come *in*, darling.'

A small girl with white curls rode into the room on a tricycle.

'Sure I'm not bothering you, Mr. Simpson?' she asked, pedalling round the room.

'Of *course* you're not, darling.' He was really delighted to see her.

The little girl rode round and round. Simpson watched her

from his high chair, a vacant beam on his kisser. The barber snipped, and the hair flaked over the huge bib. Some of it fell upon the floor.

The little girl said: 'This afternoon I went to sleep, and when I woke up my feet were tingling. It was lovely.'

'Oh, it *was*?' Simpson said interestedly. 'That means they had also gone to sleep. Didn't you mind?'

'No,' she said. She cycled round him several times.

'In fact, do you know what?'

'What, Carli?' Simpson asked.

'It's a secret, but I don't mind telling you.'

She glared at me and the hairdresser.

'It's all right, Carli. We're all friends here. Meet Carli, folks. Her family have the suite opposite.'

'Hullo,' Carli said casually, still cycling.

'What's the secret, Carli?' Simpson coaxed.

'Look, you don't have to give any presents or anything,' Carli said. 'I'm loaded with gifts.'

'But you can have anything you want, Carli,' Simpson said. 'Say, how would you like the big whale when we've finished with it? I'll give you the big whale.'

'What would I do with a big whale?'

'You could show it at fairs and make a lot of money.'

'We've already got a lot of money. My father has got so much money he doesn't know what to do with it.'

Simpson looked downcast.

'Well, if you won't have the whale, you won't. But tell us your secret.'

'Okay, it's this.' Carli pedalled towards the door and stopped cycling. 'I like it when my sleep go to feet,' she said.

'You do?' Simpson said. 'That's *wonderful*.'

'No it isn't,' Carli said, crossly. 'I like it but I don't think it's wonderful.'

'Not when your *sleep* go to *feet*?' Simpson asked. 'I'd love it if it happened to me.'

'No you wouldn't,' Carli said. 'You wouldn't like it a bit. Nor would you like it if you had eyes in your stars, or pants in your ants. *I* might like it, but you wouldn't. You'd hate it. Good night.'

Carli pedalled away.

'Say,' Simpson grinned, 'I'll give a thousand flannel pesetas to the first sane person I find on this island. The whole place is wacky.'

'I know how you feel,' I said morosely.

'Never mind, kid. We'll be going fishing soon. That will put us all back on our feet.'

Yeah, I thought. There was always that. There was always the fishing to look forward to. Mit or mittout strait-jackets.

CHAPTER NINE

Delirium

Oh, God, to sail with such a heathen crew, that have small touch of human mothers in them.

Now the sun was beginning to drive nails into all our heads; normally well-mannered cameramen became aggressive after a couple of drinks, some of the stuntment became the roaring Colossi of the brothels, a boy fell in love with a whore, a knife fight ended in tears, another stuntman crawled on all fours on the carpets of the Casa Maria barking like a dog, the Kraut took to complaining about every scrap of non-kosher food the hotel served him, Ernie took to drink, and Mimi took a great deal of time trying to convince me that I should make a special study of Gene Fowler.

Cedric shadow-boxed on the *Fishbite* and rehearsed 'The Kid's Last Fight', the song he was planning to sing in the arena before the big fight. The sea got meaner and dizzier and all the time better for the cameras. As the *Fishbite* rolled, the land on the port side and the horizon on the starboard side jumped up and down like broken window-blinds. An island girl of fifteen kissed the canvas chair Pinch had sat in for lunch. A sailor was killed in a bar in the port.

An Argentinian crew from a meat ship took over the Casa Maria for a whole night after a fist-fight with the regulars. Madame Jo Jo started putting her star performers into a limousine and turning up at the dockside, waving in the crews at nightfall. Carli's brother set fire to the six-foot wool snow-

man in the suite opposite Simpson's and almost burned the
hotel down. The cameramen crouching in little cages at the
sterns of tiny whaleboats continued to be dunked in and out
of the sea like gingerbread men, and they were getting worse-
tempered than ever. Simpson continued to brief Terrible Tom
and counter-brief his opponents.

Wherever you went the cocks crowed. My personal guitarists learnt to play 'April in Portugal' as they followed me
around the streets. One of the stuntmen was arrested and
thrown into jail for making love to a girl one night on the
beach. Pinch continued to read Proust. Ernie was busy
arranging the fight with the local fight promoters. The twins
went down with Budgerigar fever. There was a big fiesta in
the streets by the seashore, and we all joined in.

There were occasions when Simpson looked like a man who
had been told by doctors that he had only six months to live
and was making the most of his time. The palm fronds hissed,
the crickets chattered, the cocks kept crowing, and there were
times when the island seemed as large as eternity and times
when it seemed too small to hold us. Then the sky rose and
fell, and sometimes you could touch the clouds with your
hands, and sometimes you could almost see Africa, and all the
other Budgerigar Islands would lie flat on the big sea like
basking whales.

Then there was the work with the harpoons; hours of back-
breaking action devoted to moulding human figures into
plastic cinematic composition; and then the tears and curses,
the technical work, the strivings for form, with Pinch pulling
faces that became great film acting, and Ozzie watching the
sky for light and the sea for movement, and Rory Punt braving
it out for three days with a temperature of 103.

There were moments when the entire unit seemed held
together only by Simpson's crazy single-mindedness and crazy
strength. He never lost sight of his original vision, a vision of

words now dissolving into a vision on film. And in the process something was communicated to the rest of us, something indescribably intense, the true excitement of creative birth. *A madman begets more madmen. . . .*

.   .   .   .   .

One evening I was having a drink with Pinch and the talk got round to Simpson. The actor was sitting by an open window, wearing a wine-red dressing robe and cooling off after a shower. He told me how Simpson had first offered him the part.

'It was at a dinner party in London. I knew something was cooking from the expression on John's face. He was like a kid with a birthday present up his sleeve. Quite suddenly he said: "My next film is going to be *The White Whale*. How would you like to play the Skipper, kid?" I didn't hesitate. I stuck out my hand and said: "Sure, I'd love to." That was all, a handshake. We left the rest to be sorted out by agents. That night he gave me his only briefing. He said: "Jesus, kid, this part will have to be brimstone all over the deck." '

I said: 'That's one of the things I like about him. He doesn't go in for fancy talk about his trade.'

'John? No! Once or twice I've known him to edge into a discussion and drop a word here and there, but most of the time he leaves you to find your own interpretation and work it out in the acting. If it's not right he'll talk round it till you see points you haven't before, or clear up any obscurities he may have felt about the way you were doing it. But he's no prosy theorist, thank God.'

'How did *you* approach the part?' I asked.

'I had read the book at college, and I re-read it after John offered me the part. Then he sent the script out to me in Ceylon, where I was filming at the time, and that settled everything. It is one of the finest scripts ever written. I cabled

John to tell him so and that is all we ever said about the script.'

Pinch paused, then he said :

'The same goes for when John actually starts shooting. You know the old maxim in the theatre—if you *talk* a good part you cannot act a good part. It's the same with films. If you have matriculated in acting and really know your trade you don't need to talk much. John directs by example. Before taking a new scene he would act it out in front of me. I'd watch his action and it would mean, wilder. Or it meant, let the Skipper keep the obsession in front of his mind. Or he'd walk scenes, walk a few steps for me, emphasising the limp or the rolling of the ship. Or he would flash a look across at me which meant that, whatever the Skipper is doing, all the time the image of the whale is almost bursting his head. His complete grasp of the rôle is astounding. No actor could touch him in the part.'

'I don't see it that way at all,' I said truthfully. 'I think you two are complementary.'

'It's certainly working out well as far as I can judge it,' Pinch said. 'A creative director like John sets off something in an actor by example which in turn sets up a sort of telepathy. There's just the shade of suggestion at something that does not need words and something comes out. You get the same thing with Wyler, a reaching out to the stuff of life. You never get it with hack work, that discovering of something new about life. I'll give you an example. There is that moment in the story when everything is still, a sort of calm has settled over the ship's company and nothing seems to be going on. The sun is shining. It is a mild, mild day. The Skipper feels the calm and begins to wonder what it is that is driving him against all human longings and lovings to this madness of destruction. I thought this could be a moment when the Skipper shows a moment of human feeling. A strong man in a moment of gentleness. That is the way I realised it. But not John. Just before taking this scene we were sitting around the cameras very quietly and even when we started doing takes there was a hush, and John was very, very quiet after the cameras had stopped. Instinctively I felt that this was my one chance of catching the sympathy of the audiences. But after a while John came very close to me, looked me straight in the eyes, and said: "You know, sometimes I wake up very early in the morning and I wonder what all this void is around us. But I couldn't find the answer. I have been unable to find it in orthodox religion, for that kills wonderment. But I know that something is there. And I know that whatever it is I would like to make an imprint on it. So it is with you now. Bear down. Don't be reflective. Don't be a sad old man. Make an imprint on the mystery. It has teased man ever since the creation." That is what John said, and it killed my only moment of softness in the film. John plucked it out. But his words registered. They came at the precisely right moment and gave my playing a more positive attack.'

There was a knock at the door. A waiter came in with a small parcel on a huge silver tray.

'What *is* this?' Pinch asked.

'It was left at the reception desk for you, señor.'

The waiter left and Pinch began to unwrap the parcel. There were several layers of thickish brown paper. Eventually he uncovered the contents—a small sardine tin and a card. On the card was printed the name of a local professor mercantile. In ink was scrawled the message: Felizes Navidad, Happy New Year.

'Now, why in hell does a guy send me a tin of sardines?' Pinch said, puzzled.

Pinch pushed the gift aside with a thoughtful expression. He poured out more Scotch. I couldn't suppress a sudden picture of Simpson's quiet, secret way of laughing.

'His picture sense has a touch of greatness,' the actor went on. 'Going after the White Whale in the whaleboats at night, during an early sequence of the chase, the Skipper is whispering instructions to the crew. Tim, the little coloured boy, is in the boat with his tambourine. As we were about to shoot the sequence, John turned to Tim and said: "Now you go up behind Greg and stay there and beat the tambourine as the men row." The kid began to tap the tambourine softly. It sent a chill down us all. It was barbaric. Yet the picture was beautifully composed, unorthodox, and original. These things aren't in the script. They grow out of the day-by-day making of a film. John told me that he often wakes up at three or four in the morning and lets his mind wander off the script and the story, and then the ideas come. These are what he calls the good moments, when his mind is alight with scenes and images. Then he keeps whatever he has found, and saves it. Talk would spoil it. He keeps it till everything is set up, and the cameras are ready to go, and it's the last moment before beginning a scene. Then when everything is ready, he springs it and everybody is struck by it. They share the originality, and that is the moment to do it, before it is explained away.'

I asked:

'How does he keep a unit like this together for so long, when everybody—with a few notable exceptions—is coming apart at the emotional seams?'

Pinch said:

'Because he has always taken the lead. If *he* had eased up, we might have done so too. There have been times when I have felt tired and jaded, but then I'd remember that John was carrying the can for the lot of us. He has problems that we never hear about. That makes it relatively easy to put up with the occasional discomforts.'

'What keeps him going?' I asked.

'He likes people. There is an inexhaustible intellectual

energy and curiosity beneath that dried-up puss of his. If a dramatic situation begins, he doesn't let it go. He directs it. Whether they are actors or not, the people around John start acting out their emotions, and he encourages them to reach out to the extremes of their personalities. But the drama must be good. It's got to come off. Under his direction it usually does!'

He paused and looked out at the night from the open windows.

Suddenly I said:

'What is it about John that makes some people think he is mad?'

Pinch looked sharply at me.

'Do people say that? I have never heard anyone say it.'

'I have,' I said. 'Plenty of times. Cracks about the number of whales he's built. Pseudo-highbrow talk about the books that have been written about him—by pseudo-goddam highbrows.'

'I know nothing of that,' Pinch said. But he tried to answer my question. 'If a man goes farther than others, if he is unorthodox and brilliant, I suppose there are people who are baffled by him and try to explain him away by saying he is mad. But I haven't met them, and wouldn't want to. I might be tempted to reach out with my fist if I did.'

I finished my drink and went. Later, in the bar with Ernie, I said:

'I've been chatting with Grigorio. Brother, he's one of the world's best.'

'Brother,' Ernie said, 'you're dead right.'

We raised our glasses to Greg, but truly.

.   .   .   .   .

'*Do I worry?*' the Inkspots sang. '*You can bet your life I do.*'

We were at a party in a private house on the island, and the talk had turned to what we would do when the location was over.

Perdita said: 'I'm going to Klosters. Love dem skis.'

Kevin said: 'I part own a gu-garage in Morocco. Let's all look in there on the way home, and see if we've sold any tyres lately.'

The unit doctor said: 'I'm going to Rome. Why don't you all come to Rome?'

Kevin said: 'Come to Morocco. The Sultan's an old friend of mine. You'd like the Sultan.'

I said: 'We'll do that. We'll call on the old boy on the way back.'

'That's a date, then,' Kevin said. 'Unless you'd prefer Denmark.'

'I adore Denmark,' I said. 'Went there once to watch *Hamlet*. Stayed at Elsinore. Hotel Marienlust. You can see Sweden across the Sound. Know it?'

'Know it lurike the back of my hand,' Kevin said. 'That's where we'll gug-go, then. Know a lot of people in Denmark.'

'So do I,' I said. 'Met a blonde in Copenhagen. Actress. Very good actress.'

'Su-su-su-sounds like the one I met,' Kevin said, frowning.

'Best actress in Denmark,' I said.

'Thu-that's the one, then,' Kevin said, frowning some more.

'Let's not go to Denmark,' I said. 'Might start fighting over actresses.'

'No need to gu-go to Denmark to fight,' Kevin said, scowling. 'Cu-can furight just as well down here.'

'But not over actresses,' I said. 'No actresses in *The White Whale*.' Turning to Ernie, I said: 'Has John decided where he is going when he stops shooting?'

'Just fishing.'

Perdita said: 'There'll be no time for fishing, believe you me. I'm working on Johnnie's schedule right now. He must be in Calcutta by the first of February.'

'Plenty of time before then for fishing,' I said.

'I wouldn't bet on it,' Perdita said.

Ernie winked at me and said quickly: 'He's got to be in New York before he goes to India.'

I said: 'Isn't someone stopping off here to collect John for some more fishing off Cape Town?'

'There won't be *time* for that now,' Perdita said peevishly. 'Can't you guys get it into your thick heads that fishing is right out? Cooch is fixing up for him to go on safari directly he arrives in Calcutta.'

'Ah, go and type a new schedule,' Ernie said. Simpson had obviously kept quiet about his meeting with Don Pablo. Still, the chick was trying all right, all right. The chick sure was trying.

We returned to the hotel and collected Simpson from the bowling alley and went into the dining-room. The director was wearing blue jeans, a check shirt, sandals, red choker, corduroy jacket. He looked very happy.

'Dig them jeans,' a brunette yelled from her table as we crossed the dance floor. Simpson did a champ handclasp and went into a shuffling dance routine, his shoulders hunched up. The brunette applauded ecstatically, but some of the diners looked startled.

'I had news from Don Pablo,' I said as we sat down. 'He says he's found some really special tackle. He wants you to inspect it.'

'Sure, Slim, any time,' Simpson said happily. 'We're going fishing, kid. Fishing off Africa.'

'Wonderful,' I said.

We were both smiling now. It was a happy moment.

The Kraut joined us and said: 'Ess soon ess I finish here I

fly to Morocco.' To me he said : 'Vy don't you come wiss me?
We could do a picture story together.'

'We could do one here, come to that,' I said.

'Seriously,' the Kraut said, ignoring the pleasantry. 'You
come to Morocco.'

'I've a book to write,' I said.

'You could write it in Morocco,' the Kraut said. 'You could
sit in the hotel ent write book vile I go out fixing up contacts
ent shots.'

'That's not a bad idea,' I said. 'We'll do that.'

'Goot. You cable London right away.'

'Done,' I said, turning back to Simpson.

'Tell Pablo we'll see him around ten tomorrow night,'
Simpson said quietly.

'Fixed,' I said.

The table was filling up. The Sandersons, Kevin, a Greek
shipping millionaire and his wife. . . . Kevin lit two cigarettes
at both ends and chewed them until the lighted ends vanished
in his mouth.

Simpson said : 'I wonder what won the big race?'

We had been waiting for two days for the result of an
important race in England, but the aircraft with the London
papers had not yet arrived.

Kevin started lighting matches now, popping them into his
mouth and swallowing them rapidly. I asked an Italian film
star to dance with me. We smooched around for a while, then
I went back to our table.

Kevin had lit another cigarette and was now reversing it, to
light the other end.

'Never mind, kid,' Simpson was saying to the Greek. 'The
London papers should be here by tomorrow.'

'I only had fifty thousand smackers on it,' the Greek said
fretfully.

'Why, don't you trust bookmakers?' Simpson said.

'I've lost several fortunes to them,' the Greek growled.

'It's great when you win, though,' Simpson said encouragingly.

The Greek said: 'Nice to hear you being so philosophical about it. From what I've heard, you've had more than your share of bad luck with the gee-gees.'

'I've had a lot of fun, too. Don't you *like* losing money?'

The Greek shook his head moodily and turned to watch Kevin break a cigarette in half, put the two lighted halves into his mouth, and chew quietly. After a while, following the course of his thoughts, the millionaire said: 'How you making out with the film, Mr. Simpson? I hear it's costing a packet.'

'It's going along fine,' Simpson said cheerfully. 'The weather here is perfect.'

I said: 'I hear that the fishermen who operate the rowboats are planning to go on strike.'

Kevin swallowed hard and said: 'There are purlenty of scabs waiting to muscle in if they do.'

The millionaire turned green.

'Don't,' he said.

'Why, what's wrong?' Simpson asked.

'I have twenty-five ships turning round weekly in London docks. And they're threatening to start a nation-wide strike in Britain in ten days' time.'

'Say, that's tough,' Simpson said, winking at me. 'Say, how would you like to lay me another fifty thousand smackers that your horse doesn't win.'

'Are you crazy,' the Greek said. 'That horse is the favourite.'

'Sure, but favourites don't always win, you know.'

The Greek swallowed hard. 'Okay,' he said. 'It's a bet.' After all, he *was* a Greek *and* a millionaire.

'Fine,' Simpson said. 'Let's have some champagne.'

'I never drink the stuff,' the Greek said unhappily.

'If them boatmen strike,' I said, 'I'll throw them into the sea, but truly.'

'That reminds me,' the millionaire said, rising. 'I must send a cable. Come on, ducks. Good night, everybody.'

'That guy sure takes money seriously,' Simpson said, as Kevin lit another cigarette and popped the burning match into his mouth.

I said: 'How are you going to pay off if you lose—in flannel or folding money?'

'Flannel, of course, kid. We got to keep the film's finances straight. But I've got that race in the bag. Say, what's the matter. Don't you like betting?'

'Not in thousands. Having had a racing man for a father rather put me off the game.'

'I thought you liked horses, kid,' Simpson said reproachfully.

'I'll ride anything over hedge and ditch,' I said, 'but *any-where*. But I won't bet in thousands. My mother put me off. Because of what horses did to my old man.'

'What did they do, kid?'

'Apart from breaking every bone in his body, they broke up every home we ever moved into. It lost him several wives.'

'Well, kid, *I've* also lost quite a number of wives through horses. But I've *still* got horses.'

I felt crushed.

'Cheer up, Slim,' Simpson said pleasantly. 'You can come hunting with me any time.'

I brightened.

'Well, that's something to look forward to,' I said.

Simpson looked thoughtfully at me, and said:

'Yeah, I got just the horse for you.'

'Wonderful,' I said. Then I thought: Or is it? Then I

thought : Hell, quit worrying, we're going fishing soon. Fishing off the African coast.

Kevin swallowed another lighted cigarette.

.　　　.　　　.　　　.　　　.

The morning on the terrace was thirst-blue, crisp and sunny at the edges.

Ernie said : 'Will you be at the launching, John?'

Simpson said : 'If I can make it, sure. It depends on the weather and how things are going.'

Ernie said : 'The Governor's daughter will christen it with a bottle of champagne.'

'Fine,' Simpson said.

Perdita said : 'Has it been certified yet?'

Ernie said : 'What's that?'

'Its certificate,' Perdita said patiently. 'It must have a certificate of seaworthiness.'

Ernie said : 'Oh, yeah, that. That's okay. I asked Nick.'

'As long as the whale has been certified,' Simpson said, winking at me.

'Hope you *can* get to the launching,' Ernie called out as Simpson stepped into the car that drew up when he rose. Perdita followed him.

Ernie went to the desk to send off some cables. I sat in one of the swing seats and ordered breakfast. It was a beautiful morning. The sea looked like something lit by Joe Meiltziner.

Mimi sat down beside me.

'I'm not interrupting anything?' she said. 'No great thoughts? No flashes of inspiration?'

'You're not interrupting a thing, Mimi. Come and join me for breakfast.'

'I have had breakfast. Tell me, did you see my straw dress last night?'

'Yes,' I lied.

'What did you think of it?'

'I thought it was swell. Better than a hula skirt.'

'You couldn't have noticed it very carefully,' Mimi sniffed. 'It isn't a bit like a hula skirt.'

'I said it's better, Mimi.'

'I am having an entire wardrobe specially made for me in straw. There's a man in Florence who runs up the most wonderful straw creations. Straw boleros, straw skirts, straw evening dresses, straw handbags, straw dancing shoes.'

'Wonderful,' I said, looking out to sea.

Along the main road beyond the hotel grounds the trams were packed with sweating Budgerigarios going to the shops and offices in the town centre. I relaxed in the swing chair as Mimi told me more about this genius in Florence who runs up little things in straw. Then she switched to writing.

'I haven't written a line since I've been here,' she said. 'My doctor told me to have a complete rest. Besides I don't like to disturb people in hotels by clattering on my typewriter. Do you work on a typewriter?'

I told her how I wrote. She told how she wrote. It began to sound like literary ladies' night in Kenosha, Wis.

Mimi was really profound about writing. Profound, with handles.

Ernie joined us, followed by the Kraut.

'How's about a rum and hot water?' Ernie said, hissing at a waiter.

'I was just about to order one,' I said.

'Then order two,' Ernie said. 'Anyone else having rum?'

Mimi and the Kraut shook their heads.

'We're launching the whale at two-thirty today,' Ernie said. 'Coming down for the launching?'

'It is not ferry votogenic,' the Kraut sniffed.

'Whaddya mean, not photogenic,' Ernie roared. 'We're taking movie shots for the TV newsreels.'

'Det is different,' the Kraut said. 'Movink it might be interestink.'

'Hell,' Ernie said, kicking a passing pariah dog.

The waiter came up with a bottle of Bacardi rum and a silver canister of hot water and two glasses on a silver tray.

'What about the sugar and lemon slices?' Ernie snapped.

'Sorry, I get,' the waiter said.

We poured the glasses half full with rum and sloshed hot water on top. The waiter brought sugar and slices of lemon and we mixed the drink together and settled back in the rocking-chairs. Another waiter brought the Kraut his breakfast. The Kraut touched the edge of his plate and shouted, 'Frio, frio, how often do I tell you not to brink me foot served on a cold blate?'

The waiter scuttled away with the Kraut's tray.

I said : 'Did you hombres notice Mimi's dress last night?'

'Terrific,' Ernie said instantly.

'Derrific,' the Kraut said, turning his lips down à la Conrad Veidt.

'What was it made of?' I asked.

'A kinda silk stuff,' Ernie said absently.

'I don't know bud it voss derriffic,' the Kraut said.

'At least you are fairly honest,' Mimi told the Kraut. 'It was made of straw.'

'Well, whaddya know?' Ernie said, raising his glass.

'Mimi's having lots of dresses made of straw,' I said. 'They look terribly real.'

'Nudding is ferry real down here,' the Kraut said.

'I disagree,' Ernie said, looking hard at the Kraut. 'There's a lot of hard work going on, for one thing.'

The Kraut sneered. 'Vot ve are doing here hess nudding to do wiss reality.'

A slight shiver of Budgerigar fever, or maybe whale fever,

passed through me. I soused it with a few shots of hot rum. The rum went down, melting into the fever like snow on fire. Mimi started to talk meaningly about the drinking habits of dead and buried writers, tormented, thirsty souls, peaceful at last in their wooden waistcoats if only Mimi would leave them alone. But that girl has the lowdown on everyone.

Suddenly Ernie hissed: 'I got to speak to you alone, but quick.'

Excusing ourselves, we walked into the hotel grounds. Gardeners wearing white straw hats and tartan shirts were hosing the lawns and laying the dust along the intersecting pathways. The hose-water sprinkling in the morning light was cooling on the throat.

'This goddam fishing trip,' Ernie said savagely.

'What about it?'

'We got to make sure them goddam fishermen don't get carried away with enthusiasm and take John off for months. You know how it is with these fishers. Hell, the last time they went to sea they didn't show up again till Christmas. We got to watch it.'

'We'll watch it,' I said. 'We can't deprive John of his trip, but we'll watch it all right, all right.'

Ernie spat into a cactus bush.

'Okay, amigo,' he said. 'Just see you watch it. It's your turkey, you know. So remember there's millions tied up in this film and they ain't all made of flannel.'

'You sound as if you been in a huddle with the New York office,' I jeered.

'I've done no such thing,' Ernie said angrily. 'But now we're on the point of getting the last goddam whale afloat for the last sequences I don't want there to be any slip-ups, but definitely.'

'There'll be no slip-ups,' I assured Ernie.

Then the fever caught me again.

'Another breakfast?' I said.

'Sure,' Ernie said, kicking a grass snake. 'Sure, why not?'

. . . .

'What did Perdita want?' Ernie asked.

We had been reading our mail after breakfast and then a page had asked me to go over to Perdita's office.

'She wants sixty more tickets for the fight. She's had hundreds of applications and John told her to get more.'

'Impossible,' Ernie said. 'They're sold out solid.'

'Are you sure?'

'Positive.'

'Come off it, you're the big fixer. Don't tell me you can't find sixty lousy tickets for a fight you yourself have organised.'

Ernie sighed.

'All right,' he said. 'We'll see what can be done.'

Graham Greene would have got a laugh or two out of the next two hours. The only spare tickets, we were told, were in the hands of the local priests. So we made a round of the priests. Unfortunately, none of them could speak English and our joint efforts at speaking Spanish only bewildered the priests more. I thought vaguely of trying something in Catholic Latin, but how do you ask a priest for prizefight tickets in Latin? We mimed a bit, and sparred a bit, but when we found ourselves blacking each other's eyes without getting through to the priests we gave that up as a means of communication. I had great faith in a wise-looking priest with his cassock tucked up above his knees and a pair of boxing gloves on his fists, who was teaching a bunch of island kids to scrap in a church gymnasium, but we drew blank with him too. From what I gathered, between paternosters, this priest considered the local prizefights to be the Devil's work, they

were that dirty, and we narrowly escaped being slung out by
his enraged young flock. Then a simpático Budgerigario with
a beret and a lisp asked us in English-of-sorts what we wanted.
When we told him, he said we had made a mistake, the only
place to find tickets was over a grocery store. He jumped into
our car and directed us there. Ernie bought a stack of tickets.
It was as simple as that.

'Better hurry and eat, if you want to see the launching,'
Ernie said tersely, kicking a hotel porter on our way into the
dining-room.

.   .   .   .   .

*He's white! Whiter than all the snow that ever fell! Like a
great marble tombstone he is, afloat. Wherever he swims,
white sky-birds escort him—birds as white as angels!*

Immortal he is, they say.

*I say he's only a whale, bigger than most maybe and queer
coloured, but just a whale. And if we happen on him, we'll
kill him . . . like we'll kill all sorts of whales. That's our
business.*

The sun was high in a thin, blue sky when we drove to the
shipyard for the launching. Ernie, looking grey and middle-
aged after the morning's exertions with the priests, had gone
ahead with two bottles of champagne. There were people
leaning from windows and clinging to the bits of roofing and
parapets and high walls surrounding the dock entrance. The
narrow lanes on each side of the slipway were packed with
people fanning themselves with newspapers and staring at the
huge dummy whale tilting, nose downward, a few feet from
the edge of the hot oily sea. Some scaffolding on the far side
was jammed with more well-wishers, and I clambered up
and joined them on a platform of wood planks. Ernie was
pacing around with his champagne bottles. The Kraut
sauntered in, gave the whale a disgusted look, and sauntered

out again. The heat really was bad. I tried not to look at the champagne bottles as I sat on the hot wooden boards and waited for the whale to go down the slipway.

'The tide isn't quite right yet,' an engineer told me.

There was no sign of Simpson or Pinch, and when the sea had crept up a little higher the shipyard engineers decided to start the launching.

'If you don't hurry we'll lose the tide,' someone said.

A plump little girl called Amalia, daughter of the Civil Governor, walked up to the whale, and, picking up a bottle attached to a sash, hurled it at the whale's rump, shouting: 'Goot lug, Vite Vale!'

A unit cameraman called: 'Can we have that again, please?' So the little fat Amalia smashed another bottle of good champagne at the sticky-looking stern of the white monster, once more piping, 'Vite Vale!'

Everyone cheered except a local admiral.

'What's wrong with him?' someone asked.

And someone replied, 'Oh, he's as mad as hell because *his* daughter wasn't invited to christen the whale.'

That is how it is on islands.

Then the whale began slowly to move forward, and the crowd stopped cheering and watched the monster slip towards the sea like a live thing. As the flat bottom sank into the oil-thick water the whale suddenly acquired a life of its own. In that instant between leaving land and touching water, breath seemed to blow into the monster. Everybody noticed it. The whale slid into the water, and, riding the gentle swell like a veteran, turned on its own accord and we saw the thing in full-length profile. Man, I swear it seemed to sneer and turn a pig eye on us. For a moment I felt myself hating it, but hating it, but truly. Hating it blindly, with no handles.

I climbed off the scaffolding and joined Ernie.

'Jesus,' I said, 'did you notice? It's a *live* whale.'

'Come on, let's tell John the goddam thing's afloat,' Ernie said tersely. He looked a hundred years old.

Everyone moved away as if with relief to be done with the launching. It had been all right until the whale hit the water. Then it seemed as if the sun had turned black.

We drove to Las Flamenco and took a boat out to where the unit was shooting, three miles at sea. As we bumped over the waves, Eric, a technician who had also been to the launching, talked about whales in general.

'This era will go down as the time of the black whale. Hell, that guy Simpson didn't know what he was stirring up when he tried to resurrect the white whale. White whale my ass.'

'Don't talk crap,' Ernie said shortly.

'It's true,' Eric said stoically. 'We all got whale-curse on us now.'

I told him to jump overboard.

He shrugged. 'It wouldn't help one way or the other,' he said.

Stoical to the end, he said: 'At least I'll bring a few more birds into the picture,' and slipped overboard.

'Sissy,' Ernie said, spitting into the mysterious-looking water.

We drew up near Jug Ears' whaleboat.

One of the stuntmen was humped over like a dead man.

Looking up, he said wearily:

'What are we supposed to be doing now, Jugs?'

Jugs said:

'I know what we *could* be doing.' He formed one hand into the shape of a pistol and, pointing it at the distant figure of Simpson, shouted, 'Bang!'

We drifted over to where Simpson was directing shots of Rory Punt's boat racing over the sea, followed by flocks of white birds. The launch danced up and down in the breeze. It was getting chilly now as evening approached. You could see the bare hills of the island darkening and it was one of those late afternoons when the tip of a distant volcanic island could be seen rising above a wreath of clouds. I wished I had brought a jacket; an unbearable thought an hour previously. As the cameras and sound recordings were switched off, we heard Cedric throwing his voice across the waves like a man arguing with the devil.

> *Come on, kid,*
> *Come on, kid,*
> *Hit him with a left and a right.*
> *Go on, kid,*
> *Go on, kid,*
> *How were they to know it was the kid's last fight?*

And, fiercely, wildly, the Budgerigario fishermen responded :

> *Tummon, tid,*
> *Tummon, tid,*
> *Hiddum widdum leffanna rye,*
> *Tummon tid,*
> *Tummon tid,*
> *Tum ta-tum ta-tum-tum ta-ta tum-tum-tum.*

There was a strange, cannibalistic sound about that.

Then Simpson called it a day, and he and Pinch stepped into our fast launch and Ernie told him the news about the whale.

'Fine,' he said. 'Fine. It really *floats*?'

He seemed astonished.

'Goes like a bomb,' Ernie said.

'Good. Any casualties?'

'Not at the launching. Eric decided to slip overboard on the way out just now.'

'He did?' Simpson looked surprised. 'I thought he was made of stronger stuff.'

In the car to the hotel I said: 'Boy, was I relieved to see it float. I'd already sent a long cable to the States describing the ceremony. Had to, to make a feature deadline. I'd have looked a fool if the darn thing had sunk.'

Simpson grinned. He said: 'That's how Pancho Villa took Chihuahua, Slim, remember? John Reed went on a big drunk and cabled his paper in New York that Pancho had taken Chihuahua. When he came round and started sorting things out, he suddenly remembered this cable. So he went straight to Pancho and said, "I've done a stupid thing. I said you took Chihuahua." Pancho said, "You *did*? How did I do it?" Reed said, "You took the city by the north walls. Then you carried the attack right through to the main plaza and stormed the Governor's palace." Pancho said, "Jesus, did you say I did that? That's a lousy way to do it. But hell, I'll do it." He did, too, and that is how Pancho Villa took Chihuahua.'

. . . . .

Pull, pull my fine heart alive! Pull, my children, pull, my little ones. Why don't you break your backbones, my boys? Pull, then, do pull, will you please? So, so, now.

The day of the fights dawned clear and beautiful. I shaved and went up to Simpson's room early and squatted on the carpet as Simpson ate his breakfast in bed and dictated to Perdita. Sunlight flooded the large bedroom and, through the windows, beyond a tangle of tropical plants, you could see glittering strips of sea. Between dictation, Simpson, who had been reading Julius Meier-Graefe, talked about Van Gogh.

'You know why Van Gogh committed suicide, Slim?' he said.

I said, 'Yes, because he was a nut.'

Simpson grinned secretly and shook his head slowly.

'He was sane when he killed himself,' he said. 'The doctor looking after him was his friend. That clinic was one of the few places where he was understood, both as a man and as an artist. But he was getting repeated fits of insanity. So he killed himself in a lucid moment to avoid hurting the people who were looking after him. He was quite sane when he did it.'

'He was in a mess,' I insisted.

'Reading those last few pages of Meier-Graefe's is quite an experience,' Simpson said, looking out at the sea. 'Jesus, I almost cried when I read them. They made me feel like a whore at a wedding.'

'You should try reading them in the original German,' I said.

'That would be quite an experience, too,' Simpson said.

'Van Gogh would have loved a morning like this,' I said, turning to the window.

'Yeah,' Simpson said. Suddenly he said : 'How many people have you killed, Slim ?'

'Oh, I don't know. One or two during the war.'

Simpson snapped his fingers irritably : 'That's licensed killing. Is that the only time with you ?'

'Yes.'

Simpson began to peel a banana. 'I think we should each be allowed two murders. It would make life a lot more interesting.'

'Yeah,' I said. Turning, I saw Simpson's little brown eyes looking at me with a curious expression. I tried to think where I had seen it before. Then I remembered how the whale had looked the previous afternoon. I shivered, as if the morning had suddenly turned cold.

I said : 'So you're going to hunt tiger after this. You'll like India. A colonel I knew once told me it costs only two rupees to have a man murdered in Calcutta.'

'Sounds like a great place,' Simpson said appreciatively.

I said, 'What's the drill on the tiger hunt ?'

Simpson said : 'I fly to Calcutta. Then on to Assam, then

on to the shooting camp where we'll hunt tiger and leopard. We'll use twenty-six elephants and have over seventy native hunters.'

'What will you do with all those elephants?' I asked.

'Ride on two, use the rest to drive the tiger to our guns. We are also going machan shooting, going for big game from jungle tree platforms. Then we'll go ghooming.'

'What is that?'

'Roaming around the jungle on elephants, shooting whatever game you meet up with.'

'Will you go fishing?'

'Sure. We'll fish in jungle streams for the mahseer. That's a fighting fish. Weighs over a hundred pounds.'

'You'll have fun all right,' I said. 'I wish I were going along too.'

Simpson smiled oddly.

'You'd chance someone investing two rupees in having you bumped off?'

'Well, *you* are taking that chance, aren't you?'

Simpson stopped smiling. Then he fished out a grin from his stock of false expressions.

'We've a lot to look forward to here, kid,' he said. 'After all, we're going fishing off the African coast, aren't we?'

'I guess so,' I said flatly.

'What do you mean by that, kid? Of course we're going fishing. You helped fix it yourself.'

I nodded.

'It will be all right,' I said.

Simpson smiled broadly. 'Of course it will, kid. Everything will be fine, just fine.'

Perdita and I left the director to dress, and I had my breakfast on the terrace, as usual. After breakfast, I arranged to drive to Las Flamenco with Pinch. The actor was fully made up for his part as the whaling skipper.

'Don't forget Mr. Pinch's leg,' a Spanish production assistant told a make-up man as we were about to set out. 'And don't forget to bring down the cannibal's contact lenses. He's supposed to die today—with a glassy look in his eyes.'

A wardrobe man humped the actor's whalebone leg across the terrace. We stowed it in the back of the car and drove off.

Kevin met us on the beach. We stepped into a rowboat and headed for the *Fishbite*. Kevin was trailing one hand in the water as we bounced towards the reef, when he suddenly scooped out a small balloon-faced fish and held it in the cup of his hands.

'He's dud-dud-dead,' he said, after examining him closely.

The fish, all head and angry little pop eyes, had the tiny mouth of a stillborn fœtus. He was white and smooth as a duck egg.

'Nice little fuf-fuf-fellow,' Kevin said, fondling the fish.

'What is it?' Pinch asked.

'Dud-dud-don't know. Fuf-fuf-fuf-forgotten. But I know he's a gug-game little fuf-fish. Gug-gets very angry when attacked. Bub-blows himself up to this size and dud-dies. There are lots of them in this bub-bay. Makes one think of mum-miniature whales.'

'Why not collect some and turn them upside down in egg-cups and serve them for breakfast?' Pinch said.

'Gug-gug-gug-gug-good idea,' Kevin said. 'I'll gug-get the boatman to collect a few.'

We climbed on to the heaving decks of the *Fishbite,* and for an hour or two I watched Simpson directing actors in whale-boats. The sun shone, but a stiff wind raked the sea. Simpson was getting just the shots he wanted. Some of the more sensitive actors were looking green and over-fatigued; I wondered if any would jump overboard in desperation. Then I clambered into a lifeboat and slept in the sun, and the warm wind blew over my face. I woke around noon and took a

launch back to Las Flamenco and drove to the hotel for lunch.
That afternoon I went to the hotel barber shop and had a
shave and hair-cut. The manicurist was a strikingly beautiful
island girl, called Ramona. I had had a good wine with my
lunch, the sun was shining, I was happy for Simpson getting
all those wonderful shots. I had a manicure while the barber
snipped my hair off. Remembering that I had two tickets
for the fight, I asked Ramona to come along with me that
night. She nodded and looked pleased and squeezed my hands
as she pared my nails.

'Thou must dress elegantly tonight, child,' I said as she was
finishing.

'What wear?'

'Black dress,' I said. 'White mantilla. Jewels.'

'What you wear?' Ramona said.

'Bullfight shirt,' I said.

Ramona looked puzzled.

'Ho, toro,' her barber boss said, brandishing two cut-throat
razors like horns. 'Ho, ho. Dominguin.'

'Sí,' I said. 'I shall wear his shirt.'

Ramona's eyes sparkled. 'Bueno,' she said. 'You like-a the
toreo?'

'Mucho,' I said.

'Bueno. I meet thee here tonight.'

'Sí. Nine o'clock.'

.   .   .   .   .

'I'm taking a Spanish duchess to the fight,' I told Ernie
later that day.

'Has she got a sister?' Ernie asked automatically. He was
worrying about whether the contestants would stay the three
rounds.

'They've got three old men in the ring,' he said, 'and John
has briefed each one to slaughter the other.'

'It should be good,' I said.

A messenger came up.

'Señor Sanderson? Señor Grigorio Pinch send message asking if you have bought bucket?'

'Tell him yes,' Ernie said.

'Bucket?' I asked.

'Greg wants a brand-new bucket. He's going to fill it up with water and sponge Tom down all over and then sling the rest down his pants.'

That night, feeling good about taking Ramona to the fight, I changed early. I hummed the song 'Ramona' and approved my sun-tan as I tied my bow in the dressing mirror. But I forgot about the bullfighter shirt.

On my way to the bar I saw Terrible Tom pacing up and down a corridor, shaking his head and muttering to himself. I stopped and wished him luck for the fight.

'Dunno as I'll be fighting now,' Tom said.

'What's that?' I asked, astonished.

'They say I'm not fit and that Cedric will be taking my place.'

'I don't understand it.'

'Don't understand it myself,' the fighter said.

Just then Ernie came up and steered me away from Tom.

'Don't take any notice,' he said in a low voice. 'It's a gag. Tom is fighting fit all right. But Simpson's spreading it around that Cedric will be taking his place. How Cedric will be able to concentrate on singing when he thinks he's fighting as well, is going to be quite a sight. Not a word, mind.'

Ernie dashed off and I went on to the bar.

'You're a funny guy,' the shipping millionaire said as I entered. 'You've only once bothered to dress for dinner since you've been here and tonight you dress up just for a lousy prizefight.'

'So would you dress up for a Spanish duchess,' I said.

'You taking a duchess?' The Greek looked interested. 'Do I know her?'

'You wouldn't know this one,' I said. 'By the way, how's the dock strike?'

The millionaire turned green.

'Go away,' he said.

I had two Alexandrias at the bar. Then I decided to leave a message for Ramona at the reception desk, telling her to collect me at the bar. The barber shop was on the way. It was open and I glanced in as I passed. Standing by an empty chair, looking crestfallen, was Ramona, still wearing her white manicurist's coat.

'Aie,' I said, 'thou shouldst have been changed and ready long ago. Black dress. White mantilla. Jewels. Remember?'

Ramona lowered her head.

'So sorry, no possible.'

'What's wrong?' I asked.

'Thou hast only two tickets,' she said. 'Ramona not allowed go fight without chaperone.'

This was a blow. I thought for a moment.

'I know,' I said. 'Señor Simpson go fight. He can chaperone thee.'

Ramona quickly made the sign of the cross.

'Grigorio, then,' I said. 'Grigorio Pinch he go fight. Tell thy mamma, papa, brother, aunt and sister that Grigorio will be thy chaperone.'

Ramona crossed herself again.

'No possible. My brother kill you, kill Señor Simpson, kill Señor Grigorio if I go fight alone with you. Brother kill you first.'

'Then let's call it off,' I said quickly.

'No comprende.'

'You no go fight with me.'

That seemed to be wrong, too. Ramona looked fiercely at me, as if she would do her brother's killing herself.

'Okay,' I said. 'What *shall* we do?'

Ramona brightened. 'You get tickets for my brother and his friend,' she said. Then she looked at my shirt and her eyes narrowed: 'You cheat me. You bad man. You no wear bullfight shirt. I tell my brother to kill thee unless thou wearest thy proper shirt.'

I thought quickly.

'No possible,' I said, 'the laundry has ruined it. Adios.'

I hurried back to the bar, thinking I had got out of that very well. But it was not to be. You know how it is with Spanish women.

.   .   .   .   .

I was drinking an Alexandria when, on checking through my pockets, I found I had left my fight tickets in my room. Cedric's door was open as I stepped into our communal hall. Cedric was seated on his bed, his elbow resting on his knee. He was supporting his chin on one hand, exactly like Rodin's Thinker. He looked utterly miserable.

'Hi,' I said.

'Hi,' he said, terribly piano.

'What's bothering you, old-timer?'

Cedric looked miserably at me.

'Shut the door, will you?'

I stepped into Cedric's room and shut the door.

'I've got to go on tonight,' Cedric said.

'I know that,' I said. 'You've been rehearsing "The Kid's Last Fight" for the past three days. Go in and sing, champ, and you'll wow everyone tonight.'

'It's not the singing I'm worried about,' Cedric said. 'I've got to fight as well.'

I gave a low whistle. 'What, fight *and* sing?'

'That's right. Seems Terrible Tom has rheumatism in his leg and can't fight. So they've asked me to step in and fill the breach. Naturally, I said yes.'

'But sing *and* fight,' I said. 'It's an odd combination.'

Cedric beat his fists against his forehead.

'How can I put the best of myself into the singing when I have to think about fighting two men afterwards?'

'It's tough,' I said.

'It's unheard of,' Cedric said miserably. 'I can't understand Tom backing out like this, even if he had got a bad leg.'

'He's not the kind to go chicken,' I admitted.

Cedric shook his head, 'I can't understand it, I just can't.'

'Never mind,' I said. 'It will be over by midnight.'

'But I've got to *sing* first.'

'You'll sing like an angel.'

'Not when I'm figuring out the fight at the same time. I've got to go straight in and fight the moment I stop singing.'

I shook my head sympathetically.

'It's not as if I were in training,' Cedric said. 'I haven't had a scrap for two years.'

'Why don't you just go to Simpson and explain about your heart?'

Cedric shook his head. 'John expects me to fight,' he said quietly. 'That's good enough for me.'

I opened the door.

'Well, good luck, kid,' I said.

Cedric turned his face away to the wall and didn't say anything. I collected my fight tickets from my room and went back to the bar.

.   .   .   .   .

After dinner I took a taxi to the fight arena. I had given my spare fight ticket to a girl the Kraut had asked along. Simpson was already in his ringside seat. He was wearing a

white referee's pullover, sneakers and a black Spanish hat.
Pinch and his girl sat next to him, the girl bored but attentive
for Greg's sake. Perdita was there, too, and they were all
watching a very dull fight between two slow-motion island
boys. I was alone. The Kraut's girl, a Swede, did not interest
me. This was no kind of a fight at all. I was dozing in my seat
when Kevin and Britta came in and took up two empty seats
on my right, and I brightened up.

'Got a bottle with you, Kevin?' I asked.

'Nun-no, but I could use one.'

'So could I.'

'Why not go to the Casa Mump? Gug-get a bottle of
Bacardi from the barman there. Tell him it's fuf-fuf-for me.'

'No, I'll get a bottle and pay for it.'

'As you like, old man. Bub-ub look snappy.'

Stepping carefully over the feet of the watchers by the
ringside, I headed for the main gangway. The fights were
being filmed and the arena was brilliantly lighted. It was
much quieter than the last time, because this was for charity,
and the cheer-leaders had not shown up, or were overawed.
The audience was mostly a charity audience, not a strictly fight
audience. And the fighters were all punks. As I was leaving
the hall I heard someone announcing the next fight. One of
the contestants was 'El gran hero, Spinoza.

The people at the door tried to block my way. I was about
to raise my fists, but Ernie was ushering in late-comers and,
seeing me, he came over. I told him where I was going and he
fixed it with the police for me to go through. He told me to
hurry back, though, since our crowd was taking over in a few
minutes.

'Don't worry,' I said. 'Spinoza has got to do quite a powerful amount of thinking before he's through.'

The streets around the fight arena were deserted. It was
pleasant walking in the cool night, across the little public

garden with swings and roundabouts, near the Casa Mump. The fair had stopped, and you could hear the sea crashing on the shore on the far side of the park.

The bar was almost empty. A dignified bartender asked what was my desire. I told him to get me a bottle of Bacardi rum. He set the bottle up on the counter. Then I told him to pour me a large measure of rum from his bar bottle. I was watching him drawing the rum when a hand clasped my shoulder and I turned and saw a thin, spectacled man staring at me. He was a sound-mixer with the unit.

'I know you,' he said in a whisky voice.

'You do?' I looked at him. 'Well, I don't want to know you. Good night.'

'Words, words, words,' the thin guy said. He looked and talked like an English curate.

I said : 'Go away.'

The thin man did not move.

'How goes it with the gladiators?' he asked.

'A boy called Spinoza was going in to fight as I left.'

The thin guy waved his arms.

'Hooray for the pantheistic mob,' he shouted. 'There is only one substance—God. Get that, kid? Thought and extension, that's my baby.'

'You're a rummy,' I said.

'Words, words, words,' the thin guy said. 'What do you want to go slinging words around for, kid?'

'Ah, go mix some sound.'

'You care nothing for words,' Skinny said severely. 'You only use them to make money. You write whale talk. Yet words have screamed and clamoured——' He broke off and savoured the phrase. 'I like that. Screamed and clamoured. Yes,' he shouted, 'words have screamed and clamoured. And what have you done about them?'

'A damn sight more than you'll ever do.'

'Words, they have screamed and clamoured. And death lies heavy on them.' He glared at me. 'And you don't care.'

'I'll fight you, though,' I said. 'I'll fight you about words.'

He was wearing a short-sleeved green shirt.

'I'd murder you,' he said.

'We'll see about that,' I said, removing my jacket.

The thin guy suddenly shot his arm across my face. It was a thin arm, but the upper parts were curiously muscular, as if they had been tightly bound above the elbow for a blood transfusion and swollen up and stayed that way. I knocked the arm down and raised my fists.

'Come on,' I said. 'We'll see who can use words. You'll scream and clamour before I've done with you.'

'Not now,' the thin guy said, reverting to his curate's voice. 'Let us talk about words. Words that have screamed and clamoured.'

'Let's not,' I said, lowering my fists.

'Then let us have a drink.'

'Okay,' I said. 'But no more screaming and clamouring.'

We drank, watching each other warily. The thin guy told me he had worked with Simpson in Africa, Paris, London, Italy. As he spoke he shook and quivered with some profound and disturbing kind of emotion. He was an intense thin guy.

Suddenly he said : 'You want to hear a story?'

'No,' I said.

'Don't be silly,' he snarled. 'Every writer likes to hear a story.'

'I don't.'

'Now listen carefully. I will tell you a story about a man who became God. No, listen. He didn't just want to be God, or pretend to be God. He actually *was* God.'

'A Spinoza kind of God?'

'Don't interrupt. Set up some more rum. Rum, amigo, for God's sake. God? Did I say God? Well, listen, then. He

waded out of the African swamp and raised his right arm
above his head and became God. What do you think of that
for a story?'

'It's a bit thin.'

'But wait. Listen. Don't be so impatient. What do you want
me to do with this story? Wrap it up with a trick ending and
sell it to the *Saturday Evening Post* for you? Just listen, for
Holy Hepburn's sake. You haven't a clue about what you're
really tampering with by coming here on this location. I have
been on others. To you, I suppose, it seems just like any other
location. *Seems,* mark you, ha, ha. There are signs and
wonders, amigo. Signs and wonders undreamed of in your
philosophy. Believe me, kid, I know what I'm talking about.'

'The story,' I said. 'Where is the story?'

'Ah, you begin to show interest. You smell a story. You
have a nose for these things, yes? Well, I shall tell it to you in
its entirety. But do not quibble with me if it is too long or too
short. I care nothing for such matters. Now, where was I?
Ah, yes. God. Spinoza. Africa. Swamps. The man. He looked
down at the primeval microbes in the mud and knew that he
was God. There was no madness. No megalomania. No para-
noia. He was not a-Freud, ha, ha. He was God. And on
becoming God he gathered around him disciples, destroyers,
dabblers in the black arts. Well, I tell you—he was God.
Was, past tense.' Angry tears stood in his eyes. 'Was, was, was,
was, was. I am a broken man.'

'Cheer up, brother, we are all broken,' I said. 'We were
broken before we were born. I know a girl called Mimi who
wears straw clothes.'

'Listen, listen, listen,' the thin guy yelled. 'Pray do not
interrupt. So he was God. And then, lo and behold, he was
not. For there is the true irony of this story, my muddy slinger
of words. Ha, ha, my wordy slinger of mud. My mudlark.
My ode to a mudlark. Here's richness, friend. Words that

scream and clamour. He *was*, and then he was not. As suddenly and startling as was his becoming, so also was his
unbecoming sudden. Ha, ha! *un*becoming. Words, words, my
friend. And I warn you. Disaster will come to you as soon as
you step out of here. The Black Ones have marked you down.'
He coughed for a minute. Then he said, more calmly: 'So
there we are. Was that not a splendid story, brother?'

'Terrific, brother,' I said, picking up the rum bottle. 'Good
night.'

'Good night, good night, ha, ha, ha, ha . . .' I could hear
his voice trailing away like a siren. A screeching, curatey voice
thick with Scotch and sorrow.

I was walking up a narrow street leading to the fight
arena when three guys wearing big Spanish cloaks and
Cordobés hats overtook me. One caught me by the arm.

'Excuse, señor.'

I grasped my rum bottle by the neck and waited.

'Well?'

Someone shone a torch on my face.

'It is the one,' a guttural Budgerigario voice said.

'Say, what *is* this?' I said.

'Silence, señor.'

'I'll give you silence,' I said, taking a firmer grip on the
bottle. 'I'll silence the lot of you if you don't beat it.'

One of the three pushed his face up to mine and said:
'You have insulted an island woman. We have come to tell
you that you will pay for the insult. We curse the fishing.
We curse all gringo fishermen!' The guy spat. 'There, tell
that to your Señor Simpson. Tell him we have cursed the
fishing. Come, we go.'

And they went.

By the time I got back into the arena the fights were over
and a Budgerigario in a silk shirt was in the centre of the
ring playing a guitar and singing.

'Where have you been?' Kevin said, reaching out for the bottle.

'Fishing,' I said. 'Fishing in dark places.'

'You're cut,' Kevin said sorrowfully.

'I must be,' I said wonderingly. 'Yeah! Come to think of it, I must be.'

Oh, that fishing. Oh, those fishermen. Oh, those cute, crazy, mixed-up, goddam Budgerigario fishermen!

CHAPTER TEN

Bueno Nuevo Anno

IT WAS NOW the last day of the year. But as I drove in the morning to Las Flamenco with Pinch, our driver missing other cars by inches, the sun outshone the dying rhythms of that enormous, crazy year.

Death hovered.

'No wonder they're always having funerals on this island,' the actor said as we shaved the right cheek of a tram.

'At this rate we'll be lucky to see the new year at all,' I said, nicking a lump out of the rear wing of a superannuated Oldsmobile.

'Life is cheap here, amigo,' Pinch said.

Yeah, I thought, and let's quit hamming. Forget the paella parties. Forget the whales. Forget the controlled flow of visual imagery. Forget the dames. Forget the fishing. But that's one you can't forget, amigo. Simpson has set his mind on the fishing, so that's one thing you cannot forget.

'But honour is all,' I replied, getting back into the act. 'Take the señoritas. You offer to buy a nice one a pretzel, what happens? Up bobs a small army of aunts and brothers, each one just crazy about pretzels. And if you say, Sorry, no pretzels, then, brother, you're in trouble. Big trouble. Heap big trouble.'

'You don't say. Then how do you account for so many of our lads sagging at the knees every morning?'

'Ah, señor,' I said sadly. 'You must not ask so many questions. This is a land of contrasts, didn't y'know?'

I thought of the autographed publicity stills of Pinch the boys had been trading in at the Casa Maria, and how he now hung over all the whores' beds beside the sacred pictures. That was a laugh, all right.

We passed a battered taxi hauled up on the sidewalk with a long, thin Budgerigario stretched horizontally beside it. What was left of his head lay in a puddle of blood.

'That's the stuff for you,' Pinch said. 'Any book with the word "blood" in it is sure to become a best-seller. *Blood and Sand. Captain Blood. Blood on the Moon.* The only other word to beat it is "love"!'

'Seems I'll have to write a book called *Love and Blood.*'

'Or *Blood and Love.*'

'Or *Bloody Love.*'

'Or *Love is Bloody.*'

We worked out a few more book titles, and then were at Las Flamenco and Pinch stepped into the bright sunshine. A hundred or so Budgerigarios were waiting to see him stride across the beach and step into a rowboat. He clambered aboard the *Fishbite*, and I decided to get a less exalted view of things from a tug. I found a crowd of stuntmen and technicians aboard, waiting for Simpson to start the day's work.

The technicians' dialogue was scintillating.

'Wot's Simpson finking up now?'

'Gawd only knows.'

'Cards and booze, booze and cards.'

'And to fink we could av spent the new year at home. Why didn't they get a move on and finish the picture on time?'

'I don't fink it will ever be finished.'

'They better get crackin' or there'll be a mutiny.'

'My missus is sending me stinkin' letters. Anyone would

fink it was my fault that I'm stuck dahn here waiting for
Simpson to float his lahsy whale.'

The stuntmen were slightly more articulate.

'How much you winning at poker now, King?'

'Sweet all!'

'But you *are* up on the deal?'

'A quid or two, maybe.'

'Don't try and kid us. We know you've made a stack. We
also know you're planning to settle down here and set up as a
banana millionaire.'

'I might at that. It's better than acting.'

'Acting? Did you say *acting*?'

'Yeah, *acting*. Anybody want to make anything of it?'

I moved over to the *Fishbite* and idled through the rest of
the morning, smoking and sunbathing and watching the unit
bobbing about in small boats for yet another smashing-up
sequence.

Clouds were gathering like rubbernecks round a street-fight
when Simpson, Pinch, Rory Punt and the Kraut climbed
aboard for lunch.

'It doesn't look very promising,' Punt said, sniffing the air.

'You have the choice of two kinds of weather down here,'
Pinch said. 'Whaling weather or gin rummy weather.'

We went below.

'Where's the whale?' I asked Simpson over the card table.

'Where's the whale, Pia?'

'He's being hauled round from the other side of the Isletta,'
the continuity girl said. 'He should be going round the bend
right now.'

'So long as we don't all go round the bend with it,' Simpson
said, winking.

Over lunch we talked about horses, painting and Chaplin.
Then over coffee the talk switched to French literature.
Simpson said he had once fallen in love with a Balzac heroine.

The Kraut asked vich vunn. I did not catch the answer. I had got to worrying about the fishing again.

The weather was very bad now. The table was cleared and some of the eaters settled down to play gin rummy.

About an hour later the sun returned and Simpson immediately headed his flotilla out across the choppy green sea. I remained on the *Fishbite*. Cedric's voice came faintly across the water, singing 'Once I had a Secret Love.' There were occasional shouts of agony from Jug Ears and Rory, and then, on a higher register, Connor's scratchy Dublin falsetto urging the rowers in his whaleboat forward. I pushed snugly up against a canvas windbreak with Barbara Ward's *Faith and Freedom* and sank quietly into a comforting and comfortable dream world of law and logos, work and wealth, welfare and world order, with grateful acknowledgment to Jacques Maritain, Reinhold Niebuhr and Arnold Toynbee and the hell with whales or fishing or Spanish curses.

Then I dozed, warm and sheltered, while the actors shivered and shouted in the chill sea. No wonder some of the more hysterical ones were beginning to hate my guts.

.   .   .   .   .

That night there was much gaiety and back-slapping. There was a party in a sick man's room and another in the Sandersons' suite.

I was quietly drinking a pêche champagne and juggling with a dozen raw eggs when Dill perched herself on the arm of my chair.

'Oo, Slim,' she said suddenly. 'There's a wonderful moon outside. Do come and look.'

'Forget it,' I told her. 'Have another sip of champagne.'

Dill shook her head.

'Oh, please. You'll be sorry to miss it.'

'No, I'm perfectly comfortable where I am.'

'*Please.*'

'No. Run along now.'

'Be a sport. Just once.'

'Oh, all right.'

The twin went over to the open french window and stood looking yearningly at the moonlit tropical garden. I followed over, and she caught my hand and led me out.

We had barely passed through the door when the screaming began.

'Help! Murder! Oo, Slim, *don't*! Murder! Murder!'

I began to drag the twin back and bumped into five or six people rushing out towards us. We all staggered into the room together. The child skipped away, doubled up with laughter.

'What's the matter, baby?' Ernie asked anxiously.

'Oo, nothing, Daddy. I just wanted to see what would happen if I screamed.'

Ernie looked steadily at me. 'I guess it's time to take the twins off to dinner,' he said severely.

Shaken, I went up to Simpson's suite. I expected to find the place packed. It was about twenty minutes to midnight. But Simpson was sitting quietly in an easy chair. Pinch, his girl and the Kraut were talking in a corner. Pinch was wearing a tuxedo and a bullfight shirt. The Kraut was ogling the girl and pulling Conrad Veidt faces.

Simpson, who was wearing the corduroy suit and red choker, looked up.

'Why, hello, Slim. Come in, kid. You know where everything is, help yourself.'

I poured some brandy and settled in a deep armchair. It was like a wake, apart from the Kraut. He had had several lucky strikes in the bowling alley, and it was playing hell with his ego.

'You're looking very pleased with yourself,' I said.

The Kraut looked at me through an invisible monocle.

'Em I?'

'Yes, in fact I'd say you're looking goddam smug.'

'Komm, led us not argue. It is almost time to sing "Old Leng Syne".'

'Ya, let's have some music,' Simpson said briskly.

'Where's the orchestra?' Pinch's girl asked.

'Combs,' Simpson said. 'Combs and paper.'

'Vot a splentid idea.'

As we rummaged around for combs and thin paper I said to Pinch: 'Why is everyone so quiet tonight?'

Pinch said: 'John had a call five minutes ago to say that all the fishing tackle had been stolen. Don Pablo is furious.'

'Hell,' I said, 'that's real trouble.'

'Never mind now,' Pinch said. 'John is seeing Pablo later.'

We pieced our orchestra together and started up with a few hill-billy numbers.

Perdita came in, wearing a crinoline and poke bonnet. We opened a bottle of champagne. I helped Perdita with the glasses, and then, at two minutes to midnight, we put our combs up to our lips and played 'Auld Lang Syne'. Perdita, who had also found a comb and some paper, joined in, blowing happily.

Pinch looked at his watch.

'Midnight,' he said.

We raised glasses and toasted one another. There was a commotion at the doorway and King Connell entered, his cheeks glowing like a toy department Santa Claus's over the edge of his curly beard. He stopped short when he saw the tableau.

'Sorry, John. Sorry, folks. I just came to wish you all a happy New Year.'

'That's real nice of you, King,' Simpson said affably. 'Perdita, give King Connell a glass of champagne.'

'I don't want to bother you——'

'It's no bother at all, King. Come on in, you're real welcome.'

This was New Year, all right; the time, or at least the occasion) for calendars have changed), when the ancients chased old Daddy Death out of town and welcomed in the fresh young Prince of Life. The time when the Old Bull of the year was poleaxed and the New Year's Bull-Calf took its place. When in the thirteenth, unlucky month the old king yielded his sovereignty to the surrogate boy-king, and the short-lived monarch was hacked apart and his blood sprinkled across the fields to fructify the crops. Well, the year had just died; and some of this atavistic instinct had survived into this fresh year, and in this place, and Simpson was the old king who had been ritualistically murdered. By the absence of his followers.

Only Greg, the essential other hero-figure, had remained. Greg and his girl, the two-in-one caught by the centrifugal pull of the old king. And Perdita, the essential high priestess. And King, the jester banging his bladder of banalities. And myself, the historian with hooded eyes and built-in tape-recorder, poised for an ultimate betrayal. And the Kraut, crippled by the fact that he was not even carrying his camera, the only thing which justified his being around at all. That is how it was. But for one thing. In this case, the ritualistic killing was being equated by a ritualistic resurrection. In fact, the old king was in excellent form.

'Johnny, did you get through to your family?'

'What's that, Perdita?'

'Did your call to Ireland get through on time?'

'Oh, sure.'

'And did you remember to——'

'More champagne, Connell?'

'Thanks, John. I was——'

'Johnny, did——'

Simpson gave us a comprehensive wink.

'Nag, nag, nag,' he said.

'Okay,' Perdita said. She poured more champagne.

King said : 'Life's a funny thing, John. Last New Year at this very moment I was standing on the balcony of an hotel in Gibraltar with a pal. He committed suicide.'

'What, right there, on New Year's Eve?' Simpson's mouth was a leathery pouch of surprise.

'No, John, but shortly afterwards. He's dead now.'

'Is he, by Gard.'

'He's dead, all right.'

'You don't say, kid. Well, are we ready to eat?'

Simpson clamped on a black Cordobés hat, Perdita plucked daintily at her crinoline, and we followed them out to the corridor. Two startled chambermaids genuflected, crossed themselves quickly, and scurried out of sight as we appeared. The combination of Simpson with his hat and red choker, Pinch in his bullfighter's shirt, King with a bullet-proof vest, the girls, looking like a pair of Brontë sisters, in their wildly Victorian rig, and me in canvas slacks, tartan shirt and old solar topee, must have given passers-by a slight impression of our being comparatively *je ne sais quoi*. Everyone else around the joint seemed to be wearing white ties and tails or Givenchy and Balmain creations, with satin handles.

A table of honour was being set up for us in the little Green Dolphin Bar, down by the bay, and we were about to leave the hotel when the manager clasped Simpson by the sleeve and (looking at Pinch) asked if we would like a table in the dining-room.

'We have a special festivity tonight.'

Simpson shook his head.

'Sorry, but we have arranged to eat elsewhere.'

'Then' (still looking at Pinch) 'would you all care to have

some champagne before you go? It would only be for a short time. Please, Señor Simpson, por favor.'

Simpson looked at Pinch. Pinch bit his lip. The manager bit the bullet.

'All right,' the director said, 'just for a few minutes, then. Ernie has a table. We could go over and wish him and the twins a Happy New Year.'

The manager looked radiant.

'Thank you, sir. Thank *you*.'

But instead of leading us, he skipped along behind. The maître d'hôtel stood at the entrance. The door was slightly ajar and you could see the guests dancing around in fancy paper hats and throwing streamers. We were about to go in when the head waiter blocked our way. He took one quick look at Simpson's red choker and turned pale.

'Sorry, gentlemen, but there is absolutely no room. Not a single table left.'

'But we have been asked to come here,' Simpson said.

'Sorry, no room.'

Simpson turned away.

'Let's get the hell out of here before we break up the joint,' he snarled, and stalked away.

We left with him. The manager ran after Simpson, plucking his sleeve and talking at the double, but the director shook him off like a terrier puppy. As I turned in the foyer I saw the manager rush up to the head waiter and bring his fists down in a rapid tattoo on his bald Spanish onion. That, my good gossips, is why Grigorio failed to appear in that hotel that night, por favor, and that's that.

The sky was jammed with stars.

'It's a good sky,' I said, as we drove towards the bay.

'Wonderful, kid, really wonderful. Have you ever seen stars *underneath* you, Slim?'

'No.'

'I have. In Italy. Not during the war, but after, when I was filming there. It was in Ravello, in the Amalfi area. There's a bay there, kid, and one night the sea was so still, that the stars seemed to have fallen into the bay. That was something.' He stared moodily away into the darkness.

'Yeah,' he said, after a long silence. 'The stars burned cold that night.'

We sat down at a long table covered with paper cloths. The Green Dolphin Bar was pleasant, particularly after the hotel. The entrance was open to sky and sea, and far out you could see the lights of small fisher-boats. A Budgerigario fisher had just come in with a basket of dripping seafood caught specially for the restaurant. This was to be our first main dish. Other fishers were still out catching the rest of our meal. While all this was being prepared we were given large plate-fuls of fish soup as good as any Marseilles bouillabaisse I have ever tasted. The sea air blew in like a cosmic kiss. We kept our hats on through the meal.

King Connell suddenly remembered about our drinking bout.

'Let's have it now,' he said.

'Mañana,' I said. 'I got work to do tonight.'

'You're chicken,' King sneered.

'That's right, I'm chicken.' I turned to Perdita.

'He's chicken, John,' King complained.

'Oh, I wouldn't say that,' Simpson said soothingly. 'It's just not the right time for it, that's all.'

'You'll have your contest,' Pinch said. 'So why don't you just relax now, eh, Connell?'

But King couldn't leave it alone.

'Hell, I could drink him under the table any time,' King growled. 'What do you think, John?'

Simpson paused, 'It's hard to say, King.'

'No, tell me. Who would you back?'

Simpson turned to Pinch.

'Well, Greg,' he said slowly. 'Shall we bet on it?'

'Sure. A thousand pesetas stakes?'

Simpson paused again. 'Well, if you want me to place my bet, I would say...' He paused again. 'I would put my money on Slim.'

'Okay,' Pinch said. 'It's a deal. My money's on Connell.'

King doubled his knees up to his beard like a fœtus in the fifth month, and groaned.

'Oh, my God, this is terrible.'

'What's bothering you, King?' Simpson asked softly.

'Hell, John, what a thing to do to a guy. I know I can win this, but it takes all the kick out of it if my winning will make you a loser. Not that I want Greg to suffer by it, either, but——'

'We quite understand, King,' Pinch said reassuringly. 'You don't have to bother to explain.'

'No, but——'

'There are no buts about it,' Pinch said. 'All I want is to see a nice, clean contest.'

'Without anyone pulling any punches,' Simpson added menacingly. 'No fiddling with measures. No secret puking.'

'Oh, my God,' King groaned again.

There was a commotion at the entrance. A waiter flew in the air like a softball. Women screamed, with that odd note of ecstasy, that supersonic whine they put into a scream when they're on the fringe of a rough-house. A cat scorched across the restaurant—panic in its eyes, a fishbone sticking out of its mouth. Several Budgerigario eaters lit out quietly for the hills. Then the cause of it all swaggered in, Man Mountain Pablo Ruiz Polianski-Smith. The Big Budgerigar Fisherman. Boss of the neighbouring seas. Punchy Pablo. Rash Ruiz. And he was heading straight towards me, pushing away his hoods who were trying to hold him back.

Ignoring Simpson and the rest he caught me by the collar and began to shake me slowly, with great expertise and without the aid of handles.

'Is it true?' he asked.

The table was between us, so I could not bring my knee up in self-defence. But I picked up a fork and stuck it into the big fisher's wrist. I distinctly heard him say *ouch*, in good American, and remember marvelling that a Budgerigario should have such a sweeping command of language.

'Animal,' the fisher said, releasing me. 'Pig. Dog. Goat. Camel. Palæontological anachronism of the early cainozoic period or maybe at a pinch the mesozoic.'

'Steady, Gus,' I said. 'I prefer mine without custard.'

'I tell thee thou art a tough cookie,' the fisher snarled, 'but if thou triest any more of thy commando tactics here thou shalt be thrown to the sharks.'

'What's on your mind, bub?'

The fisher scowled as two of his hoods stitched up his wrist with green catgut.

'Tell me,' he said. 'Is it true that thou hast violated one of our island women.'

'So that's what's bothering thee,' I said. 'The answer is no. But I sure gave one the brush-off.'

The big man's moon face regrouped its craters into the shape of a vast incredulous grin.

'Thou *didst*?'

'Sure, I didst.'

'But—but how?'

The fisher drew up a chair and sat down and looked as if he was about to pin a medal on me.

'Well, what doest thou know,' he said when I told him. 'Well, bloweth me down. This calleth for a drink.'

And waving his hands, and shouting in the guttural

Budgerigario patois, he had the waiters rushing around bringing kegs and bottles and glasses and huge platters of hot,
wriggling octopus. This was a good eating house, the Green
Dolphin Bar, and we resumed our eating happily and in terms
of high comradeship. The other fishers turned up and regaled
Simpson with vinous anecdotes of fishing. The director was
happy again, there with the fishers. It was a good feast, with
much talk and laughter and fundador. When, at last, Don
Pablo rose he was in great good humour.

'Mañana,' he said, bowing to Simpson. 'Tomorrow, which is
today, we show thee such fishing as even thou hast never
dreamed of, ole. See, we wax poetic. Fish. Dish. Dish. Fish.
What is a fish without a dish? Ho, ho—semantics have always
been a special study with me. Good night, children, everywhere. Ho, ho, ho.'

The fisher fell backwards, laughing. His hoods caught him
midway and humped him on their shoulders and carried him
out into the tropical night. We finished our fundador, watched
by a crowd of local rubbernecks. But they were good, true
Budgerigarios. They did not come over, or try to muscle into
our talk, and as we rose to leave there was that low liquid
sound of applause only the Budgerigarios make. Nobody
followed us out. Pinch and his girl went off together along
the empty moonlit beach. The sea crashed along the shore,
it was good to think of people being in love, and the year
turned mysteriously in the night sky.

'We go whaling tomorrow, kid,' Simpson said as he got
into his car. 'Good and early.'

'Fine,' I said, looking out to sea. 'It is a good beginning for
the year, Juan.'

'Couldn't be better, amigo. Good night.'

I found myself alone with King Connell. A few hundred
yards along the bay was one of the smartest bars on the island.
You could hear the dance band throbbing faintly above the

sound of waves and gulls. We looked at each other, nodded, and headed for the bar.

'This is it, Connell. Drink for drink. Measure for measure.'

'Okay. We might as well settle it.'

We went through the swing doors, pushed through the crowd of upper-crust Budgerigarios and anchored ourselves to the bar. I signalled the bartender over and told him to set up four large brandies. When they arrived I poured the contents of two of the glasses into the other two, and pushed one over to King.

'Right, Pantagruel,' I said. 'We begin with double-doubles.'

'Okay, brother. If that's how you want it.'

'That's how I want it.'

He gulped his brandy in one swig.

'Same again,' King roared. 'Four brandies.'

That is how it began. It was a good bar. A bar bar. A bar is a bar is a bar, bar. And King Connell is one of the finest characters I ever met. Also a writer. One of the best, *the* best since Saroyan was a stable lad. I said *Saroyan*. Seventy Thousand Assyrians, Our Friends the Mice, London, Ah London, Sweetheart Sweetheart Sweetheart, Ever Fall in Love with a Midget?; yeah, and Christians Singing, Locomotive 38, the Objibway, Johnny the Dreamer, Mary the Model at Magnin's, Plato the Democrat, At the Chop Suey Joint on Larkin Street at Two Thirty in the Morning, No that's the title. Sure, it must be about that now, or three. What a boy that was, that Saroyan, looking like several violinists out of work, I'll never forget the impact that boy made when I first read his Seventy Thousand Assyrians; enough to turn you to drink, *he'd* done it so how could you do it. Give it up, brother, stick to journalism, write for the slicks and read Saroyan in your spare time to purge your soul. A writer's writer with handles, ask his cousin Dikran the Orator.

And King is another such writer, though you may never see

his stuff. Take Saroyan, take Christians singing, boy, you should
have heard those Christians singing. It was beautiful, all right,
all right. Double-double doubles are not in it. And King had
that kind of stuff running out of his ears. Then this being
here in the Budgerigars. What makes Simpson different to
the intellectual bums and artistic layabouts in the Village, in
Bloomsbury, in Saint Germain des Près? Hear me, brother,
I'll tell you. It's stamina. It's concentration. It's application.
He knows more about the mechanics of film making than any
film mechanic. It's all very well for the critics, poor spiritually
undernourished bastards most of them, to yap about the controlled flow of visual imagery. Sure he's got it under control,
but he's got something else. Stamina plus concentration plus
know-how plus intuition adds up to—what? Genius? Why be
afraid of the bloody word? It won't bite; and it fits Simpson,
if you really know him, that is. Nothing else will do, whether
you are directing it through the diatonic scales, or oils, or with
a pencil on the backs of envelopes. Or whether you use all
three and press them on celluloid.

Harmonise. Synthesise. Externalise.

We go to sea. These are treacherous waters. Storms, many
fishermen sail out and are drowned, they just disappear. And
these are the elements being caught on film by a sophisticated,
world-weary man, his head amongst stars, his boots kicking up
dust-clouds. That time in the whorehouse, going there with
a basket of wine as a gift for the girls on a courtesy visit to
thank Madame Jo Jo for looking after the boys. The madame
showing us round the kitchen, the communal eating room,
the laundry. The whores ironing their smalls, and then coming
into the private room, one by one, shy as schoolgirls, the
great director watching them, trying to make them feel at
ease, offering wine from the basket. Madame stern, cross about
their shyness and the gawky, awkward way they stood in their
lace pants. And, afterwards, Simpson chuckling and saying,

'That was a fine house, Slim. I've always liked cathouses. When I was a kid I used to save up for them.' And you saying, 'They were shy, though. Hell, they almost ended up reciting "Twinkle, twinkle, little star".' And all that not mattering because you knew that, whatever happened, wherever he went, Simpson would never lose sight of those stars, and somehow push a cluster of them into whatever he was making.

You still there, King?

Okay, push it over, and listen. Hear *me*.

Art is not just something pretty with a frame round it.

It is a disturbance, a dislocation of the senses.

Producing elation or illumination, take your choice, gentlemen.

And some artists are unorthodox because for their kind of art they need to take an attitude, create a pose, to save them from a conformity which will stifle, *not* their art or talent, but their opportunities.

And now a new year comes walking into the world, a little-boy year asking for information.

'What's that you say, son?'

'I said, "Where are you, Dad?"'

'Right now I'm whaling, son. Whaling with John Simpson and a guy called King.'

'Dad, do whales eat men?'

'Sometimes.'

'But before you left for the Budgerigars you said they can only swallow little things, like shrimps. You said they have a sort of curtain of stuff like seaweed that stops anything big going through to their belly. You said that is why Jonah couldn't possibly have passed into the whale like it says in the Bible.'

'I said that the Bible story of Jonah was written symbolically.'

'So when you just said that whales eat men, you were speaking symbolically?'

'That's right.'

'That's a funny way to speak, isn't it, Dad?'

'It's no way to speak, really. No way at all, unless you can't express it any other way.'

'What is a symbolic?'

'A symbol, son? It's like your friend Mister Oo-Oo, real and yet not real.'

'Mister Oo-Oo *is* real. He's high as ten million mountains and he speaks eighteen billion languages and has killed millions of whales.'

'Well, I hope to kill a whale soon.'

'Pooh, that's only a *stuffed* one.'

'There are other whales around, apart from the stuffed one.'

'And sharks? You said there would be lots of sharks.'

'There are plenty of sharks. The sea around here is thick with sharks.'

'Will *you* kill a shark?'

'I might, if one comes too close.'

'Where exactly are the Budgerigar Islands?'

'Off the coast of Africa.'

'I'd like to go to Africa and shoot lions.'

'Lion. Perhaps you will when you are older.'

'I am old now. I'm nearly five. Dad, what is John Simpson really like?'

'That's hard to say.'

'But you *know* him. What is he *like*?'

'He's tall.'

'Not as tall as Mister Oo-Oo.'

'Almost.'

'*Really*, Dad? Then he must be a very big man.'

'He is.'

'As big as God?'

'No, not quite that big.'

'But pretty big, just the same?'

'He's pretty big.'

'Say, Dad. Are you all right? It's pretty late at night and I've been in bed for hours. Guess it's all right for you to be up, though. Tell me more about John Simpson and whales and the Budgerigar Islands.'

'What do you want to know?'

'Are there pirates on the islands?'

'Not any more. There are smugglers, though.'

'Smugglers are *quite* interesting. Do you and John Simpson chase smugglers?'

'John Simpson is too busy chasing whales and fine weather. Besides, I don't think John Simpson would enjoy chasing smugglers.'

'Why, Dad?'

'He is too simpático towards them. He is a sort of anarchist.'

'An anarchist? Are you being symbolic again?'

'No, there are all sorts of ways of describing anarchists. I see them as people who look beyond the law for a personal freedom that will serve them in dealing with life and other men.'

'Oh, just now I thought I could see the dawn through the window. But it's only the moon still. Go on about John Simpson and anarchists. Does he break the laws very often?'

'Not really. How can I put it to you? When men work with him, or are his friends for a while, they somehow feel and act a little bigger than they really are. If they are the right sort of men they benefit from it. For a while, at least, they are better actors or better writers or better boom operators or better bookmakers or better horse-dealers or poker players (even when they are losing to him) or better hunters or better drinkers or better fighters or better fishermen. After they are no longer with him some scale down to normal size again, but the right ones go on being better than they were.'

'Good-o.'

'But that alone doesn't make John Simpson an anarchist. That comes through his creating conditions for himself in which everyone else with him can operate on this level. You see, son, there are lots of men in this world who don't like to see other people enjoying themselves, or being bigger or happier or crazier or richer than they are. Some even appear to be quite big themselves. Bankers, senators, or teachers at school. Well, John Simpson goes about making conditions for himself and for other men to feel good in and realise some of their dreams and capabilities. On the surface he does this by making films. He doesn't make films, mind, just to create an anarchy for himself and his immediate following. Out of all the nonsense and small-talk and frustration and ballyhoo that goes into films, occasionally something comes out that will thread together the people watching it and make a bonfire of their emotions and illuminate dark places. And, for an instant, they release us from such everyday humiliations as swallowing foul goddam brandy instead of standing on a beach and watching the stars.'

'Mumma said you are not to use so many bad words when you talk to me.'

'Mumma doesn't know. There's nothing wrong with bad words so long as you don't use them in place of better ones. But give her all my love; and yours too, squire. She's worth it, worth all the rest of the junk put together.'

'Go on, Dad, tell me more about John Simpson and whales and lighting bonfires inside people.'

'Well, to do the sort of things a John Simpson does, and go where he goes, you have to be a kind of anarchist. I would call John Simpson an aristocratic anarchist.'

'I know what an aristocrat is, Dad. Like in stories you've

told me about the Scarlet Pimpernel. They are an—oh, what is the word, an alight?'

'You're close, son. You're thinking of an élite. It's a French word meaning the pick or flower of anything. The word is not popular among the little men I mentioned, because they want everyone to be on one dull level. But it's a good word to remember.'

'An élite, I'll remember.'

'Used carelessly, it can be a horrible snob word. Used in connection with John Simpson's kind of anarchy, it works its passage. It involves certain obscure forces, and moods, and codes of behaviour. If you care about them, you don't try to explain them. You'll find them, son, if your nose is in the right direction at the right time. It's like you not having to be reminded when it's wrong to gallop a horse or shoot a partridge.'

'Is John Simpson very good at knowing when, and where, to do things?'

'Jesus and Mary, no. He makes all sorts of mistakes and breaks all sorts of rules. Doesn't he, King? Okay, okay. So you don't know who I'm talking to. Get on with your drink. What's that, son?'

'I said why exactly *is* he such a big man?'

'I don't quite know, and I wouldn't really want to know *exactly*. Right now he is coming to the end of making this film about chasing the White Whale. He has spent a great deal of time on it. Other men have spent a great deal of money. It is said that he is a procrastinator, a time-waster. That the film could have been finished in half the time. That is wrong. He has waited twenty-five years to make this film, and he intends to make it *his* way if it kills him and everyone connected with it!'

'You'll kill a few sharks in the meantime, won't you?'

'Of course.'

'Promise?'

'Promise. We're going fishing tomorrow night.'

'You are? I wish I were coming with you. Look, what a big bright moon. I hope it shines like that for you tomorrow night. Tell me about the fishing, Dad?'

'Not now. It's time you had more sleep.'

'Promise you'll try and kill a shark, Dad.'

'It's a promise.'

'And bring back a shark skin?'

'Yes.'

'And really kill the damn thing?'

'Better not let Mumma hear you say a word like that while I'm not there to argue with her.'

'I won't. So long as you really try and kill something.'

'There'll be a killing, son. *Some* kind of killing.'

'Good-o.'

The new year slipped away and King was missing.

I waited a while, watching the Budgerigarios living it up. They were tilted at a Carol Reed angle mostly, but they looked good. That was different to drinking green wine at the Fontoria dancing bar, in Lisbon, or seeing that sign on the road to the hotel, here on this island, reading JOSE GONZALEZ SOCORRO, FUNERIA SERVICIO PERMANENTE, or encouraging the twins to adopt a leprous fisher boy they saw at Las Flamenco, and rushing up to me and squealing, 'Oo, Slim, you must find a vet for poor Pepito, you *must* find a vet, quick, quick.'

Next to this bar is the local museum containing fifteen thousand skulls, bones, and mummies, the mummies stitched together; but in many cases the leather coverings have decayed and reveal viscera, brain, muscle, skin and withered flesh still attached to the hands. '*King, King, where are you? Where am I?*' Of course, some people prefer it to living in caves and it was different in the war. It's the cochineal cactus flowers you squeeze to draw the blood-like liquid. Jesus, they are religious down here. The poor, anyway. They go to the festival in honour of the Virgin del Pino, the Virgin of the Pines, on their hands and knees. They crawl literally on their hands and knees for several kilometres, uphill and over rough country. No wonder Simpson brought us here. I hope he gets his fishing tomorrow. *King, where you hiding?*

John said: 'Have you ever seen *Hamlet* performed in Swahili?' Greg said: 'No. How do you say, To be or not to be in Swahili?' And John mumbled some gibberish and we all laughed. That was at the Yacht Club on one of the good days, when the fishermen had stopped being troublesome for a while. Then there was that night in the dining-room when one of the Sanderson twins passed us a note saying WE ARE MAKING ALL THE OTHER NUTS HERE THINK THEY ARE SANE! Then there was the smash on the road to the airport with ten dead Budgerigarios lying in the sun, and the drunken doctor speaking into his stethoscope. And the rich, mixed-up girl quoting Keats and having an affair with the waiter. And Rory and Jug Ears playing cricket in the hotel lounge with an orange, using a marble pillar as the wicket. And the actor from Dublin losing his temper and telling everyone he was playing in a film called *The Pale Sardine*. And Dede Weston flying in and saying: 'Oh, boy, this location is going to do us a lot of no good!'

Insults at poker. People going down with typhoid. The nymphomaniac from Alabama making a pass at Simpson, and settling for a stunt man. And Greg being dragged through the sea near the harbour, then sitting in a boat with a blanket over his shoulders and wiping his mouth and saying, 'That oil tastes good.' And all the others in the sea, and Snorts Valentine having his heel chipped off and shouting in agony and Simpson saying, 'Keep him in the water while we re-take.' And Rory Punt with a high temperature, his eyes fevered, going into the water day after day. And Bernard, one of the Shakespearian actors, having his smashed arm strapped up in the seamen's hospital and insisting on going back to work. And the unit doctor saying: 'You can't expect to walk *and* talk at the same time on this location.'

Then hiring the whores and guitarists and the drum and fife band and the broken-down bullfighters and getting them to stage a cabaret at that little run-down café-bar on the other side of the island. And Simpson insisting on bringing that Spanish whore to dinner in a smart mountain-top restaurant, and, when Greg came in, introducing her as an eminent Flamenco dancer. 'We might almost be at Chasen's.' And then falling asleep at the back of the car, his head on the patient whore's shoulder, snoring contentedly.

That was right, and everyone was happy that time. And then you trying to write it, trying to live the sad lonely introvert life of a writer in the middle of a tropical madhouse, with all this happening around you. Try doing that some time, Oscar. *And* Mr. Edmund Wilson, and the rest of your tribe. Try it some time. And there, as I was looking around for King, the brandy a ton weight in my fist, there in the *Spanish-American Courier* dated this day, December 31st, or last night now, they had quoted Hemingway's acceptance speech which had just been read at a Nobel Foundation banquet by U.S. Ambassador John M. Cabot, with that piece going: 'How simple the writing of literature would be if it were only necessary to write in another way what has been well written. It is because we have had such great writers in the past that a writer is driven far past where he can go, out to where no one can help him.' And you feeling ashamed of not being that good a writer, or that kind of writer, and then getting angry with yourself for feeling ashamed instead of getting on with whatever there is for you to write. And then remembering Simpson summing up your clumsy attempts, that time in Paris, to find point of unity between Waugh and Hemingway. Him saying: 'But they are really *very* different, Slim. Waugh's leading characters are always complete shits. Papa's characters are incomplete heroes.' And you being unable to laugh that one off, or trying to clown about it the way you clown about most things you feel truly about. And goodbye to all that, anyway, because new performers with fresh tricks are knocking at the years. And there was that paper from Madrid, crumpled and sweaty, sticking in your pocket, *and where in hell was King Connell anyway?*

And then the glass falling from your suddenly paralysed hand.

I left the fashionable bar and walked slowly along the seashore, the sea looking like moonlit Guinness, till I came to the narrow streets leading to the place which seemed most like home. Raquel came across as I entered and put her arm in mine. We sat at a table away from the band. Spender brought champagne. The band played 'Besse-Me Mucho'. We danced, and the new year in its hiccuping infancy seemed good, very good.

CHAPTER ELEVEN

The Storm

THE SUN FLASHED over the mole suddenly, an electric torch probing, shining on trash-bins, sea-wrack, shingles.

I had been watching the sea from a parapet near the hotel, seeing it turn from mushroom grey to limejuice to the colour of a properly mixed Bloody Mary. I saluted a passing goat. The morning air was cold and damp, and I hunched my shoulders into the corners of my suede jacket and walked briskly into the hotel. The night porter was sorting postcards behind his counter and scrubwomen were sluicing cloths across the uncarpeted bits of the foyer. Bonjour, señoras. Bonjour tristesse. I nodded to the porter, collected my key, went to my quarters and undressed and took a shower. I dried off, flopped on my bed in my bathrobe, and picked up the telephone and got through to the night porter and ordered breakfast for nine. Café complet and bananas mashed in rum and milk, the liquids to be brought separately for me to mix myself.

'Sí, señor. At nine. Sleep well.'

'I will if I can rely on being called at the right time.'

'I will see to it personally.'

'Good.'

The porter was, by nature and training, just another hypnotised sunstruck, timestruck Spanish gremlin. But over this matter of breakfast our rapport was established. We had soldiered in the same bottlefields and you know how it is with old soldiers. It was seven-fifteen. I slept deeply and profoundly until the breakfast was brought in at nine. By nine-twenty I was dressed and shaved. I reached Simpson's suite as he and Perdita were about to set out for Las Flamenco.

'Hi, Slim. Happy New Year.'

'Hi, Perdita. And to you.'

'Did you sleep well?' Simpson asked.

'Excellently,' I told him.

The director looked at his Rolex watch.

'Okay, kids, let's go. We're shooting the whale today.'

The drive to the bay was, if anything, more hazardous than usual. The fiestas of the previous few days were beginning to catch up with the Budgerigarios, but in a big way, and the streets were full of slap-happy drunks, lurching and singing. It was a gay sight, all right, all right, and Simpson grinned whenever any pie-eyed Budgerigarios got in the way of our car. The drunks, noticing our grinning faces, would wave and cheer and blow kisses at Perdita. It was cloudy and windy, with patches of sunshine, and the thin Budgerigarios, gathered around as usual to watch our departure in the small boats, flapped in the wind like bleached washing on clothes-lines.

We arrived at the same time as Pinch.

'Mind they don't pick your pocket,' I told the actor, as a swarm of elated Budgerigarios crowded round him.

'It's only happened to me once in my life,' he said. 'That was in Newmarket. I'd won over a hundred pounds in notes. Someone must have seen me stow them in my pocket. I never saw them again. Thank God most of them were flannel.'

'Well, don't take any flannel pesetas,' I advised.

We got into rowboats and went bobbing round the reef. The rocks were looking particularly ugly that morning, snarling wetly out of the racing foam. With the sea heaving and hawking like a chesty opera singer it was a relief to come alongside the tug and climb aboard. Everyone on the tug seemed to have done a man-sized amount of celebrating overnight, the crew and some of the unit technicians still wearing coloured paper hats and moving around the boat with fixed, dehydrated expressions.

The whale wasn't quite ready and Simpson spent an hour or so smashing up row-boats, dragging boatloads of actors at speed over the choppy sea. I remained on the gently heaving tug, watching the deck seeming to bend like rubber as offshore rollers smacked against the sides. A tough-looking technician standing next to me was staring ahead with the steady, bug-eyed look of a man who does not like sea water in motion.

'Mucho fiesta?' I asked.

'It's not that,' the technician said. 'I get this every time I come aboard. Can't stand the rocking at any price.'

'How did you survive the North Sea?'

'God only knows. It was murder.'

'Didn't you know this was going to be a sea film when you signed on?'

'I didn't know a goddam thing. It was just another job of work.'

I looked at the sky.

'Cheer up,' I said. 'The weather seems to be clearing.'

How wrong can you get? Man, how wrong *can* you get?

. . . . .

Around eleven o'clock, the whale was towed into the centre of the bay, and now everybody began to move in for close shots. I got into a rowboat which I shared with Perdita, Greg's girl, Snorts Valentine and Connell Connor. The two Spanish fishermen who owned the boat pulled fiercely away from the tug, hating having to do so, and we headed briskly out towards the whale. Connell curled himself under a tarpaulin shelter, stretched across the bow, and went smack into Celtic twilight. The waves began to chop over the sides, drenching me. So I took off my shirt and stowed it under a seat and sat in a pair of white shorts, letting the sea splash all over me and water the hairs on my chest. The girls kept their clothes on.

As we drew close to the whale, Connell woke up, and without a word left us to board another craft. We drifted round the whale for a while, watching it roll in the heaving sea.

'It doesn't look much like a whale,' the French girl said.

'It does in camera,' Perdita said loyally.

'It looks so clumsy. I'm sure it's terribly slippery and dangerous.'

'Maybe it's got a headache,' Perdita snapped.

Simpson, Pinch and Kevin climbed on to the whale, followed by the Kraut and Stephen Chimes, the artistic wizard responsible for the making of all Simpson's whales. Simpson was like a general inspecting a new bomb, tapping here, twisting bits of rope there. Then Pinch leapt back into a small boat, standing by, ready to clamber on the whale for his sequences as soon as whatever was holding up the shooting was settled. You could not hear, from our boat, what Simpson was saying. But it seemed pretty technical, judging by the way the others cocked their heads and listened, occasionally checking a point of the whale's anatomy.

Meanwhile, the flotilla stood by, small fishing craft, launches, the camera boat, and the mother tug to which the whale was attached by a long umbilical cable of steel. This was a big day for the Catagonian Consul, who, as a director of the island shipping firm which had built the whale, was standing by on the tug to see how the monster worked at sea. For a while we drifted in circles round the whale, sizing up the half-menacing, half-comic contraption.

The biggest tug, the *Gran Budgerigar*, lay apart from the other vessels, but the crew were cutting meat to throw into the sea to attract gulls. You could hear them singing. Someone did a tap-dance on the coffin on which Snorts Valentine is finally washed up as the only survivor of the fight with the whale.

'That's sacrilege,' I told Snorts.

'Whassat?'

'They're dancing on your coffin.'

Snorts spat into the sea.

'Judas priest, the whole thing is sacrilege.'

We had been drifting in large circles round the boats, now we drew close to the whale again. It sure looked as if it had a headache, rolling around with the waves washing over its big blind eyes.

'Isn't it just the cutest whale you ever seen?' Perdita said delightedly.

But the French girl shook her head.

'I still cannot make head nor tail of it,' she said. 'Where *is* the tail?'

'At the back,' Perdita said firmly.

'But where *is* the back?'

'At the opposite end to the head. See where it tapers off?'

'I see. But I don't see any tail.'

'You have to imagine that,' Perdita said. 'It'll look terrific in the picture, believe you me.'

'I hope so,' the French girl said dubiously. It didn't need any two-bit analyst to diagnose that what *she* was worried about was Pinch having to work on the whale. And she was right to worry. Man, that whale was a death-trap.

The fishermen rowing us now began to talk excitedly in Spanish, shaking their fists at the sky between angry tugs at their oars.

'What's eating *them*?' Perdita asked.

We listened carefully.

'They say there's a storm coming up and that we should get back,' Snorts said.

'Tell them to stay where they are,' Perdita said.

We looked over towards where the neighbouring volcanic island shows on a clear day, and saw the horizon closing down fast, with a dark curtain of rain marching slowly towards us.

'Tell them to move in closer to the whale,' Perdita commanded.

'Let me get across to the tug first,' Snorts said. 'I got the runs.'

I noticed his eyes for the first time: they were fogged with fever. And his teeth were chattering like castanets.

We got the actor aboard the mother tug and steered back over to the whale.

'There's gonna be a storm, John,' Perdita called into the wind as we drifted into earshot.

'Fine,' Simpson called back cheerily. 'We'll be able to test the whale for seaworthiness.'

Perdita shrugged, and we drifted away again.

'Isn't that Simpson all over?' she said in a resigned voice.

'It makes sense,' I said.

'Oh, it makes sense,' Perdita said. 'Everything he does makes sense.'

She plucked a few straws from her hair. Then she got out a green watering can and started spraying the sea.

'It still doesn't look like a whale to me,' the French girl said.

'Whales don't look like anything,' Perdita said shortly.

'They just roll around,' I said. 'I hope no one falls off!'

'Slim!' Perdita said severely, swinging her can across the French girl's ear. 'Don't *say* such things. We just can't afford to tempt Providence. Not any more!' After a pause she said: 'Do you know, I really think that some evil force is at work on this picture. Call me crazy if you like, but whenever we get a boat or whale ready for shooting, something cockeyed happens. Away goes the sun, up comes the wind, and—bingo —that's the end of shooting for another day. My guess is, the original author touched off some force of Nature in his book about his misbegotten white whale that's bin stirred up all over again. By *us*. By us making this goddam film.'

I shook my head.

'Steady now,' I said. 'We must be rational about this.'

Perdita stared at the sky, an El Greco storm sky.

'Brother, I wus rational once. But I ain't any more. There been too many screwball things happening to us for me to take it all as pure coincidence. And how be rational if you're likely to be at the bottom of the sea before lunch-time? Look at our rowers' faces. They're scared silly. And why? Because they know this rotten sea inside out!'

We were closer to the whale now; the wall of rain was only half a mile off. Simpson was lying on his back on top of the whale, smoking a cigarette. Suddenly he leaned on his elbow and called over to Perdita.

'Send for a harpoon, honey. There's a harpoon missing.'

'Now what does he want with a harpoon?' the French girl said.

'I don't know,' Perdita snapped, 'but if he wants a harpoon, then he'll have a harpoon if it kills us.'

'It probably will,' the Gaul said gloomily.

A boatload of technicians drifted by and Perdita told them to fetch Simpson a harpoon.

Now the storm hung over us all; a tiger about to pounce. If we had been on land we would have felt the raindrops by now.

A moment later I heard Simpson call over to a passing boat: 'This is the wrong harpoon. Get me the Cannibal's harpoon, *and* a broken lance.'

He sounded good and angry.

'The Cannibal's harpoon and a broken lance,' an assistant director shouted out over the smashing waves.

'Judas gold,' Perdita said, 'can't they get a single thing

right? All the guy asks for is the right harpoon, so they get him the wrong one. Jesus, Joseph and Mary, I give up.'

Suddenly the French girl yelled :

'Sacré !'

We turned to where she was looking. Brother, it looked just as if the whale had come to life.

'Holy Hepburn, the whale's broken loose! Perdita screamed.

She was right. Picking up speed, the whale was drifting swiftly out towards the blackest patch of the storm, the gap between whale and parent tug growing wider, but fast.

'Oh, God, follow it,' Perdita shouted. 'Tell the boatmen to keep close to the whale. If we lose this one, it's curtains.'

I urged the boatmen to move after the whale, pointing at it and making quick rowing motions and shouting, 'Rapido, vivo. Rapido, vivo.'

We caught up with the whale and I called to Simpson : 'Looks as if the cable has broken.'

'That's precisely what's happened, kid,' the director said calmly. Turning to Perdita, he called : 'Situation normal, hah?'

'You crazy coot,' Perdita called back, half laughing, half crying.

'What's happened to that harpoon?' Simpson suddenly snarled. 'Do you mean to tell me they haven't found the harpoon yet? And what about the lance? Can't they break a lance?'

'One broken lance coming up,' a technician shouted, and passed a harpoon and a broken lance up to the director, who carefully stuck them into place on the whale. Over on the tug, the Consul was frantically directing operations to retrieve the cable. There was nothing Simpson could do until that end had sorted itself out.

'Some of us are going to get pretty wet and cold,' Simpson

said calmly. 'Will you kids go over to the *Gran Budgerigar* and fetch blankets and lifebelts?'

'Right,' I said. 'Anything else?'

'A bottle of Scotch whisky.'

I prodded the boatmen and pointed to the big tug lying half a mile inshore. The old fellows brightened when they saw the direction I had indicated. I did not complicate things by telling that we would be coming back. It was quite a sea now, you could feel the wind and rain lashing at you as you bounced over the waves.

As we passed one of the launches I heard a second assistant director say :

'All we need now is to have Snowball coming out of the whale's mouth, singing "The Kid's Last Fight".'

'I take that back about being rational,' Perdita called over to me.

A huge, green wave drenched us as she pointed a forefinger at the low, black clouds.

'That's where it's all coming from,' she said tersely. 'Someone up there is good and mad with us.'

'The boss will be even more mad if we don't get that bottle of Scotch,' I said. 'Ho, ho,' I shouted, prodding the fishermen. 'Rapido, vivo.'

The boatmen rowed rapidly, glaring and muttering, but going fast because of going inshore.

A dozen faces peered over the rails of the tug as we approached, anxious for news.

'What happened? Has this one got away too?'

'It's snapped its cable,' I told them.

'Bang goes this location.'

'I knew nothing good would come of this trip.'

'Ah, pack it in. Give these kids a hand.'

Perdita shouted : 'Never mind about a hand. We want lifebelts. As many as you can spare. And blankets.'

The faces disappeared.

'Snap into it, boys,' a voice above commanded. 'Collect as many lifebelts as you can.'

'Call the cook,' Perdita shouted as a technician threw over the first batch of lifebelts.

Others began to pelt down lifebelts. It was like cushions being tossed into a bullring.

The Spanish cook appeared.

'Whisky, por favor,' I shouted. 'Let us have a bottle of whisky.'

The cook shook his head.

'Whikkee,' I yelled. 'Rapido.'

The cook just stared.

'Whikkee, you cockeyed half-caste son of a Budgerigar sea-cook,' I shouted.

The cook stared, and shrugged.

'Flattery will get you nowhere,' Perdita said. 'Ask for Doc Magee.'

'Get Doc Magee,' I called to a technician.

After a long wait the doctor appeared.

'Doc,' Perdita shouted. 'Johnny needs a bottle of whisky. There's some in the cookhouse store. Write out a prescription for a bottle if you have to, but for pity's sake let's have it pronto.'

Doc disappeared.

More lifebelts flew down.

Then the doctor returned, with whisky. It was three-quarters full.

'It's the best I can do,' he called, and lowered the bottle over the side.

I stood in the boat and heaved up and down on the waves, reaching for the bottle. I managed to grab it on the seventh heave.

'Want me to come along?' Doc shouted.

'I think you better stay here,' Perdita replied. 'We'll bring the bods over to you if we have to.'

'Right, good luck.' The doctor disappeared. He was used to crises by now.

The fishermen started rowing towards the shore.

'Not that way, meatheads,' Perdita shouted. 'Back. Back to the whale.'

The fishermen went on rowing stolidly towards the shore.

'Judas cabbage, Slim, shake some sense into them, can't you?'

I shook.

'Apoyer,' I snarled. 'Apoyer hasta ballena.'

The fishermen showed their yellow tooth-stumps and pointed angrily to the shore. I pointed angrily back to the whale. My anger was greater than theirs, and they turned and rowed sulkily, but fast, towards the whale, which seemed to have settled down now to a steady circular course. But as we drew nearer I could see that the tide was taking the whale closer towards the reef. Simpson was still sprawled on the top of the whale with the tug following close behind and the Consul shouting his head off in Budgerigario-Spanish. Simpson had been joined by Isidore Fandango, a Spanish swimming champ. He and Kevin were both diving in and out of the water after cable ends, Kevin in his underpants, Isidore completely naked. The Spaniard looked funny, naked. Like a baby. Or a body on a battlefield. He should not have been there at all; he was riddled with Budgerigar fever.

'What's he doing here?' Perdita exclaimed, seeing the Spaniard. 'He should be in bed nursing that temperature!'

'I suppose he is like the rest of us, suffering from whale fever,' I said. 'Ready to die for Simpson if necessary.'

He was a funny sight, that Spaniard. The French girl and Perdita started giggling. You couldn't blame them, the way that boy looked was a scream.

We passed the lifebelts up to Simpson. Then I handed him the whisky.

'Thanks, kid.'

'Want any help?'

'Just stick around.'

'Oke.'

The Kraut was fiddling around with harpoon ropes.

'Where's your camera?' I asked.

'Back on the *Fishbite*. Nuds to kemeras. I help viss vale!'

'Why in hell did you leave it there? You must be crazy. This is something worth shooting.'

'Nuds.'

'No, not nuts. Look, come aboard our boat and we'll fetch your camera.'

'Nuds.'

'You give me the——' I began and then broke off.

Isidore had plunged back into the water. He did not come up for at least three minutes. When he did, he was holding a bit of cable. Kevin clung to the tail-end of the whale, rising and falling into the water, with one hand extended to clutch cable strands as Isidore fished them up. It was a back-breaking business, and Kevin's perch was almost as exhausting as the Spaniard's diving. Then he would heave over and the white strip of his non-sunburned rump would bob up and then disappear underwater again. He risked death every time he dived.

The flat-bottomed boat on which the whale had been built was plunging wildly in the stormy sea, and if the ledge where it joined the whale had crashed down on the Spaniard—and sometimes he was within inches of it—he would have been caved in like an eggshell in a child's fist. The rainstorm was beating down on us now and the sea was in a dark green turmoil. Once Isidore went under it was impossible to follow his movements. He made a dozen dives, fixing wires. Then another dozen. And another.

Of course, he was quite mad. His eyes, filmed with Budgerigar fever, saw no one or nothing. His nerves and muscles were entirely concentrated on securing that whale to the parent tug. His frenzied plungings went on. Several times we hauled him into our boat and pumped water out of him. Reverting to his mother tongue, he would gasp out: 'Agua, agua, agua,' the words coming out rhythmically with his breath-beats. A boatman gave me his water-flask, and Isidore would swallow a mouthful and then quickly plunge back into the sea. He was truly courteous about his nakedness with the women, always drawing a piece of canvas across his hips whenever he slumped into the boat.

It took over an hour to secure the whale. Sometimes the Spaniard would surface after a successful mission with a radiant expression, at other times he came up angrily, his eyes murderous and his teeth wolf-like. He drank his water greedily, lovingly, recklessly, soberly, wildly, cautiously, desperately. He surfaced sadly, he surfaced proudly. Sometimes he beat his chest like a bear and rolled blindly and drunkenly on the waves, shouting mindless, atavistic curses at his enemy, the whale. At the same time, he was incredibly funny. There was something irresistibly comic about his bare behind, his fever-blinded eyes, his insane anger. You know how it is when a dog chases its tail or a kitten jumps after a wasp.

A new danger set in, as the whale started drifting inland, towards the reef.

'Jesus, I hope they hurry and fix it soon,' Perdita said.

The Consul was charging round in a motor launch, shouting angrily at Isidore.

The Spaniard shouted angrily back.

And the fisherman cursed darkly, inwardly. They kept striking their chests with their fists.

Maybe they were praying.

Simpson retained his slippery perch on the whale. He remained calm, pulling at cords, the Kraut in attendance.

Kevin kept sliding up to the whale's back, shaking himself like a drenched puppy before going back to help Isidore.

The Consul started shouting more. Isidore shouted back.

Boatloads of technicians circled round, helping where they could, splendidly.

And then suddenly Isidore is out of the water for good, his job done. And he isn't funny any more, just drained out. And the reef doesn't look dangerous any more, even though the sea is still rioting around. And then Simpson winks and raises a whisky bottle and drinks. He passes round cigarettes to the others on the whale, his whale, his goddam whale. And he starts making wisecracks, soothing everyone down. The jabbering Consul, who did a really splendid job. The nameless grumblers who did well. The braggers who were useless all through the crisis. Then it hits you with the force of a wave: if the whale *had* gone on to the reef it would have been the end of everything for us. This was the last whale anyone would let Simpson build. We suddenly realised we were wet and cold.

Opening the hatch door, Simpson stepped into the whale. Raising the whisky bottle in one hand, and holding his nose between the forefinger and thumb of the other, he said:

'So long, kids. See ya next year.'

There was a devilish twinkle in his flat, brown little eyes as he slowly disappeared into the belly of the whale.

.　　.　　.　　.　　.

We got everything together and hauled the whale into a sheltered part of the bay, the director remaining inside the monster's belly. Perdita and I kept our rowers close to the whale, and when at last everything was fixed Simpson emerged, a happy grin on his indiarubber face. We hauled alongside and helped him into our boat, and the fishers were told to row us to the *Fishbite*.

'Happy days, Juan,' I said, looking at his whisky.

'Happy days, Slim.'

'Anything left in that bottle?'

'Help yourself, kid.'

'Thanks. Wonderful weather we're having.'

'Wonderful. Swell.'

'Well, you've had a fine day to test the whale.'

'Wonderful. Just perfect.'

It was too early to talk about Isidore, so I passed back the bottle and stared at the water. The clouds were still overhead, but something had gone out of the storm. It was almost as if it was sulking at having failed to smash up the whale.

We boarded the *Fishbite*. The Consul followed. His wife and daughter were already aboard. We went down into the stateroom, and settled in chairs, forming a circle round Simpson. The director was grinning amiably at nothing in particular. For a while no one spoke. Kevin found a half-full bottle of vodka and poured out tots all round. The *Fishbite* rocked wildly. The captain lurched through, too pie-eyed to notice any of us. We sipped vodka without saying anything until Britta turned up with a tray of hot coffee. She looked neat and hygienic and Scandinavian and cool in a white tropical outfit, like a nurse.

'I know what,' Simpson said, suddenly gay. 'Let's all talk about art.' He turned to the Consul and asked: 'What do you think about art?'

The Consul looked startled. He puffed out his cheeks.

'I know what I like,' he said cautiously.

'What *do* you like?'

'Constable, Turner——'

'Have you ever met Picasso, John?' I asked.

Simpson shook his head.

'No.' He paused. 'Now, there's a guy I would walk a long way to meet,' he said.

After a while, Simpson said :

'What do you think of Renoir, Slim?'

'He's fine. All flesh and sunsets and real breasts with real breath in them.'

Simpson said :

'He worked best in pastel. What do you say, Consul?'

The Consul shook his head. He was watching the skyline heaving and dropping beyond a port-hole.

'Have you seen his "Steeplechase", Consul?'

The Consul shook his head again.

'People dancing,' I said, breaking a silence, 'In clip joints.'

Simpson nodded appreciatively.

'He was good with criminals too,' he said.

'*And* on the racetracks.'

'No, he was not so good there, Slim. He was more interested in the people than the horses. What do you think of Pointillism, Consul?'

The Consul shrugged.

'Seurat's "Baignade" will always stick in my mind,' I said. 'It was one of the first things I ever saw.'

Simpson took up the dialogue again :

'But do you really warm to it, kid? All that obsession with technique.'

'No, I guess not. Artistic discipline is necessary, but it can become a strait-jacket. Give me a slap-it-on painter any time. But control still impresses me.'

'By control, meaning—wut? Mastery of form?'

'Yeah. I loathe the near-miss, half-assed artist. Any sonofabitch can paint, but how many can paint something that becomes part of your experience the instant you see it?'

Simpson nodded thoughtfully. The Consul yawned.

'Seurat had it all worked out,' I said. 'His creed was simple.
Art is harmony, period. How right he was! Can anything
beat that feeling of knowing that you've caught something
perfect? It even beats being shacked up with a dame.'

The Consul winced and looked away from his wife.

'Mu-mu-mu-more vodka, anyone?'

Nobody stuck out his mitt. So Kevin finished the bottle.

'Modigliani,' Simpson said 'Ever fall in love with a
Modigliani woman, Consul?'

The Consul shook his head. He was still breathing heavily
after the exertions with the whale.

'I knew a Modigliani woman,' I said. 'She's old now. But
what a wonderful woman! Modi once said to her, after a
row, "My love, you are a whore." '

Simpson leaned forward.

'What's that you said, Slim? I didn't catch that last bit.'
row, "My love, you are a whore." '

The Consul, his wife and daughter looked at the ceiling.

Simpson turned to the Consul's daughter, a kid around
fourteen.

'Have you ever been to England?' he asked.

'I hope to be going in a few weeks' time,' the girl said.

'You *are*?' The director looked delighted. 'Will you be
visiting Ireland?'

'No, I don't think so.'

'Aw, that's too bad. Do you *know* Ireland, honey?'

'No.'

'Why, that's *terrible*. Do you ride?'

'Yes, sort of.'

'She rides quite well,' the Consul said.

'She does?' Simpson turned to Perdita. 'You hear that,
sweetheart? The little girl *rides*. She must come to Ireland
and hunt with us. As my guest. I've just the horse for her. Is
your outfit up to date?'

'Well, my jacket is a bit small now,' the girl said.

'You shall have another one,' Simpson said grandly. 'We shall have one cut for you while you are in London. Have you a hard hat?'

'No.'

'No? Then we'll get you a hat as well. Perdita, before we leave I'd like you to make a note of the little lady's measurements. Then we'll have her fitted the moment she arrives in London. Is that all right with you?'

'It's very kind of you,' the Consul said. 'But——'

'Then that's fine,' Simpson said. 'You'll love Ireland, honey.'

He turned and looked at the sea through a port-hole, the girl and Ireland forgotten as he brooded about the whale.

'One of the stuntmen set fire to his bed last night and nearly bub-burnt his room out,' Kevin said, after a long silence.

'Who was it?' Simpson asked, interested in his surroundings again.

Kevin told him. The director chuckled. To the Consul he said :

'Mattress fires are the worst of them all. Have you ever set fire to one?'

'Yes,' the Consul said. 'In Lisbon. I'd had a few.'

Simpson beamed happily.

'Swell, swell,' he said. 'At least two of my friends have died in mattress fires.'

'They can be tricky if you're not very alert,' the Consul agreed. 'I've always managed to avoid actually setting the damn things on fire. Except that once. Never again.'

A dark horse, the Consul, I thought. Good in an emergency.

After lunch, Kevin said :

'Wurell, shall we all push along? There's lots to do ashore.'

We rose. There was nothing more we could do with the whale that afternoon. Not in that weather. We went ashore and drove to the hotel to prepare for the fishing. I hoped the weather would clear up before nightfall.

I didn't want anything to go wrong with the fishing.

CHAPTER TWELVE

The Night Fishing: Fadeout

THE THREE DRUNKEN fishermen squatting like monkeys outside the Green Dolphin Bar in the port discussing the big
fight were drunk because the winds of the night had driven
them ashore and the morning winds had kept them there,
even when the Americano's whale had come loose and gone
drifting towards the barrier reef.

The winds had driven them ashore, away from the fish and
the dangerous waves, and when the Americano's whale had
drifted away then they had not helped and now they were
ashamed. They had drunk deeply in the down-town bars
and then come back to their wall in the lee of the Green
Dolphin Bar, away from the fish and waves and close by
their small wooden boats, shaped the shape of boats Homer
had known, white boats drawn close to the entrance of the
Green Dolphin Bar, to be guarded by drunken eyes; and
some boats were even hauled into the narrow side-streets
outside the fishers' homes where the women and ninos could
guard the small craft, the shells that were their life and death,
whenever the fishers were blinded by drink or their vision
was obscured by drunken thoughts and feelings of shame.

The fishers were quite drunk; weather drunk, shame drunk,
drunk drunk, and fight drunk. Also they were drunk because
they liked it, but they were more drunk because of shame and
the weather, and the fight, and the whale, than because of

all the fiesta drinking. And now they were speaking of the fight, since talk of fighting made them feel back to the place where their manhood was hiding in shame, back to feeling that their cojones were still intact.

The first fisher said :

'Listen, amigos, this Señor Juan Seem-son is mucho fino hombre and mucho loco. I tell thee that he and the starfish Grigorio Peench go to the boxings at our blessed arena of heroes and so mucho like what they see that they wish to arrange boxings of their own. Among Señor Juan's actors who have come to chase the strange white whale in our waters are several heroes of the boxings. And Señor Juan himself, in the strength of youth, was lightweight hero in the State of California, which is in the Americas discovered by our revered Christophe Colombe.'

The fisher belched comfortably and continued :

'Now, the primo hero of boxing amongst Juan's crew of cannibals, Red Indians, Negro Princes, flannel millionaires and heroic drunkards is a fierce Indian named Tommahawk, also known as Tomasio, who is an outstanding fighter for many years amongst the gringos of the northern continents. This Terrible Tom, billed as the Ultimo Mohicano, fought *two* other heroes of Señor Seem-son's crew, Jeem Spellman, who has boxed exhibitions with the fabled Joe Louis, and Joe Pavlov, who only two days before lost many teeth falling from the mast of Don Juan's whaler.'

The fisher stopped to pump his wineskin, and the second fisher said :

'It is significant that Terrible Tom was seconded by the starfish Girgorio. This Peench packs a truly mean punch, and is truly heroic, as any fisher will agree who has seen him swimming strongly in our turbulent bay for Don Juan's cameras.'

The other fishers nodded agreement and the second fisher continued :

'It was good, on the night of the fight, to see so many heroes working so brilliantly against one another. Aie, I tell thee there was mucho excitement in the arena that night.'

The third fisher, who had not been to the boxing, said :

'Milk on the excitement. These boxings were made by actors and everyone knows that what actors do is not real. The blood was paint, the agony was learnt at the gringo drama academies.'

The first fisher said angrily :

'Always must thou doubt, Tomassio Secundo. It was thou that doubted that summer when the fishing was good off the Volcanic Island, and thou wouldst only fish between here and the Lizard Islands which are for baby fishers. Thou wouldst not listen to us, who went to the Volcano, and that is why thy wineskin was empty that season when ours were full. Be silent now and listen to us who were there at the boxing !'

The third fisherman said sulkily :

'How was it that thou wert there by the ringside at all, with seats priced beyond a month's income and selling for five times more than the price in the thieves' market by the Cathedral ?'

The first fisher said proudly :

'It was the starfish Grigorio Peench. He have tickets for amigos and want to be sure that we fishers have seats beside the Governor of these islands, and the Government ladies for whom he also place as companion Madame Jo-Jo of the well-blessed cathouse. But a sly one amongst the ushers has switch our seats. We are still close to the ring, though, and truly we see the true blood drawn from Don Juan's heroes. Is that not so, amigo ?'

The second fisher nodded over his wineskin, and said :

'Whilst an actor of Shakespeare is speaking in Spanish more atrocious than that spoken on the mainland, this actor being the fight announcer, Señor Seem-son is strolling coolly about the square ring whistling contentedly to himself. He is as if in a quiet room. He mucho, mucho at home in the square ring. Then that great volcano of song, Cedric Donnell, walks into the ring as a fighter in bathrobe, but instead of putting on gloves he sing "Tum on tid, Tum on tid, Hiddim widda lef anna ride." This he sing with strange choking sounds till he drop exhausted, the song we fishers now sing as we row into the waves. Then there is mix-up when Spellman, billed to fight first round, is replaced by Pavlov.'

The fisher pulled at his wineskin and continued :

'Don Juan then give him and Terrible Tom instructions that set them doing the wrong things very comical until they draw blood, then they fight truly and forget what Juan has told them. There is now mucho excitement and at the end of the first round the starfish Grigorio pours water down their fight pants and Terrible Tom hops on one leg like circus clown, ho, ho. Pavlov leaps in like a bull, fights hard. The Tomahawk breaks skin on his head, Pavlov splits Tomahawk's nose. Tomahawk opens Pavlov's cheek. Blood flies across the ring and lands on our laps. There is much shouting in the ring. Then more blood. I dipped fingers into blood patch on canvas near rope and it tasted true. There is much further exchange of blows but Terrible Tomahawk, Il Ultimo Mohicano, play with opponents like we play fish. Their mouths lose shape. Their eyes go white. In come the fresh Spellman and pummels Tomahawk's heart. But the Indian continues to fight heroically to the end. Both are blinded with blood as the bell goes, and the excitement is now a great wave.'

The fisher scratched himself all over and went on :

'Don Juan now steps forward and, after checking points,

with the audience now wild and crazy and shouting and fighting amongst themselves—Juan brings together Spellman, Pavlov and Tom and, stretching out his arms like one crucified, shouts in a voice that stills the arena: *Equallo!* Jesus and Mary, it is true! For that moment we were all equallo. The Governor. The generals. Their wives. The ladies from the blessed cathouse. The starfish. All, all equallo. Aie, the excitement.'

'It is true,' the first fisher said. 'All that he said is true.'

'What kind of man is this Don Juan,' the third fisher said, 'that he should make all feel equallo?'

'He is a mucho fino hombre. He is a giant and a true fisher highly spoken of by Don Pablo.'

'Aie, and we have failed him by not helping with his whale this morning.'

'We shall not fail him if he wishes anything more from us.'

'True, true.'

'Then, amigos, let us do justice to this new skinful of good Budgerigario wine before the weather changes and drives us back to work on the female-fickle waves.'

Thus the fishers.

Everywhere on the island the fishers pumped their wineskins. You know how it is with fishers when the waves are high and it is a time of fiesta. I did not look forward to nightfall.

.   .   .   .   .

'Where in the name of hell is Don Pablo?'

Simpson was half dressed, in fishing rig. He crashed a bottle of Scotch down on the table and looked angrily over to where I was sitting. The bottle did not break.

I shrugged.

'You know how it is, John,' I said. 'These goddam Budgerigarios are always an hour or two late for any appointment.'

'What time did you say he would collect us?' The director's voice sounded like a snake sliding through rough grass.

'Six.'

Simpson looked over his shoulder.

'What time is it now, honey?'

'Close on eight,' Perdita said.

'Hell,' the director shouted, smashing down the whisky bottle again. This time it broke. Perdita fetched another from the liquor cabinet. Simpson did not look at me again.

Ernie Sanderson came in wearing a sou'-wester, yellow oilskin and high waders. He carried a net over one shoulder and in one hand he held a harpoon lance.

'Sorry,' he said, turning back towards the door. 'My mistake. I didn't realise they'd directed me to a morgue.'

'Wait,' Simpson said.

Ernie leaned his lance against a wall and waited.

Simpson spoke quietly, pausing between each word.

'You—seem—to—be—the—only—sane—guy—around—this—place,' he said quietly. 'Get a car. Drive to the port. Find Don Pablo. Pablo, the—fisherman. Got it? And take Slim along. To interpret. He's the expert.'

Ernie looked at me and jerked his head towards the door. I finished my Scotch, but slowly, and walked out after Ernie.

We did not speak during the ride to the port.

No one had seen Pablo at any of the bars and clip joints we called in. Don Smeet? A shake of the head. Sorry, you like-a señorita? They very clean. You like a nino? But one thing was sure. They had not seen Don Pablo Ruiz Polianski-Smeet for days. No one had. We found Pia Viertel and Snorts Valentine eating paella in one joint. Snorts was Holy Hepburning and Judas golding about the whale. They had not seen Pablo either. Then we went to the Crazy Coconut. Spender rushed up and fussed over us and said, O young men, young comrades, what doest thou seek, seek what? or some such mushy stuff. And then Raquel appeared wearing a long white ballroom dress worth a mint of flannel in any currency.

She rushed over and clutched my arm and said, don't go, don't leave me, please, please, please, don't ever leave me, and I said:

'I got to find Pablo.'

Spender and Raquel turned pale, then green, then yellow. They stepped aside and talked quietly for a minute, then I saw Spender shrug and they came back and Raquel said: 'Come, follow me.' We were almost at the door when the boss of the joint came over and pushed his gut between me and the door and said, 'Joost a minute.' I smacked both my fists down on his bald head and he collapsed like a tree. He was just a fat Budgerigario gone to hell with late nights and too much drinking.

'To the Isletta,' Raquel told our driver.

.   .   .   .   .

We got there in seven minutes flat and pulled up in the driveway of a white floodlit mansion with green-tiled roof. There were palms hissing. A flunkey tried to stop us, but we pushed through.

We found Pablo in a big room with rugs and divans; a dozen underdressed women filtered around the joint. He waved at us with an arm so weighed down with Scotch it looked like it had elephantiasis, and told us to siddown. I went over to him and shook him by the collar and told him to snap out of it. A Nubian guard tottered over to help his boss, but half-way across fell flat on the floor. The women looked on with suppressed joy and interest. I guess they were hoping I would slap Pablo right away.

'Come on, Pablo,' I said. 'You got a date, remember?'

'Go 'way.'

The punk was drunk.

'Rapido amigo,' I said. 'We're going fishing.'

'Go 'way.'

Ernie stepped in and said: 'Come on, Pablo, Señor Simpson is waiting for you.'

'Who?'

'Señor Simpson. Your friend. A fellow fisherman.'

'Milk,' Pablo said. 'I desecrate his mother's milk. Who didst thou say it was?'

'Simpson. Señor Simpson.'

Pablo began to blubber like a whale. He was just a drunk punk.

'Aie, I remember. I am desolated. It is too much to bear. Drink?'

'Thank you, but no thank you,' Ernie said. 'Just get up on your dogs and drive back with us.'

'No possible. We have let you down. My brother fishers have let you down. I am ashamed for them. I am ashamed for myself. We did not help with the whale.'

This punk was a drunk punk all right, all right.

'Ah, forget it,' Ernie said. 'We managed okay, didn't we, Slim?'

'Sure,' I said. 'Don't let us down now, Pablo. We need you.'

Pablo blubbered some more. Man, he was slobbering drunk.

'No possible. Too late, too late. I have demolished the twelfth, the lethal bottle. After twelve bottles of the Scottish whisky it is impossible even for Pablo to move.'

'Sure you can,' I said encouragingly.

'No, I am rooted. I cannot move.'

It was true. Even as he spoke Pablo toppled sideways and went into a coma on the floor. The women rushed up and dragged him to a corner and rolled him on to a divan. Pablo began to snore, a smile crawling over his face that would have made a mortician purr with joy.

'Hell, let's go,' Ernie said, tearing up a telephone directory which happened to be lying around.

'I know,' Raquel said brightly as we drove down into the port. 'I find three fishers for you. They will not be completely sober but they will work for me.'

'Any sailor three bottles behind this punk will do fine,' I said.

'And I'll shake up the crew of the *Fishbite* and we'll use that,' Ernie said, perking up. 'Will your guys have nets and tackle?'

Raquel nodded.

'I see they have *everything*,' she said. 'Meet me at the jetty in half an hour. Bring everyone. I get Santos to cater for you all. Champagne, chicken, caviare. Everything.'

'Good kid,' Ernie said.

I kissed Raquel on the forehead, but like a father.

Ernie went off to round up the *Fishbite* crew. I got into the car and told the driver to break all the records. We were back at the hotel in three minutes, driving like crazy through flocks of sheep, goats, chickens, and Budgerigarios who shook their fists as we streaked past. I skidded into Simpson's room like a spear carrier in a Shakespearian play.

'Well,' the director said, 'where is he?'

He looked like a hunched tiger about to spring.

'It's all fixed,' I said quickly. 'We're using the *Fishbite*. The fishers are shipping their tackle aboard now. And we've got a gastronomic wizard in charge of catering.'

'Okay, kids,' Simpson snapped, rising, 'Let's go.'

We jumped into a fleet of cars. Simpson, Perdita, Cedric and Kevin o' the Bog in one. Pinch, his girl and King in another. I led the way in the first car with Britta, Mimi and the twins. King wore the biggest Mexican sombrero I ever saw. Everyone else was rigged out in heavy fishing outfits, and there was barely room to move. Mimi wore a straw wind-cheater. We were a bunch of true fishers, but truly.

The three limousines screamed to a standstill on the edge of the jetty. The place was deserted.

'Well,' Simpson snarled, 'where—*are*—the—fishers?'

'They'll be along any moment now.' I said.

'Where's Pablo?'

'He's on the Isletta. Passed out. Finito.'

The way I figured it, if Simpson had had a revolver handy he would have shot me on the spot.

'What *is* this?' he said. 'Are you trying to make a monkey out of me, kid?'

'No, Pablo got ashamed the way the fishers didn't help with the whale this morning.'

Simpson kicked a yellow dog. These dogs are constantly passing to and fro down there in Los Tropicos.

'The hell with that. I could have hauled the whale back with one small rowboat if that Spanish kid and Kevin hadn't fixed the cable.'

'That's what I told Pablo. But by that time, the poor jerk was too far gone to do anything about it. He's a twelve-bottle man.'

Simpson looked interested.

'Wine or spirits?'

'Whisky,' I said. 'Scotch whisky.'

Simpson gave a low appreciative whistle.

Just then a row of lights turned in at the beginning of the jetty. A fleet of taxis rolled up. Ernie jumped out of the first, holding the skipper up by the scruff of his white jacket.

'I got the lot here,' Ernie said cheerfully. 'Skipper *and* crew, except for the so-called watch aboard. They were all in the Green Dolphin Bar.'

He propped the skipper against a post. The crew formed a

ragged line. The mate stepped forward, saluted. He said : 'All present and correct, sir.'

These were true sailors, but truly.

Then two more taxis rolled up and Raquel pushed three pie-eyed Budgerigarios out. They sprawled across the plankings of the jetty, at the feet of the skipper, who appeared to have taken a one-way ticket to oblivion. As she hurled tackle out after them, Spender jumped from the second taxi, followed by two dazed-looking Budgerigar waiters staggering under a load of wicker hampers.

'Santos bring wonderful food and wine and waiters,' Raquel said happily.

We loaded everything into launches and pushed off. Raquel snuggled against me, out of the night dampness and sea spray. Even in the harbour the Atlantic water had a lively roll.

'Are you sure you want to come?' I asked her. 'How about your boss.'

'Boss very happy. Raquel very happy. Raquel say Señor Simpson pay for catering. It come to many thousand pesetas. Boss cleaned his joint out of food and drinks. Santos bring a week's stock of liquor. And the food—aie, wait till Santos serve it up !'

Spender and his waiters had caught what Raquel was saying and nodded happily. They had brought guitars along, and now they started playing and singing. Simpson stared into the dark sea, saying nothing.

It took several minutes to get aboard. The sea was quite wild at the harbour mouth where the *Fishbite* was anchored, and sometimes the launches were almost up to the level of the ship's deck and sometimes they would slap down into a trough and suck up close to the keel. It was a truly badly ballasted boat. Two of the crew fell into the sea but managed to catch a rope ladder and clamber aboard. No one bothered;

they were smugglers with prices on their heads from Tangiers to Takoradi.

Raquel squeezed my hand and said : 'I help Santos organise the kitchen.'

'What, in that dress?'

The girl looked at her elaborate gown.

'So sorry,' she said. "Scusa.'

She unzipped it and it fell crumpling on the deck. She wore a thin black sweater and tennis shorts underneath, but cutely.

'I find somewhere to hang this,' she said, picking up the dress and going.

We were moving out of the harbour now. A lantern at the stern lit up a vast patch of water, and under it Raquel's three fishers were fixing up the big net ready for casting. They lurched a bit, but the ship was rolling badly and when we hit the open water beyond the harbour it was as if we had passed into a wind tunnel. Sometimes the boat listed so heavily you could hang your feet over the side and drag them in the water. I passed the fishers a basket of wine and they smiled courteously and hoisted the wine to the side and jammed it between the strut of a lifeboat and a lashed-down box of bait.

I went below. Simpson had scratched together a poker school in the stateroom and was absorbed in the game. King Connell had already collected a pile of pesetas, which he kept, with his reserve chips, in the brim of his sombrero.

Simpson grinned over at me.

'How's it going, kid?'

He was happy now we were really under way, and I think he would have truly regretted it if he had shot me earlier that evening.

'Fine,' I said. 'I've deployed the fishers and they are quite content.'

'Wonderful, kid. Let me know the moment we get anywhere near some fish.'

'Sure,' I said happily. We were friends again. I would write him some really fine whale dialogue, I told myself.

Perdita and Pinch's girl sat in deckchairs lashed against the side of a cabin, the night wind and spray twisting their hair and driving into their faces. They were giggling like schoolgirls at a midnight feast. I lashed a chair up beside them and reached into an icebox and hauled out a flagon and poured some wine into a glass held out by a grinning waiter.

'Santos say me to look after thee until he is free to do so himself,' the waiter said. 'Santos say thou art his brother and I must guard thee with my life.'

'Thou art well instructed, amigo,' I said. 'Santos is indeed my brother.'

The waiter squatted at my feet and watched me and the girls drinking with great dog-like eyes. He was a fine Budgerigario waiter, with a white jacket and tar on his bare feet.

'Sing,' Perdita said.

'Yes, Slim, give us a song,' Pinch's girl said.

'You sing,' I told them.

They did. They sang the old ones. 'Kitty from Kansas City.' 'Ain't She Sweet?' 'If I had a Talking Picture of You.' 'Tiptoe Through the Tulips.' 'You Oughta be in Pictures.' 'Blue Skies.' 'My Blue Heaven.' And then they sang real blues. 'The Graveyard Sure is a Mean Old Place', they sang. 'They Dump Ya in the Ground and Slap Dirt on Your Face.' And they sang 'The Blues is a One-Way Ticket from my Heart to Nowhere.' Man, those chicks were just chicks but somehow they knew all the oldies. Don't ask me how. Then Cedric loomed up and lashed a deckchair alongside and started to sing. He sang 'Ol' Man River'. He sang 'Bless This House'. He sang 'Once I Had a Secret Love'. Then he sang a jungle jingle from the Caribbean, and we joined in every other line. It was called 'Hill and Gully Rider'. We sang it dozens of times, and each time Cedric changed the pace a taut, crazy excitement ran through us. The singing got wilder and some of the crew joined us, chanting and clapping their hands together. The waiter at my feet jumped up and shuffled round with the crew, hitting heads with his champagne bottle. It was a wild dance out there in the wind on that rolling deck, everyone responding to the coaxings and urgings of Cedric's deep rich voice. The crew looked like something washed out of the sea, dancing in the lights of the ship that showed up the yellow funnel above us and made a circle of light around us in the Atlantic darkness. When Cedric stopped I asked him what the song was about.

His chuckle was like a tropical cloudburst.

'The hill is the crest of the wave,' he said. 'The gully is the trough. You ride them both, man. Hee, hee, hee!'

.   .   .   .   .

The lights of the island were far behind now, they were not even a glow in the darkness.

Spender brought up a dish of steaming chicken.

'Is that all you have?' I asked.

Spender clapped his hands and the second waiter stepped forward.

'Ah, turkey,' I said. 'Fine, thou hast done well!'

'This,' Cedric said, chewing happily, 'reminds me of my friend the Calypsonian back home in Trinidad. A lot of Calypsonians live with girls in so-called sin, you understand. My friend spent Sundays lying in bed after being up all night singing calypsos. Sunday is the day when everyone eat. My friend's girl cooks him chicken every Sunday till at last my friend gets fed up and says, no more fowl. So next Sunday she gives him turkey. Hee, hee, hee.'

Cedric's huge frame shook with delight. The boat rolled on towards Africa. Dill and Doll went past with Kevin and the drunken skipper, singing 'Getting to Know You'. The skipper suddenly did a hornpipe and threw his cap overboard. The twins blew kisses at me. I shook a champagne bottle at them, happily. The boat rolled on and we talked about people we liked. Audrey Hepburn. Ken Tynan. Chaplin. Orson. Ava. Count Poklewski. Fernandel. D. Betty and Bogie. Peter Ustinov. Royal Dano. Papa. Marlene. Brando. Billy Wilder. Ben Benci. Suzie Flon. Willi Frischauer. Aubrey Verrall. Paddie Brosnan. Satch and Lucille Armstrong. It was good being out there in the Atlantic talking about people you had all at some time kicked around with, or worked with, or played with, or fought. Some knew some, and some knew others, better or worse, or for better or worse even, and the wind blew, the ship rocked, and the champagne passed round smoothly.

It was good being there and thinking of those other people, and good to be with the people you were with, and the waiters were good and efficient. The poker school had left me with an overflow of women. Mimi came over and pushed her fingers through my hair and I told her she was a fine woman and a brainy blonde. And the twins brought me a newly opened bottle of brandy, and I thanked them and told them they were fine women, too, even if they were only twelve. And Britta brought me a peach, and I thanked her and took it and told her she was a fine woman and a fine Swede. And then I told Pinch's girl she was a fine woman, and a damn sight more attractive than the Mona Lisa. And I told Perdita she was a fine woman and a damn fine dish of paprika goulash. And then Raquel took over from the waiter and sat at my feet, passing up bottles and singing Flamenco songs, and I told her she was a damn fine tramp and she smiled happily and blew kisses. And I blew kisses at everyone and

felt like the dying Toulouse-Lautrec in that colour film someone made about him a few years ago.

Then we all started throwing champagne and chicken. We
threw as much as we could lay our hands on into the sea, for
the hell of it. It took a long time and it was very funny seeing
all that stuff vanishing like that. And then I decided to have
a sense of responsibility about the fishers, and went aft to look
for them. The boat was rolling very badly and it was heavy
going, and for minutes at a time I would find myself leaning
against the rail watching out for waves coming in over that
side of the deck. The duty waiter followed me, watching my
progress anxiously.

The fishers were crouched under their lamp drinking wine
from out their basket.

'Merde,' I said. 'They should be watching out for fish.'

They looked at me calmly and when I spoke to them they
shook their heads and said, 'No comprende.'

I sent the waiter for Santos and when he arrived told him
to make those jerk fishers get on with the fishing. It was late
in the night now, I said, and the fishers were wasting time.
Spender talked in the guttural patois to the fishers, who continued to shrug. Then they turned back to their wine and
Spender looked away to sea, avoiding me.

I caught him by the shoulder and asked: 'What is it,
Santos? Do not fear to tell me anything. We are brothers.'

Tears the size of Maryland grapes stood in the rims of his
eyes.

'It is good that we are brothers,' he sobbed. 'For the news
is very bad.'

'Go on,' I said dully. 'I can stand anything now.'

'The moon,' Spender wept. 'It has failed to appear.
There is an unusual amount of cloud. And in such darkness as
there is tonight the fish do not come near the surface. We are
now in one of the best areas for fishing anywhere. But

the fish remain below, away from the nets. It is a tragedy of Nature.'

'Okay,' I said, releasing him. 'Thanks for telling me.'

The fishers looked up and smiled and waved their flagons and resumed their grunting, Budgerigario chatter. Santos stood beside me, waiting. I shook my head.

'Go,' I said. 'See to the catering. See that everyone is happy.'

'But what willst thou do, amigo?'

'I must talk with Señor Simpson.'

'Aie, that is sad.'

I went below. Simpson had fallen asleep at the table, cards in hand, the game continuing around him. I noticed he had very few chips, or money. This was a special game, not part of the marathon, and all were using real money. King Connell and Ernie Sanderson had most of the winnings, and Simpson was almost cleaned out. I shook him and he woke immediately.

'Okay, kids, let's play,' he said automatically.

He looked at the chips in front of him, at the piles elsewhere, and frowned. Then he looked at me with flat eyes.

'What is it, kid?'

'Come up on deck,' I said. 'I got to talk to you.'

'Just a minute, fellers.'

The poker school gave a collective grunt and went on with the game.

On the way up Simpson knocked his head on an iron crossbeam, and cursed in Mexican-Spanish for two minutes.

'All this talk about the free life you lead at sea is so much cojones-talk,' he said, stretching up as he stepped on to the upper deck. A gust of wind caught him and spun him round and he cursed again. He coughed like an old man between curses. Then he turned to me.

'Well?'

'I've bad news.'

'I guessed that already!' he said impatiently. 'What *is* it?'

'There isn't a moon out tonight.'

He looked up. A few faint stars were forming fours in a drunken sky. Mostly it was the thick darkness of piled-up clouds.

'So, *wut*?' he snapped.

'So the fish don't bite,' I said. 'They need to be coaxed up by the moon. No moon, no fish.'

He looked murderously up at the sky. If, right there, he could have projected himself into space, he would have done so—and dragged the moon hissing down into the sea. This is what drove him always, this wild impulse to push beyond the cramping irons of physical being, beyond personality, beyond thought, to the vast always-receding spaces of eternity.

I was shaken when he turned back to me and said: 'It doesn't surprise me, kid. I didn't really expect it to work out.'

He spoke quietly, without rancour. I swallowed some iron-flavoured spit, and wondered what to make of it. Was I relieved? Or sorry? I didn't know. It didn't somehow matter. He leaned against a rail and stared out to sea. There was nothing for me to say. There never is, with him. He knows it all. Talk is so much superficial noise to him. Unless it's written dialogue, or an actor speaking lines, pushing towards Form. Hell, I can talk for hours with lightweights. But not with Simpson. Not about the empty things. I leaned against the rail also, and waited for him to break the moment.

'It's that goddam whale,' he said at last.

This rattled me too. I remembered Perdita earlier that day, now become yesterday, pointing to the storm clouds as we had rocked in that small boat and watched the whale drift loose. I didn't say anything.

And then it happened. For a moment I thought I had got

the screaming heebies. A large white mass was coming out of
the darkness towards us. *The whale.*

'Holy Hepburn,' I said. 'Look!'

But Simpson was already sprinting across the heaving decks.
I followed quickly, turning to look from time to time at the
approaching monster.

Simpson shouted down the companionway: 'Kevin. Greg.
Ernie. King. Quick, the whale is going to ram us!'

There was a scuffle of chairs, a sound of incredulous voices.
Someone laughed uncertainly.

Simpson rushed to the bridge with the rest of us close
behind him. The master of the ship was lying on a bench,
dead drunk. His mate nodded over the wheel, humming an
old drinking song about a cellar cool and clear. The director
pushed him aside and took the wheel. It was hopeless, with
the whale rushing at us at about six knots.

The way it was coming it would ram us amidships.

'Get the women over to the starboard lifeboat,' Simpson
shouted.

Kevin was beside him now, and Ernie. Pinch began mar-
shalling the women to lifeboat stations. Cedric started singing
a spiritual. King Connell was booting the crew into action.

The whale was almost upon us.

'I'll beat you, you bastard,' Simpson shouted crazily. 'I'll
beat you yet, you dumb white ugly bastard. I made you and,
so help me, I'll tame you!'

Kevin and Ernie joined Simpson at the wheel, getting a
hold and trying fiercely to turn the ship away from the
oncoming whale. The monster was growing bigger every
second, rolling towards us with a killer's lurch. It grew like
something in a terrible dream. (Thing rolling and leering in
deadly waters. Eye dead, eye evil. Thing malignant. Thing
white and lethal. Why this madness of the chase, this cold

wild sea in a dark world? Thing monstrous and hard to hold, impossible to catch and conquer. Ah, I feel old, kid, and bowed, as though I were Adam staggering under the piled centuries since Paradise. What is it? What nameless, inscrutable, unearthly thing commands me against all human lovings and longings to keep pushing and crowding and jamming myself on all the time? Is it I, God, or who that lifts this arm? Say, Perdita, send a cable to the new York office. Ask *them*. But if the great sun cannot move except by God's invisible power, how can my small heart beat, my brain think thoughts, unless God does that beating, does that thinking, does that living and not I? What, though, if it is true that God is dead? No, no, no, no, no, no, no, I'll never believe in disbelief. Cage me a peacock, pour me a shot of Jack Daniels' Tennessee Sour Mash. This must not destroy us, this thing with fangs, with hate, with dark marine power. Pass me over the box of Sherman's Havana cigarillos. Water generates sparks, sparks generate fire, fire generates heat. Heat, then, strike sparks of fire in sleeping muscles sleeping. Strike! Strike! Strike!) Then King and I hurled ourselves at the wheel, and our joint weight turned the ship just as the whale smacked into us. There was a crunching sound, as of bones being chewed, and the decks shook with sudden concussion. Then the whale rolled away and slipped back into the darkness.

Our first impulse was to turn and chase the whale, but we had no equipment to make it captive even if we caught up with it. King and Kevin volunteered to swim after it and board it, but Simpson shook his head.

'Where's the radio room?' he asked.

Kevin led the way down to a cupboard equipped with radio transmission apparatus.

'Where's the wireless operator?' King shouted.

'Du-du-du-du-drunk in the scuppers,' Kevin said contemptuously.

He squeezed into the cubicle and took control of the instruments. Kevin had been twice torpedoed on wartime service with the merchant marine and knew all about emergency radio transmission. After a minute he turned to Simpson and said:

'It's all under cu-cu-cu-cu-control. The Budgerigario Navy has been flashed and a cu-couple of gug-gunboats are heading towards us now. They turied to contact us earlier but couldn't get a reply. Gud-goddam radio op wasn't at his post, as usual. They've got the whale's position now.'

'Let's go chuck the radio op overboard,' King growled.

'Keelhaul the entire goddam crew,' I said.

We turned to Simpson. He looked blankly at us, then walked slowly over towards the companionway and sat down. His long thin figure swayed with the movement of the ship. He stared ahead for several minutes, not seeing anything.

'Better keep in touch with the gunboats, Kevin,' he said at last, briefly, and relapsed into silence. The radio made atmospheric noises. Fifteen minutes later we received a message from the admiral's flagship telling us that the whale had been caught, and was being towed back to Los Tropicos.

'Ask if we should join them,' Simpson told Kevin.

A minute later Kevin said: 'It's all right, John. They are making for harbour as quickly as they can and say there is no pup-pup-point in our contacting them again until we get ashore.'

'Fine,' Simpson said. He looked at King and Ernie. 'Well, let's get on with the game, fellows!'

.   .   .   .   .

The poker school was just getting under way when there was a clatter outside the stateroom and Perdita rushed in, her almond eyes shining like horse chestnuts.

'Quick,' she shouted, 'we've just spotted an enormous fish!'

Cards fluttered across the table and there was a rush to the deck. The fishermen under the stern lantern were hopping mad, shaking their fists and threatening people with wine bottles.

'Where's the fish?' Simpson said impatiently.

Perdita pointed to a spot a few yards out.

'There,' she said. 'See that silver flash? Look, it's following us.'

I looked hard. The water was like a broken chandelier, chopped up by the lamplight. Something flickered briefly.

'I saw it,' King yelled excitedly. 'It's a fish all right, all right.'

Simpson leaped forward, pushing the rest of us away. His hands grasped the line but the Budgerigario fishers clawed at his wrists and tried to pull him back. He shook them off. One fell overboard. The others cringed away under the lantern, muttering. Simpson was about to haul in the line, but the fishers yelled sharply at him. Their companion clambered back up the net, with Simpson furiously shouting at him to get out of the way. Seeing Spender hovering amongst the crowd behind us, I called him over.

'What are those fishers saying, Santos?' I asked.

Spender looked scared. He mumbled something I could barely hear. I asked him to repeat it. This time I heard, but could not believe what he said. But it was true.

I tapped Simpson on one shoulder. The director looked fiercely at me, and turned back to the line. I tapped him again.

'What the hell do you want now?' he snarled.

'You better drop that line,' I advised.

'Why should I? That's a fish there, isn't it?'

'Yes.'

'Then stand back. It's my fish, goddam it.'

'That's the trouble,' I said. 'It isn't your fish.'

Simpson turned and glared.

'What — are — you — trying — to — tell — me?' he asked angrily.

'It's not a live fish.'

'What the hell is it, then? I swear I'll knock you down if you're kidding me.'

'No,' I said sadly, 'I wouldn't kid you.'

'Okay, go on—what *is* it?'

'Bait,' I said.

Simpson went slack. For a moment he looked like an old man, grey and limp on a deathbed.

'Okay, you bastard,' he said softly. 'That's fine. You sure fixed things fine. That's just about the best night's fishing I ever had. Thanks, kid. Thanks a lot. You've been a great help—a terrific help all along the line.'

'Sorry,' I said. 'It's just the way things have worked out. I'm truly sorry.'

'Sure,' he said. 'Sure, you organised it fine.'

He walked away. The rest dispersed after him. I felt quite alone. A smudge of dawn was streaking in from the east, and I went over to a rail and watched it grow as the sea changed from mourning to morning. It was cold, but I did not want to move or see anyone. After a while I calculated that, if I were standing on the other side of the ship, I would be seeing the island coming up over the horizon. But I still did not want to move. I didn't care how long I stayed there or how cold I got. Then I became aware of Simpson beside me. We leaned on the rail for a while, not talking.

'I reckon the whale must have got a few dents in that collision,' I said at last.

'Yeah.'

'What will you do?'

'Shoot actors smashing up in whaleboats till the whale is seaworthy again.'

'Yes, I suppose you can always do that.'

'Sure, and we'll do gull shots and you can throw meat, kid.'

'I like throwing meat,' I said listlessly. 'I'll help cut it up, too.'

'No, that's a technician's job. You can't do that. It would be bad for your prestige.'

'Does that matter?'

'Sure, kid. Of course it does. Besides, it's against union rules.'

A few minutes later I said: 'I think I'll be able to give you some fresh whale dialogue in a day or two.'

'That's swell, kid. Really swell.'

'To integrate the whale more, you understand.'

'Sure. Keep working at it that way.'

'I'm glad we spotted the whale,' I said 'It might have gone adrift if we hadn't located it.'

'Oh, easily, kid. It's as well we were there when we were.'

'I guess so.'

Simpson looked amazed.

'You *guess* so? I *know* so! It justifies the whole thing. Last night we killed that whale for good. *Killed it, I tell you, kid.* He'll behave now.'

'It's a point.' I began to feel slightly better. 'I suppose it *would* have been hell if that whale had just drifted away, like the other, without our spotting it when we did.'

'*Sheer* hell, kid. It's the only whale I got left.'

I brooded over this awhile, staring hard at the silvering sea.

'It's a goddam hell of a whale,' I said.

'You're right, kid. But it's all we got.'

'Yes,' I said. 'It's all we got.'

'When this is over, we'll go hunting,' Simpson said after a while. 'We'll hunt tiger.'

'Will we?'

'Sure. And lion. And rhino. We'll have a swell time. You will help organise a safari.'

'I *will*?'

'Sure, kid. Why not?'

I didn't know the answer to that. Before I had time to say anything, there was the sound of a gong being hit below. Breakfast. Simpson moved off, his mind already on other matters. The whale meant nothing to him now. He was already exploring vaster mysteries. The whale was tamed. It did not mean a further God-damn.

As for me, the safari would never happen, not the way he said it would. But, suddenly, I found that I had an appetite. Another bright Budgerigar day was beginning. The wind had dropped. The sea was behaving. I followed Simpson down to the stateroom without another word. We sat down to a truly fine breakfast. Eggs. Bananas. Fundador.

I ate a lot, knowing there was much work ahead. Straightforward work with a tamed whale. With actors. With whaleboats. With spears and harpoons. With Simpson. But without handles. Completely without handles.